ISBN 978-1-330-99145-9
PIBN 10130726

1 MONTH OF
FREE
READING

at

www.ForgottenBooks.com

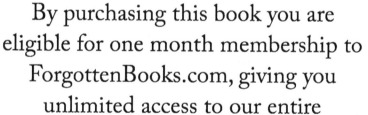

By purchasing this book you are eligible for one month membership to ForgottenBooks.com, giving you unlimited access to our entire collection of over 700,000 titles via our web site and mobile apps.

To claim your free month visit: www.forgottenbooks.com/free130726

English
Français
Deutsche
Italiano
Español
Português

www.forgottenbooks.com

Mythology Photography **Fiction**
Fishing Christianity **Art** Cooking
Essays Buddhism Freemasonry
Medicine **Biology** Music **Ancient
Egypt** Evolution Carpentry Physics
Dance Geology **Mathematics** Fitness
Shakespeare **Folklore** Yoga Marketing
Confidence Immortality Biographies
Poetry **Psychology** Witchcraft
Electronics Chemistry History **Law**
Accounting **Philosophy** Anthropology
Alchemy Drama Quantum Mechanics
Atheism Sexual Health **Ancient History**
Entrepreneurship Languages Sport
Paleontology Needlework Islam
Metaphysics Investment Archaeology
Parenting Statistics Criminology
Motivational

THE
LITTLE SUFFERERS

A STORY OF THE ABUSES OF
THE CHILDREN'S SOCIETIES

BY

G. MARTIN JURGENSON

Author of "The Social Mirror"

BROADWAY PUBLISHING CO.
835 Broadway, New York

BRANCH OFFICES: WASHINGTON,   BALTIMORE
INDIANAPOLIS,   NORFOLK,   DES MOINES, IOWA

TABLE OF CONTENTS.

CHAPTER   PAGE

I.   A Story of the Abuses of the Children's Societies 5

II.   The O'Neils in the Cell 13

III.   A Racket at the Flanagans' Home . . 24

IV.   The System's Agents 35

V.   In the Magistrate's Court 48

VI.   The Critical Dilemma of Lankey George 58

VII.   Jack Stevenson Reduced from Ranks 67

VIII.   The Kidnapping of the O'Neil Children 75

IX.   Mrs. O'Neil's Visit at One of the System's Homes 84

X.   Lankey's Arraignment of the System 95

XI.   A Visit to Hastings Farm 106

XII.   Red Hook Dan Connors' Letter . . 122

XIII.   Harry O'Neil Disappointed 134

XIV.   Jack Stevenson upon the Juvenile Question 151

XV.   A Light-Hearted Dinner Party . . 172

XVI.   The Defeat of Jack Stevenson . . . 190

XVII.   May Thornton's Appeal to her Old Lover 202

XVIII.   The End 218

The Little Sufferers

CHAPTER I.

A Story of the Abuses of the Children's Societies.

"Truly, Harry, I'm very happy that you got that job, even though it is a few dollars less a week. No matter, dear," said Mrs. Harry O'Neil, as she helped her husband to a breakfast of liver and bacon. Taking a seat beside him, she continued: "By and by, dear, you'll get a position like the last one; anyway, twelve dollars a week is not so bad, though everything is expensive. I'm not extravagant, nor do you spend anything for drink, so of course we'll get along nicely. Besides, perhaps Willie can sell a few papers and, in a pinch, once in a while our Louise can stay home from——"

"You are awful good, Nelly," broke in her husband, "but it must come hard, my child, for you and the children to get along on so little; it means just two dollars a day, including carfare and——"

"I know, Harry, I know," she exclaimed. "But did we not figure out last night that by moving to South Brooklyn, where you are going to work, we could save a few dollars a week in rent? And besides, you'll have no carfare to pay; so, after all, dear, it is not so much of a difference, and soon we'll get used to it. Truly, Harry, we'll be as happy as ever. Where mutual love exists, no matter what befalls, all other troubles can easily be overcome. You were always so good and willing, and have tried so hard to please me and have our home so pleasant, that surely now I can help you a little, and we can perhaps save a few dollars. I can't do anything too much for you, and, as I said before, Louise once in a while can mind the baby so that I can take in a little sewing and washing. Every little helps and does no harm."

Endeavoring to conceal his emotion, Harry arose and, embracing his wife most lovingly, said in a tremulous voice: "Thank you, Nelly, but you shall not, as long as I have all my limbs, do a stroke of work to earn a cent."

Harry now hastened to his new job as teamster in a South Brooklyn planing mill, which lay close to Gowanus Canal.

After having completed her household duties, Mrs. O'Neil, with her three children, left for South Brooklyn, in search of a cheap apartment convenient to her husband's work. As she passed up and down the dirty avenues of that part of Brooklyn, the contrast to what she wished to find was so great that she suffered intensely. A fear came over her, as she saw women and children carrying cans of beer from the saloons which were run by some of the aspiring politicians in that ward. Her route lay directly past a resort frequented by political aspirants, ne'er-do-wells, ward detectives, and other law-breakers, who leave their tainted money at the bar, and in return look for the favor and protection that a saloon-keeper's influence or pull can provide.

"I'll bet my last nickel that that piece of calico and

the fine kids are something new about here," said one of the gang.

"Just look at her, Jim, she'd have made a fine policeman, had it not been what failed her," said another.

"Ah, let her chase herself, we're all right," drawled a sleepy-looking individual sitting on the sidewalk.

Mrs. O'Neil paid no attention to these idle remarks, although they added to her misery.

Finally, worn to a compromising frame of mind, she got suited, in a way, in the lower end of Bond Street, within a couple of blocks from where her husband was employed. There she engaged four fairly decent rooms at a rental of ten dollars a month.

Having completed her task, Mrs. O'Neil started for home. On passing the ice-house, she saw at a corner about two dozen idlers lying about with some beer cans, and among them stood a policeman. Being a stranger in that neighborhood, she asked the officer how to reach the cars for East New York.

"Well, well," drawled the officer, fumbling his boyish face, "I'm on my vacation; and, anyway, I'm not a street directory. I am assigned to catch——" Before he could answer, a boy offered for a cent to guide her to the nearest car.

She gladly accepted, and within an hour she reached home. A more unhappy woman than Mrs. O'Neil could hardly be imagined. The thought of leaving her quiet surroundings and cosey home to dwell in a locality where there was neither law nor order, discouraged her and nearly broke her heart.

A month and a half had now elapsed since the O'Neils moved into their new home in Bond Street, and those few weeks had seemed years to sensitive Mrs. O'Neil. Indeed, she had ample reason to feel badly, for the children thereabouts were totally deprived of training and the merest infants were left running about the streets without proper oversight. The O'Neil children from their earliest infancy had been properly trained, but it is easily conceived that children as young as they may be readily led into the habits of their fellow-playmates. At first the little girl and boy consulted their mother as to the impropriety of the remarks heard in the streets, but they became inured to the life into which they had been thrust. Twelve-year-old Willie soon fell victim to the cigarette habit, and, although not practising it openly, with the boys of his own age he would frequent alleys and hallways in order to smoke, gamble, and use profanity. His mother openly tried to influence him to retain his former good habits, thereby causing other mothers of the neighborhood to ridicule her.

Her neighbor, Mrs. Flanagan, tried to placate her by saying: "Sure enough, Mrs. O'Neil, boys will be boys, and my Jimmie, as smart a lad as ever was reared in the Tenth Ward, and fit to be alderman in the best ward in town, can smoke with any grown man in McGarry's district. Sure he's only the age of your Willie, and could smoke cigarettes ever since he was weaned."

Mrs. Flanagan was hopelessly vulgar. Her husband drove a coal cart, and they lived on the same floor with the O'Neils. Both drank and encouraged their children to do the same. When too far in arrears in rent, they would move to other quarters, and continue to practise their habit. They had a large family of dirty children; their little girls were sent out to beg, and the boys to plunder passing carts and wagons, stealing food and fuel for the use of their parents. After church on Sunday the children were

8

sent out with the black bag in which the beer can was hidden, as was the custom in that neighborhood.

One Sunday morning, while the children were still in bed, Mrs. O'Neil said to her husband: "Well, Harry, here is twelve dollars which I have saved up, without having earned a cent of it myself."

"Nonsense, child, though you do no washing for others, you earn that money as much as I do, and perhaps more so. I probably would spend it all, were it not for you, my dear."

"I would like you to spend a few cents now and again advertising in the paper for a better position," said Mrs. O'Neil. "You can meanwhile hold on to your job, and I'll attend to seeing the persons who answer your advertisement, so you needn't lose your present position until you get one to suit you. I'm sure, Harry, this one must be hard for you, who have been used to a position as foreman. When you have a better job we can live in a nicer neighborhood."

"It would, perhaps, be a good way to better ourselves, but I'm all right where I am if you can stand it here. The wages are rather small, but I'm not worked so hard, dear, nor are there so many cares resting upon me as if I were looking after a gang of men."

Harry O'Neil proceeded to the stables to look after his horses, and Mrs. O'Neil went to mass, leaving the baby in the care of little Louise. On her return from Father Duffy's church, upon entering the hall, she found her Willie with the oldest Flanagan boy, Jimmy, sliding down the balusters and smoking a cigarette. Mrs. O'Neil felt that she ought to punish the boy, for long since she had suspected that he smoked cigarettes and told her falsehoods to keep it from her.

Willie said that Jimmy Flanagan had begged him to smoke, and Mrs. Flanagan, overhearing this without any provocation whatever, laid violent hands upon her neighbor. Mrs. O'Neil was younger and stronger than Mrs. Flanagan, and broke away from her after a slight scuffle. Mrs. Flanagan rolled into the street just as Officer O'Sullivan, whom she knew, passed the house. The officer, refusing to hear Mrs. O'Neil's explanation, promptly. arrested her for assault and let guilty Mrs. Flanagan go. Then calling for a patrol wagon, he took the shrinking and protesting woman to the station house. When they reached their destination the policeman found that his prisoner had fainted from fright and mortification, and the officers had to carry her in.,

Officer O'Sullivan said to the sergeant: "This woman is only shamming, or else she is drunk. She nearly killed a respectable woman comin' home from church, and sure enough a murder would have been committed if I had not been attendin' to me duty."

Mrs. O'Neil revived in a few moments and, rising to her feet, cried: "Oh, please let me go home to my children. I am innocent of any wrong."

"Shut up! Give us none of that," growled the official in charge, as he ordered the two officers to put her in a cell until morning.

Just then Mr. O'Neil entered and, going to his wife's side, he said excitedly: "Leave her alone; she's my wife, and is guilty of no misconduct."

The doorman, who stood by, attempted to come between O'Neil and his wife, but Harry, who had almost lost his senses through what had happened, gave the officer a stinging blow and knocked him down. Then, turning toward O'Sullivan, who was holding Mrs. O'Neil, he struck him and also knocked him down.

"Why don't you use your clubs? We can't have ruffians come to the station house and do us up at their own liking," said the sergeant, in no mild tone, leaning over the rail. Officer Jack Stevenson, who was attracted by the scuffle, rushed from an inner room and with a wrestler's grip laid the infuriated man on the floor. O'Sullivan, angered by the blow he received, hit him several hard blows upon the head, lacerating his cheeks. The doorman, too, prepared to avenge himself, but here Officer Jack interfered and tried to raise O'Neil upon his feet.

This beating not only took the fight out of Harry, but it dazed him. The officers could not support him on his feet, and he sank helpless to the floor.

Scratching his head, the sergeant said: "You landed him pretty tough, all right. Throw the gent into the cell, and be quick about it, too, as he might die on our hands."

These brutal occurrences occupied but a few minutes. Mrs. O'Neil had become frantic, and was now wildly fighting to assist her blood-smeared, dazed husband. Upon the sergeant's assertion that he might die upon their hands, she uttered a loud screech and dropped to the floor.

While the doorman and Officer O'Sullivan dragged Harry, helpless and stupefied, into a cell, Officer Jack picked up the poor, unconscious woman whom he carried into a separate cell and stretched upon the floor to revive as best she might.

The officers then returned to the desk, all of them looking somewhat disturbed, and the sergeant most of all. This condition was not to be wondered at, as he was on the promotion list for Captaincy, and, though a strong favorite of the chief, he could not afford to be publicly criticized or investigated.

Looking at the three officers, the sergeant said: "I wouldn't care if you had killed the dog (meaning Mr. O'Neil) if it had been near the canal where you could have kicked him in, but every reporter in town is down on us; they'll roast us in the papers, and we don't want no investigation, see?" In a cautious tone he noted: "Them folks in the pen got more'n what's good for 'em, and we must fix up things so the job looks straight. You, Officer O'Sullivan," he now directed, "go down to 'Pikes' McGinn's distillery and get two flasks of his rankest booze. Then you go into their cells and if you can't get the stuff down their throats, souse it all over 'em, so they smell like a rum shop. I'll ring up the hospital so they can come and give us a clean bill of our duties."

In a few minutes O'Sullivan returned with a couple of flasks, each containing a quart of whiskey, and with his brother officer proceeded to the pen of Harry O'Neil, who had not yet come out of his stupor. They managed to pour down the helpless man's throat fully a pint of the stuff, the remainder they spilled over his clothes. As he lay there he truly appeared a helpless drunk. Mrs. O'Neil, wretched and semi-conscious, was still stretched on the bare floor, and she was subjected to the same ordeal. "This is good stuff fer ye, me gal," crudely joked one of the officers, as, despite her protests, he forced a good part of the contents down her throat. The balance of the vile brew was dashed upon her face, hair, and clothes.

Meanwhile, the sergeant had noted the occurrence upon the record in two separate paragraphs. The first read: "Unknown woman too intoxicated to give any address, brought by Officers Jack and O'Sullivan; besides being intoxicated, she created a disturbance."

The second consisted of these words: "An intoxicated unknown man, terribly bruised and cut, followed unknown woman to the station house. Upon his entering he fell down in a drunken stupor."

Beneath both of these entries was marked "Ambulance call required by cause of their apparently extreme intoxicated conditions."

CHAPTER II.

THE O'NEILS IN THE CELL.

Some little time passed while the officers were in the cells of the unfortunate couple. The sergeant spent these moments walking up and down behind the desk, apparently speculating. Was it possible that within his guilty self he nourished a feeling of cowardice to look on and encourage three strong, brave officers to attack an unarmed man and so severely beat him while he was down?

He had become a police officer after a three years' sojourn in this country, having managed to secure witnesses to testify to a five years' stay. Like some of the coarser of his race, upon finding certain powers vested in himself, he had allowed his love of authority to run riot.

"Well, fellers, did you make a good job of it?" he asked, in an encouraging tone, as the officers returned from the cell.

"I bet yer me brass buttons and three days' pay that dem folks never had such a soaking before. The ambulance surgeon will 'diocese' it to be perfidious drunkedness, and in last stage, at that," reported O'Sullivan learnedly. "They'll be sure livin' grog shops in any sober man's eyes. But what I have fear o' most, sergeant"—he drew in partial whisper—"they won't live the day ter tell their story."

"Oh, hell, we only done our duty," quickly entered

the sergeant, in a matter-of-fact way; "should the junk die on our hands, our record will show clean."

"Sure, sure," corroborated O'Sullivan, throwing his chest forward proudly.

The sergeant went on: "We have bums enough in this ward, anyhow, that would be a good way to git rid of some of 'em. I bets you a platoon if I get my promotion I'll jest make an example of the rest of them!"

While Officer Jack made no reply, O'Sullivan agreed: "Sure on yer life, sergeant, Brooklyn is a bum town, and there ain't a dasen' man livin' in it, but we'll soon cervilize 'em."

Barely had the speaker finished when the ambulance clanged up in front of the station house, and there quickly alighted a dapper young doctor with a satchel in hand.

"Hallo, Cap," he saluted, with pleasant freedom, "what's the trouble?"

"A couple of the finest drunks you ever seen, Doc. Since I took to my uniform, I never seen the like," announced the sergeant soberly.

"Yis," promptly corroborated Officer O'Sullivan, "what they have drunk would float a vessel, and it smells loike nicotine," he ended, in a wise assurance.

"Whew! I guess by that I'd better get my cork-screw," answered the doctor, as he returned to the ambulance, where he removed from a chest certain implements. "This will do some little sipping out," he said assuringly, as he showed the stomach pump.

"Where are the creatures," the doctor now asked, preparing for duty. "Let's go and take their index," he added, throwing away the butt of a cigarette. "Show me the woman first; she is probably the weakest from the effect of drink."

The officers thereupon led him toward the cell occupied by Mrs. O'Neil. But to the surprise of both officers and the doctor, when the door was opened, leaning against the partition, stood Mrs. O'Neil, looking sternly calm. She had much the aspect of a martyr. Stepping toward the incomers with dignity, she said, in a tense tone: "Where is my husband? Let me get him and go home to my children, and I shall forgive all."

The doctor looked greatly astonished as the beautiful, clear face and eyes gave no sign of dissipation. The officers, disappointedly surprised, had to cling to each other for support. They now realized that the whiskey with which they had saturated the woman had been only a means of reviving her.

However, the doctor kept on stirring. Finally he said to one of the officers: "Haven't you brought me into the wrong cell? This woman is no drunkard, nor does she appear to need medical attention of any sort."

Officer Jack looked greatly ashamed, while Officer O'Sullivan said: "Upon me oath, doctor, she was as drunk as a beet when we brought her here, or else she was shammin'. Jest smell at her garments, if they don't smell loike real fire brand I'll never draw another pay."

Here Mrs. O'Neil broke in: "I remarked some peculiar odor about my person, and I, too, felt that some one had given me something strong internally which has brought me out of my fainting spell. But, truly sir"—she now addressed the doctor—"I never drank a glass of intoxicating liquor in my life. If some one has given me something now, it has perhaps aided me. If you will only just let me go home to my little children I shall be happy," she ended her appeal, with a strain of strong self-possession in her voice.

The doctor was deeply touched by her purity and

sincerity. He realized that a good woman had been wronged for some cause. Of course, he was not called to look into details; she needed no aid from him. In a tone of strong sympathy he said, as he prepared to leave: "I am sorry, my good woman, it is not in my power to release you and send you home to your children, though I will vouch for your ability to look after them. I am but an ambulance surgeon and not a magistrate. I will say, though, that should the charge of intoxication be brought against you in the morning, I'll take the stand in your behalf——"

"Oh, in the morning," here broke in the poor mother, with a wild cry, "but what will become of my poor children all night? All—alone—all—alone! Oh, my husband! Oh, my children! Oh, what shall I do?"

The poor, wretched mother sank back upon the hard floor and piteously wept and moaned. The surgeon who could vivisect both humans and animals and listen to cries of suffering without any great show of pity, here felt tears rush to his eyes. Mrs. O'Neil soon faintly leaned back; her moanings and whisperings for her loved ones grew fainter; the pupils of her eyes began to set, and she seemed to undergo a process somewhat akin to death. The good doctor, with a strong emotion, pleaded: "Cheer up, madam, it will all come out right."

The doctor now felt her lowering pulse, and at once removed some stimulant from a vial which he carried in his vest pocket, and, after some persuasion, he finally revived her. "For the sake of your children you must live. If you succumb now what will become of your home and little ones?"

This little cheer and strong suggestion did much toward stimulating her. She arose to a sitting position; sending the doctor a feeble look of thanks, she said weakly: "Yes, that is true; I shall try to be brave."

It was without a doubt the most touching scene the doctor had ever witnessed. Pain of the mind, of the heart, and a mother's feeling and a woman's love for husband and home spoke through it all. Its true sincerity could not fail to awaken the coldest of spectators.

The police officers felt very uncomfortable at witnessing this tragic scene, and if it gave them no warning for future, it at least made within them a mark that now and again would be touched. In their uncomfortable position they felt much relieved when the sergeant poked his head in and asked and demanded to know what all the fuss was about. He had become alarmed at the doctor's unusually long visit. His guilt nagged him, but he had to show a brazen spirit in order that at least his outer skirts should appear clean.

However, the doctor, in a like brisk tone, returned: "This lady is not intoxicated, and in my opinion never has been. She needs most of all to be released and sent home to her children. I own no real estate to pledge as bond, but will you parole her in my care till morning, and I'll see that she answers the call in court, and——"

"Here! Here! Here!" abruptly broke in the sergeant, in strong ill-temper. "Your duty has ended if she does not need your assistance, so you may go."

"I am very sorry for you, my good woman," sympathetically remarked the young doctor, as he was forced to depart. The officers, much pleased to have an end to the scene, locked the cell door, leaving poor Mrs. O'Neil alone in torture.

As he thought of the situation, the doctor had become touched with anger, both in the treatment of the unhappy woman and the sergeant's rough answer to him. "Where is that other drunk that you said you had?" he roughly demanded.

The sergeant had motioned his men not to lead the doctor to O'Neil's cell, for he feared that a similar result would follow.

"Oh, the fellow is sobered up, and don't need nobody," answered the sergeant abruptly.

Whereupon, the doctor, who felt grieved, replied: "It don't cost anything nor does it harm, while I am here, I might as——"

"Here, that'll do!" cut in the sergeant savagely. "I don't want to stand for no ruse from any of yer ambulance fellers," he returned, with a strong glance.

Upon this ultimatum, with a disgust upon his face, the doctor departed with his unused stomach pump and surgical outfit.

As the ambulance clanged and rolled away, the sergeant remarked: "I'd leave off my vacation if I could nap that cheeky ambulance pacer and chuck him in my woodbin fer a week's spell. I will bet he'd soon learn ter mind his own business."

"Hey you, Jack," he now instructed the officer, "go and see how the feller is getting on with his booze; maybe the stuff woke him up, too."

O'Sullivan followed Jack. As they reached the cell they breathlessly opened the door and peeped in. The whiskey had had a similar reviving effect upon O'Neil, but his whole face showed unmistakable effect of ill-treatment. The injured man noticed them, and said: "Officers, I'll be willing to stay over night in the cell and face any charge you may prefer against me, but permit my wife to go home. She has three children, the oldest but twelve and the youngest a baby. We are entirely without friends and acquaintances here, and it is within human reason that you cannot permit those little ones to be alone."

"Well, we'll see what we can do for you, though you was pretty fresh," replied Jack, in a conciliating tone.

"Perhaps I was," answered Harry. "But I was drawn into it; I knew my wife was innocent, and——"

"That'll do ye," broke in O'Sullivan pompously. "We're officers of the law, and act according to our sworn duties. Had yer wife bin innocent, she wouldn't hive bin arrested; it ain't fer yers ter lay rules fer the perlice."

It was evident to Harry that there would be nothing gained by pleading for clemency or his wife's innocence. Controlling himself, he said: "It may all be true as you may say, but I am sure you'll not see those innocent children punished and deprived of care."

"If it was in my power, I would free her, all right, but the best I can do for you, friend, is to speak to the acting captain," consoled Officer Jack, as they left the cell. Upon reaching without, Jack remarked: "I'm awful sorry for this couple. The sergeant has made a blunder of it, and I'll have to confess I lent my hand to it, too."

"Ah, ye're a molly Jack," was all that O'Sullivan answered, and they proceeded toward the desk.

"The stuff we gave him took the fight out o' him, but it made him as sober as a teetotaler," reported O'Sullivan. Whereupon, Jack added pacifically: "He wants us to leave his wife go home to her children——"

"None of that," interrupted the sergeant, with a chastising look; "we have made a job of it, and must stick to the bluff. The entry is made upon the blotter, and I won't stand for no softin' up."

At this moment the door of the main entrance opened, and a respectable looking workman entered. Before he had reached the desk, the sergeant, in his customary "bulldozing" tone, accosted him with: "Well, what do ye want?"

"Well, well, I——"

"I asked what do you want?" the sergeant snarlingly interrupted, before the incomer had been able to explain.

"I came to see about Mrs. O'Neil, who was taken away from her home in the patrol, and also to inquire if her husband is here. They have little children home, and——"

"Hey, not so fast, you!" broke off the sergeant. "Who are you, and what's your name?"

"My name is Tom Ryan. I work in the Planet Mill with Harry, and live a block away from his home. He has no friends around here, but from my short acquaintance with him I learned that he's a decent fellow, and I want to help him if I can."

"I know none by the name of Harry or O'Neil, but I have some drunks in the cell too soused to give their names, so you better not bother yerself about it. Go home and mind your own business. To-morro' the judge will act accordin' to his duty."

"Well, captain, you wouldn't for a moment think of leaving that woman in the cell over night with her little——"

"Here, here, damn you; I'm running this precinct, and won't stand for no meddlin'!" snapped the sergeant.

"You must hear me. That woman you brought in your wagon is Mrs. O'Neil. She just came from church, and as I understood it from inquiry, she does not drink, and I know Harry, her husband, don't touch liquor at all, so there——"

"Have you got any real estate property to go on their bail with?" demanded the sergeant sarcastically.

"No; but—but——"

"But—you git out of here or I'll clap you into a cell till mornin'," cried the sergeant angrily, as he partly arose from his seat.

For fear the sergeant would carry out his threat, the interceder in the unfortunate couple's behalf retreated. He gained courage enough as he reached the outer threshold to hurl back: "You people here have made a miserable blunder, and though I have no bonded real estate to pledge for their release, I'll have his boss and others who know them in court to-morrow to expose your shameful actions."

"If I had that dog back again I'd fix him up so he'd get a six months' stretch on the Island. I'd give him a lesson for sassing back an acting captain," snarled the sergeant, as Tom Ryan closed the door.

"Well, I'll mighty quick nab him fer yer, sergeant," responded O'Sullivan, as he hurried to intercept the departing one. But the sergeant quickly reflected and called him back.

"No, it won't do, 'Sullivan; we must be a bit careful, though we have the law with us; but," he added, vindictively, "if any of youse meet that young upstart in a dark alley, don't fear to bale him with your nightstick and haul him along so we can get the feller mugged and have his likeness tagged in the gallery."

Jack meanwhile looked rather absorbed in thought, and the sergeant noticed this, and in no mild tone exclaimed: "Say you, Jack, you'll never make yer mark on the force; you'd be better fit fer police matron. I ain't got no use fer, that kind ov men weakin' in the middle of a job."

"I ain't going back on no job, but I feel for the couple. I have three little children and a good wife, too, and can't help feeling their position," answered Jack sadly.

"Say, ye are a beeswax, Jack, and should be made ter trot post on the cemetery and weep o'er the dead," returned the sergeant in ridicule.

Barely had the sergeant spoken the last syllable when the telephone rang. Reaching for the receiver, a voice was heard: "This is the juvenile system. We have a report that you have in your lock-up the parents of three little children."

"Maybe we have, and maybe we ain't," answered the sergeant, not wishing to commit himself. However vulgar the sergeant was, he felt that the pair had been punished enough without taking away their children. He knew the practice of this alleged humanitarian society, which describes itself as the juvenile system, a chartered private incorporated company. He was also aware that when this system once gets children within their clutches, no judge in the country can release them. But of course, like a good, true officer, sworn to law and duty, he could not go back on his own report on the blotter.

As he prepared to hang up the receiver he said: "I'll look into it and let ye know."

The sergeant did not feel altogether at ease. For his own sake he would much have preferred that those arrests had not been made; it began to dawn upon him that something unpleasant might arise from it. Though he had the backing of the commissioner and all his precinct men, withal, such brutal treatment of a good couple might work him an injury.

After a little deliberation and fumbling with his red mustache, he said to his officers: "You needn't push the case for the judge in the morning unless it comes to a strong test. Then ye must stand by the charge and you put the two empty whiskey flasks in evidence which you must swear to that you took out ov their clothes. And get a couple ov more officers to swear that the pair were drunk and disorderly." In a threatening tone he added: "That ambulance surgeon may be there in the morning. But I'll bet yer me buttons he'll lose his job if he does."

After another pause, he continued: "You, 'Sullivan and Jack, bundle off yer uniform and git inter plain clothes and go ter Bond Street and get some evidence that the pair were disorderly and drunk. I don't care where or how ye gits it, either."

"Sure I'll scare half ov the ward to swear ter what I say," answered Officer O'Sullivan with a wink, while Officer Jack said nothing, but reluctantly went along, according to bidding.

A few minutes afterward that pair of officers were on detective duty. As they reached Butler and Bond Streets, Jack was heard remarking firmly: "I'll not for all the police jobs in the country help to plot up any further than I have. I'm going to see if I can get some kind neighbor to look after the unfortunate children till morning. Just suppose these poor children should be abducted by the Juvenile System?"

"Oh, ye should be in petticoats, Jack!" replied O'Sullivan, who looked for great fame upon the police force.

Upon this they turned and walked toward the lower end of Bond Street. Officer O'Sullivan said: "Say, Jack, let's take a spin up to Flanagan's and we'll find enough ter clear our record."

"You do as you like, O'Sullivan, but if I want evidence I want it from a different source. But candidly there could be no evidence strong enough to satisfy me that those people in our lock-up are anything but respectable," answered Jack firmly. "I do not hold myself above going a little out of the way where no one is to become the sufferer, and I'll do anything to aid my superiors in posing strong, but I'll mangle no souls in order to do so."

"All right, Jack, ye know best," returned O'Sullivan, with a mild scorn, as he turned on his heels, walking toward Flanagan's.

Officer Jack remained standing on the corner for a few moments, speculating upon what course to take in order to save those unfortunate O'Neil children from the System's claws. He had learned from the telephone conversation that this organization was upon their tracks.

His thoughts were suddenly interrupted by loud clanging and soundings from gongs and clattering hoofs, which came from the direction of lower Bond Street. His brother officer was only a few paces off, so hurriedly Jack turned and followed him. Both walked quickly to the point to discover the cause of the commotion.

CHAPTER III.

A RACKET AT THE FLANAGANS' HOUSE.

None in the neighborhood of the O'Neils, beyond the fact of a patrol wagon having carried away Mrs. O'Neil, had any knowledge that her husband had suffered a similar fate; nor did the fact awaken any unusual interest. Fights, disturbances, and police 'buses, in this and similar sections, are daily occurrences, though more particularly so on Sundays and holidays, when the habitual roughness and coarseness have opportunity to run riot.

However, this O'Neil couple were comparatively strangers, and not, by any means, favorites; so, while they suffered in the lock-up, their little ones were left entirely to themselves. Of course, Mrs. Flanagan and her pals in the same building knew it, but their spirit of joy ran in the vein of punishing any one belonging to the O'Neil family, and so they took no heed concerning the fate of the little ones.

When the wagon took Mrs. O'Neil away, her boy Willie ran into their home and hid away, crying; this no doubt being the severest punishment for any of his deeds. While his sister sat trembling, weeping, and hugging the baby in her tiny arms, her poor little brother piteously cried and pleaded to be given back his mamma, and loudly promised that he would never swear or smoke cigarettes again if only his mamma would come. But alas! his sorrowful heart in begging forgiveness had no one to offer consolation, but his little sister, who also suffered as keen a pang. Thus, while these children despaired in tears, their mother was kept in a cruel cell, suffering a similar torture.

Of course, the two larger O'Neil children knew that their father had gone for their mother, but they could not grasp so cruel an idea as what had happened, nor the cause of their desertion. At last, after suffering long distracted absence from their parents, the children became faint and weak. In their helpless plight they twined themselves close together in a corner of their front room and cried themselves into a sweet, forgiving sleep.

Across the hall from the O'Neils, the Flanagans were having a "racket," this being their term for the debauching revelries common among that class. Mrs. Flanagan had gained a trump and she truly was proud. And to add strength to her honors, she carried this day's festival to the height of fashion.

The general feeling in the neighborhood naturally ran for Mrs. Flanagan. She was of the general cast and was looked upon in their standard as a decent woman. New arrivals to their section must step down to their level before such can become generally popular and be permitted to live in peace. The inherent finer qualities of the O'Neils could not be lowered to mingle with these coarser natures, and thus they had been constantly annoyed. More than once had Mrs. Flanagan attempted to provoke them to quarrel. That she had gained her contention this day and in so manifest a manner that her enemy had been cast into jail, gave her an enviable social prominence among her pals.

As soon as the patrol had carried off the unfortunate innocent woman, the Flanagans sent out word to their "cronies" around the ward to join them in a "racket." As a matter of fact, the Flanagans held a revelry on every Sunday. It always had been their custom after mass to begin to "rush the can," and with the willing aid of their neighbors carried on until long after midnight one continuous round of beer drinking and horseplay. This evening's festival, in consequence of the day's happenings, was to break the record. They had laid in a full keg of beer, and any of their clan were welcomed.

These people, regardless of scale of wages or amount earned, are "broke" in the beginning of each week. In order to maintain existence they commence on Monday, and on each day following till Saturday, to despoil their homes of all chattels from that of wearing apparel to kerosene lamps and holy pictures, leaving them in pawn to be redeemed on the nearest pay-day.

To all of the set word had been sent that Mrs. Flanagan had upheld the prestige of the ward by showing newcomers that they must act according to established customs or leave the ward, and soon friends began to pour in and offer congratulations.

The few living rooms of the Flanagans were packed with visitors, and some of the near neighbors brought their own chairs. Girls were held upon the laps of young men, and seats for the elders were provided from soap boxes, the edges of beds or window sills. The keg of beer was placed upon the kitchen table, and the beer was drawn into all kinds of vessels. Now and then, between their drinks, some of the younger members would play a jig upon a harmonica, and the gay ones would stamp upon the floor to follow the tune. There was no dancing room, but there was merriment enough.

While the O'Neils upon this day were suffering a torture of existence, the Flanagans were having "the time of their lives," and between draughts of beer they would comment the difficulty, but the praise was all centred upon Mrs. Flanagan who accepted it with satisfaction. With mingled joy and satisfaction, she would remark: "Sure, a stuck-up woman with her braided kids have no business ter live 'mong daicen' people."

After some little discourse continuing along this line, one of her pals proposed: "I have the foinest schem' in the country that'll settle them stuck-up O'Neils for the rest o' their days, and let's work quick."

"That's a go," responded all in glee.

"We'll send word ter the Juvenile System that three children are left alone and their parents are in the lock-up fer drunkenness and disturbin' the pace——"

"Sure, sure, sure, Mrs. Merlone; ye'r alright," cheered all.

"I'll let me brother Mike go an' phone up the System and tell'm the three little ones are alone."

As a tribute to this excellent suggestion, each had a refilling from the diminishing contents of the keg. "That's a good way ter fix them parents what thinks themselves more'n us ole warders," agreed Mrs. Flanagan. "Sure, an' she sid my Jimmy spoiled her kids there's none finer boy then moin in the whole ward," she concluded boastfully.

"The Juvenile System closes their shop at six o'clock, and now it is ten minutes off, so we better make the job quick," remarked one who all along had sat currying love with a couple of young girls, one of them being his betrothed. The speaker was Dan Connors, better known as Red Hook Dan.·

"Ye'er all right, Dan," agreed the first speaker. "If we want the System ter take the kids it must be this noight, fer ter-morro' the Judge will have her out o' jail and she'll fight for them. Ye'r mor' edjercated ner me brother Mike, so ye better spake in the 'phone, Dan."

"Sure, I can speak in the 'phone," responded Dan, feeling proud of being looked upon as educated. "It'll but take me three minutes to get the 'perceiver' a-goin', and that'll finish the job," he added, emptying his vessel of beer and preparing for the street.

Here the girl, May Thornton, drew him towards her and whispered into his ear, upon which both walked into the front room. Looking straight into his face she said: "If you have any love for me, Dan, don't send for the System's agents. Those poor children will never——"

"Ah, forget it!" broke off Dan impatiently. "You're a big toad bothering yourself about some little brats." Then, in a conciliating tone, he added, "I'm trusted with the job and wouldn't for all the rags in the ward go back on my word. You'll like me the better for it," he ended in little self-assurance, to which the girl replied·that he would see. Upon this Dan departed to attend his mission.

May Thornton, like her lover, had been born and

brought up in Red Hook section. He was twenty-three years and she was twenty. May was a pretty little blue-eyed lass, and looked upon by all as the belle of the Erie Basin and Red Hook Point section. Her father had died while May was a child of six, and she now worked at the handkerchief factory at South Brooklyn. There were, besides May, several brothers and sisters, all of them aiding their widowed mother to keep the house and attend to household duties. The Thorntons were a respectable lot of poor people, and held themselves above the average Flanagan class; but through Dan, whom the girl so blindly loved, she had of late been frequently brought into relation with this lower element.

Dan Connors, or Red Hook Dan, was of the Flanagans' set. He had been permitted to grow up without schooling and in idleness, and even among the worse element he was looked upon as a bad character. Long before he was old enough to vote he would lead gangs of repeaters to the various polling places and be of much political use .to whichever party required him. Just now he had reached a stage at which he could qualify for the police, an appointment which he, owing to the merit of his pull and his influence he had just received. He was now an officer on probation, and two weeks hence would be awarded the regular uniform of patrolman.

That Dan Connors always had many girl admirers is not to be wondered at. He was well built, stalwart and strong, and a bully naturally carries considerable force with inexperienced hearts. Truly, very often the best of girls fall victims to this sort of character. Very often this trait is the cause that many a good little mother is pining away her life and suffering endless torture. It is easily understood that May Thornton should love Dan, and now that he was about to become a uniformed officer, she reasonably should love him the more.

Dan soon returned from the telephone booth, followed by Lankey George, a man of odd jobs. Lankey found a seat upon an upturned bucket and Dan joined his sweetheart, who had remained dejectedly seated in the same place. In a mildly bullying way he approached her. "Well, aren't you over your grouch yet?"

May remained in same position and gave no reply.

Seating himself beside her Dan reached his arms to embrace her, but she removed herself and looked as though she were offended. "Ah, you only want to be coaxed," he sneered, "and you can bet yer rats I coax no hairpin when I needn't go further un' to any factory, and I'll get the whole bunch pegging to get at me. And two weeks from now, when I get my uniform, the whole Point will want to marry me."

"But I will never marry you," announced May, rising and entering another room.

"Two weeks from now, when you see me in my uniform, you'll do some whining for this, my job lots," returned Red Hook Dan, the probation officer, with a light scorn as he walked into the kitchen. There he leaned against a window-sill, where he began to carry on with a couple of Baltic Street belles.

Dan and May were to have been married upon his first pay-day. Of course all their girl acquaintances looked upon it as a lucky catch for May, and naturally, in consequence, were jealous of her.

The Flanagans' festival went on in this manner of raw carousing, unharmonious singing, harmonica playing and stamping upon the floor. Their keg of beer had been renewed and every one appeared happy, except May Thornton, who gloomily sat in the corner of the adjoining bedroom with her cheeks buried in her hands.

Her girl friends, envying her luck, though concealing their jealousy, now pretended to encourage her. "Don't have the blues for such a little spat as that; it'll be all right again with you and Dan. Sure he thinks his life of you, but he's just like all the fellers—they want to use their rough edges on us girls once in a while."

"Yes, indeed, May," elucidated Lizzie Tims, a Warren Street damsel. "You're beating us all with your good catch. Should you be left a widow the city'll pension you."

Here the girls' attention was drawn to the kitchen, where strong words and argument were heard.

Lankey George had upbraided Dan for sending for the Juvenile System's agent. "Why, ain't the poor children and the parents punished enough as it is," he exclaimed, "without breaking up their home? Nobody understands the ill cause and effect of this Children's Society better than I do. That Juvenile System is the cause of my misfortune. It robbed me of my children, it broke up my home and drove my wife to drink. She is now dwindling her days in the Kings Park Hospital, hopeless and demented. It brought me to where I am to-day." Here Lankey's voice faltered a moment in attempt to suppress his emotion, and the tears glided down his worn face.

"This Juvenile System is terrible, really it is. What he says is all true, so it is," sadly murmured May Thornton as she heard part of George's tale, while Dan jeered him with taunting slurs. "I'll forgive a set of petticoats to soften up and bale out dewdrops, but it ain't for a man to show tears for nothing," he said, looking contemptuously at Lankey. "Anyway, I don't see why a feller should be chicken-hearted for these little brats what don't belong 'round here."

Dan Connors was of a quarrelsome disposition, and would nag at any one not agreeing with him, and was always ready for a fight. While under the influence of intoxicants this disposition was even more pronounced. He had drunk a good deal of beer this evening, and, aided by his growing police spirit, it urged him on to emphasize his own conviction.

The rest of the Flanagan party remained silent while Lankey and Dan quarreled, though most of them, of course, agreed with Dan. He was both feared and admired, and his promotion from civilian to police weighed vastly in their respect.

Lankey George, however, made no reply to Dan's sarcasm. He still sat as though absorbed in deep thought.

"I never took you for much of a man, anyhow," continued Dan in a quarrelsome tone. "I 'phoned for the System's man, and he's going to take away the kids as sure as I'm going to trot in my uniform two weeks from now. And if you don't mind your own business I'll show you what kind of a hitting cop I'll make. If you wasn't an' ole man I would throw you down the two flights of stairs right now," he ended, having worked himself into a fighting mood.

"Well, I fear you'll never wear your uniform, then," coolly replied Lankey with a sharp gleam in his eyes, and arose. "As to being a hitting cop, you are, in my opinion, only a stuffed cop. The agents of the Juvenile System will never kidnap these children so long as I have a spark of life. And if I am to go down two flights of stairs, you'll follow me. A man who has no regards for women and children, has no regards for age, so you need not consider my age," he finished in so strong a note of defiance that it momentarily thwarted the bully probation officer, and partly awakened the Flanagans and their guest out of their maudlin state.

Fights and squabbles were customary, and as much a part of these poor people's festivals as were the refreshments. It was only natural that such outbreaks became free, rough-and-tumble until one or the other was beaten. Of course there were none among them who would not have staked their all upon Dan. George was a good deal older, and, though apparently strong and wiry, he could not be looked upon as a match for Dan, who was in his best condition, and always in practice.

Of Lankey George very little was known; but he was about thirty-six years of age, and had lived in the ward about twelve years. He did not mix greatly with people, and was not known to have relatives or friends. His acquaintance with the Flanagans had been brought about through some little favor and assistance which he received a couple of years back while laid up with an attack of la grippe. George had a furnished room next door, but out of courtesy he would pay an occasional visit to the Flanagans. While not a heavy drinker, he enjoyed his beer. Upon close observation he showed a trend of intelligence, and appeared of better stamp than the average warder; and he always carried an engaging air of mystery about him.

However, Red Hook Dan needed no further invitation for an attack. Measuring up Lankey, with an expressive contempt, Dan swung his left arm, which, to the astonishment of all, was neatly parried by Lankey. With the fleetness of a prize-ring expert, the older man returned a heavy blow, which landed straight upon his opponent's jaw, and drew blood. Dan became furious by meeting so sudden and unexpected a repulse, and rushed upon Lankey, who here showed the agility of a cat and equal cleverness, and besides proved himself a hard hitter.

The Flanagans' guests crowded into a corner and close to the wall to give room. In the tumult chairs were upset, the partly filled keg of beer was knocked off the table and rolled into the adjoining room, while the table became tilted upon its end.

It was a lively fight, but purely without prize-ring rules. Dan was severely overexcited from disappointment, and much the aggressor, but without real effective tactics, while Lankey showed more coolness and good judgment, and throughout the scuffle maintained and used his strength to the best purpose.

The Flanagans' cronies had entirely sobered up by surprise of the apparent outcome. A moment ago all would have laid down their lives on the certainty that Red Hook Dan would have finished George in a single round, and now, as it was, their champion was receiving blow after blow and gasping for wind. There was barely a scratch upon Lankey, but Dan was all cut, and his left eye had been discolored and closed.

In his disappointment of beating Lankey by fair means, Dan now picked up a heavy bowl from the floor and, with a wild curse, hurled it at Lankey, who quickly dodged. The vessel made its mark in the centre of a large holy picture adorning the wall above the mantlepiece. The force scattered the glass and pierced the cloth, throwing the picture off the hook, so that it fell in a heap upon the floor back of the stove.

Upon this arose a great commotion. "Oh! Oh! Oh! The Virgin's picture!" loudly screamed Mrs. Flanagan, with a quick flow of ready tears upon perceiving the damage to her idol. She was joined in loud cries of sympathy from the other women.

While Mrs. Flanagan cried sins upon their souls, the

combatants fought on. Lankey George, for the first time, now appeared to make real use of his saved energy. Swiftly he drew Dan out into the hall, tilted him over the baluster in order to throw him downstairs. Dan clung on to him in desperation, and the pair landed at the second floor.

Dan was biting and kicking, and it was now plainly in Lankey's mind to have his opponent upon the street and in a freer scuffle, so he managed to whirl Dan over the baluster and clear himself of his hold. Into the lower hall rolled the probation officer, Dan Connors, much bruised, and with his left shoulder-blade dislocated.

The tumult and noise had aroused the remaining tenants, and also crowds from without the street. However, as Dan lay there helpless, he sorely needed attendance. Some bystander immediately telephoned for an ambulance, and in a little while an ambulance and a police patrol rattled up.

Red Hook Dan was removed to the hospital, and, of course, Lankey George, in order to avoid arrest, had, for the moment, to betake himself to some other quarter, where he stayed until things had quieted down.

CHAPTER IV.

THE SYSTEM'S AGENTS.

Officers O'Sullivan and Jack reached this lower section just as the ambulance swung up into Douglass Street toward the precinct station.

"I wonder what can be the trouble," called Jack to his brother officer.

"I 'pose it's more ov the junk loike them folks we have in the lock-up. True ter me life, Jack, them folks in better rags are all the time stirrin' a fuss and gittin' themselves and us inter trouble. They think they're more'nd us cops. If they'd mind their own business and lave the police run things, as we find our duty and we're paid ter do, there would be less jails and perlice shake-ups," philosophically scored intelligent Officer O'Sullivan.

Officer Jack Stevenson, far superior in intellect, gave no reply to this comment upon police requirements, for though he had to take sides with all police injustices, he did so because the rules of the department demanded it. He was an American born; of old New England stock, and had sprung from an industrious, hardy people.

The two men quickly directed themselves towards where the ambulance had called, which proved to be at Flanagan's. The crowd had thinned considerably, but as the officers were on a more sacred mission than to hunt up the cause of this disturbance, they proceeded to build evidence.

As O'Sullivan turned to go in towards the Flanagans' apartment Officer Jack said: "A teamster school chum of mine lives down in Union Street; while you attend to your affair, I'll go and see if some of his women folks won't look after these unfortunate little children till morning. If I didn't live up in West Farms, where I was on duty till I was shifted to South Brooklyn, I'd have them to my home to stay over night."

"Say, Jack, I ain't your superior, but if you'll take a solid advice, you lave them kids fare their own fate," answered O'Sullivan.

"Why, man, for mercies' sake, let us not permit that!" said Jack reproachfully. "Should these unfortunate children be removed by the Juvenile System it would be a cruel outrage. You know as well as I do that once within the claws of that Human Hawk System it means child servitude at the Hasting Hills, or perhaps upon some Western farm for these innocent ones, and it will break their poor mother's heart——"

"I agree with you on all that," broke in O'Sullivan; "but I ain't goin' to take no chances of losin' my shield for the sake of any kids what's nothing to me. You know the Juvenile System has more pull an' power'nd half of the judges in the country, and they'd mighty quick git us off the force if we wouldn't work ter their loiken. But you go ahead and do as you think best; I shan't work against you nohow, so long I kin kape meself clear," ended he, and turned towards the stairway.

At the outer door Officer Jack was met by a tall, neatly dressed and slightly stooped elderly man, with hard-set features, and dull-gray eyes. The incomer did not recognize the officer who was garbed as a civilian, and thus accosted him, "Do you live in this house?"

"No, sir, upon what grounds do you ask me?" returned Officer Jack, who suspected the stranger's errand.

Here the man stepped back, compared a note with the street number and, as he passed by the officer, he said, "Thank you, I won't need your assistance," upon which he walked up the two dark flights of stairs, reaching the top floor, upon which lived the Flanagans and the O'Neils. Their apartments were divided off by a centre hall.

Officer Jack turned and followed closely, halting back of him on the upper landing. The door leading from the hall to Flanagan's apartment stood three-quarters open. Officer O'Sullivan, who had preceded them a couple of minutes, was sitting on the edge of the stove with a cup partly filled with beer in his hands, listening to Mrs. Flanagan, who, with moist eyes, sat complaining of the misfortune which had befallen her holy picture. "Sure, I could always borrow a dollar upon it at McSheeney's to buy vettels, and now it ain't worth a cint."

The tall, lean stranger walked into the open door without announcement. His dull-gray eyes lit up and twinkled as he saw the disorderly apartment and noticed a couple of the Flanagan children lying asleep upon the floor in the corner between the coal box and a dish closet. The biggest boy, Jimmy, who was partly the cause of this day's tragic occurrences, sat beneath the table, smoking a cigarette.

"I guess I'm in the right place," announced the stranger, slowly moving towards the children. "I am an agent from the Juvenile System, and I received a telephone message to call here for some children——"

"Oh, mercy!" broke off Mrs. Flanagan with a loud screech which could be heard for a half block. Followed by a couple of pals, she rushed to where her children lay asleep, picked them up and hurried into the front room, where she hid them away in a clothes closet. Little Jimmy, much frightened, dropped his cigarette and crawled back of a chair, upon which sat a spooning young couple.

Mr. Flanagan, who only spoke when his wife was not present to lead, said: "You made a mistake here, all right."

"Sure yer did; I'll vouch fer these people," added Officer O'Sullivan in a tone of authority, raising himself from his sitting position. "These people are the finest in the ward, and are only havin' a little sociability of their own this noight——"

This little incident somewhat amused Officer Jack, who stood in the doorway and viewed the consternation which the Agent had caused. He did not directly wish the Flanagans' children to be carried away from a bad home to something worse, but at least he was certain that the O'Neil children were in care of better parents.

Mrs. Flanagan, in her intense fear that the Agent would follow her and take her children by force, with her women friends, closed and barricaded the door and sat trembling within, awaiting the departure of the Agent. The mere mention of the Juvenile System will throw the average poor mother into hysterics, and very often when one of its Agents appear upon the threshold a weak mother will sink into a swoon and youngsters, like chicks before a hawk, will creep underneath beds and bureaus and hide away in the furthest and darkest corners. No "Boogy man" scares a child as does the mention of the Juvenile System. Now after a moment of speculation the Agent viewed O'Sullivan and remarked, "You appear to be a police officer, are you not?"

Of course O'Sullivan felt proud to be so identified without his uniform, and answered impressively, "Ye are sure ter that, sir. I'm a regular appointed officer," he announced.

"Well, I'm a representative of the Juvenile System," showing his badge. "We are empowered to call upon your department upon any occasion we may choose in aiding our system. I therefore want to know and demand the arrest of the ones among these people who have wilfully sent a false message to our Humanitarian System and thus brought me on a fool's errand."

"Ye are sure ter that, Mr. Agent," replied Officer O'Sullivan. "We are instructed ter assist yer upon call, and I'll do me duty if ye'll tell me who to lock up."

Here the Agent reflected a moment, fumbled in his vest pocket and drew out a scrap of paper, and in a modified tone remarked: "Oh, that's so, I am looking for the O'Neil children, whose parents are in the lock-up for drunkenness."

Of course all the party knew it, but none had felt a desire to acquaint the Agent thereof. Officer O'Sullivan would rather not have been confronted so close with the question. He had noticed his brother officer's motion of silence upon the matter, but, on the other hand, he feared to offend the Juvenile System. He would have preferred to deceive his own chief, the commissioner, than the power behind this Humanitarian System. "Ter be sure, the O'Neils are in the lock-up, and their guilt will be settled by the Magistrate in the mornin'," answered the officer evasively.

"The Agent meant the children across the hall," here innocently announced a little lass among the party.

Upon this information the Agent passed Jack and crossed the hall to the O'Neils' room. Turning the knob of the door he found it locked. He gave a few loud raps, but received no reply.

"Some kind neighbor no doubt has taken the children in charge till their parents' release," ventured Officer Jack, with a view to discourage the Agent's further activity.

Manifestly the Agent could not afford to leave the premises without being fully assured that the ones he sought were not there. Now, to assure himself, he bent forward and peeped through the keyhole and breathlessly listened, after which he also tried to force open the door.

Upon this Jack jumped forward, and with a firm hand clasped him upon the shoulder as he said firmly: "Do not step beyond your authority; you will get yourself into trouble——"

"Authority? Trouble? What are you talking

about? Who are you? Here, lock that man up for interfering with our System's right," he sharply demanded of Officer O'Sullivan.

"Here, don't talk so fast, old man, or I will lock you up," now exclaimed Jack in a serious tone.

The Agent jumped back and demanded, "Are you an officer? Show me your shield."

Jack promptly complied, upon which the Agent began to explain his rights and authorities, which he did not conceal, superseded those of any police power or judge of the land.

"We need no warrant. We can simply break into any house upon our suspicion of certain conditions existing therein."

"This has been all true to your System," replied Officer Jack hotly, "the private corporation which you represent has been granted privileges which all work against the poor, defenceless class. The privileges you there exercise are contrary to the very constitution of our land. Your authority and right would get a set back were you to attack and practise your method upon a class with money to defend themselves."

"If you prevent me or interfere with my duties, I shall prefer charges against you before the Commissioner," threatened the Agent.

"I repeat, I'll not permit you to break into homes where doors are locked and bolted, unless you have stronger authority to act from," firmly replied Officer Jack. "If you make another attempt to push in the door I will lock you up."

The System's Agent understood fully the power and position which the System he represented held. Turning towards Officer O'Sullivan he said: "As a police officer, I demand your protection in carrying out my rights. Whether it be your brother officer or not," he added, pointing at Jack, "is of no concern if he hinders me from entering that apartment. It is upon you to lock him up and I'll follow along to the station house and make a complaint against him."

Poor Officer O'Sullivan had been two years on the police force, and in all but seven years in this country, so naturally he felt himself in a dilemma. He feared the Juvenile System, but in his short experience on the force he had never been called upon to lock up one of his own class. Of course, with an ordinary citizen, it would have been entirely different. He realized that his brother officer was determined, and he felt that an attempt by him to lock him up would meet with failure, as Jack was without doubt the abler man and had an equal advantage with clubs and pistols. Deliberating a moment, and scratching his head, he said: "Sure, this is new law ter me. If you will break no door," he directed the Agent, "till I go to the 'phone and spake to the Sergeant, I'll lave it ter him."

Here Officer O'Sullivan prepared to go to the nearest telephone and call up his precinct for advice. A slight laugh escaped Officer Jack; but he said no words.

Officer Jack was becoming angry with the obstinate Agent, who persisted in forcing the door. A slight scuffle ensued, and the door into O'Neil's apartment flew open. Jack lost his grip as the door yielded, and this caused the Agent to fall full length upon the floor. Raising himself quickly, he ran through the apartment, which was dimly lighted by a kerosene lamp, but what was not his disappointment and anger upon finding that no one was there.

Officer Jack who followed close upon the Agent felt as surprised as the System's man, but he was infinitely pleased to discover that the children were removed out of the System's clutches for the time being, at least.

Flanagan's guests, who had been as neutral spectators throughout the altercation, upon learning of the
disappearance of the O'Neil children, also felt anxious
to learn what had become of the little ones.

"Oh, God, hive mercy on the poor little kids, anyhow," now begged Mrs. Flanagan, who had ventured
out from her barricaded door and felt some twinges
of conscience, induced by her own threatened predica-
ment of losing her own children. "Sure enough, the
Juvenile System is no place for any woman's children,
even fer the O'Neils."

However, upon finding that the children were not
anywhere within the apartment, the Agent began
strongly to denounce Jack as being in compact with
some clique to foil the System, and he threatened to
make a charge against him before the Commissioner.
Then he hastily left the building, much to the relief of
all. Immediately the Flanagans' party broke up for
the night, the gathering having the record for excitement and novelty of sensation.

What had become of the O'Neil children is in itself
a little narrative. When the ambulance called to take
away injured Red Hook Dan, the excitement and attention of course was directed towards him and the attending surgeon. The entire Flanagan party, excepting Mrs. Flanagan and a couple of her pals, had followed them out into the street and mingled with the
crowd there gathered.

Lankey George, upon his victory, sought a safer
quarter. On his way to escape, it flashed through his
mind to carry the O'Neil children with him. He figured that this would prove an opportune moment while
everybody's interest was momentarily secured to the
ambulance call.

Turning back into the dark hall and ascending one

flight he encountered May Thornton, who, in the darkness, he barely recognized. She stood alone, supporting herself against the baluster. A stress of sympathy possessed George's breast as he noticed little May's dejection. He knew that Dan and she were lovers, and he suspected that the girl was too overcome with grief at the humiliation of her lover to remove from her position.

"I'm very sorry for you, little girl," he said sympathetically, resting his hand gently upon her shoulder. "I was kind of forced to do it; but poor Dan will come out all right, and it'll make him a better man."

"Don't feel sorry for me, Lankey. While I am sorry for Dan, and hope he will come out all right, don't let that bother you. I hope, as you, that he will be a better man for it," answered May quietly. George now proceeded to the upper floor, whereupon again May exclaimed: "Oh, I am sorry for the helpless children upstairs, and if I could I'd love to prevent the Juvenile System from getting hold of them."

"Thank you. You are just on my turn of mind, May Thornton," responded Lankey George as he turned back. "I need a good little girl like you to give me a hand. My plan is already laid out, but we must act quickly. A moment's delay might mean failure," he added, as he took May by the hand and drew her with him. Hurriedly, and on tip toes, they reached the upper hall.

The door leading to the Flanagans' apartment stood ajar. The few sympathizers within were sobbing and crying blasphemy upon the fighting pair who had caused the destruction of the holy picture, and so no notice was paid to the light steps without. Thus, unobserved, George and May managed to enter the O'Neils' apartment. Fortunately the key was stuck in the door—it was unlocked.

A glare of light from the street without shone in through the windows and showed the position of the sleeping children, still clinging to each other. Lankey did not have to give instruction as to what part May was to take in the abduction. Gently she folded her arms about the peacefully slumbering trio and tenderly whispered, "Children, dear children."

The unhappy little ones broke their sound sleep with a suddenness mixed with fright and joy. The two larger ones cried out: "Oh, mamma, mamma, mamma!" while the baby in the darkness fumbled out and reached May's neck, crying piteously as though its little heart would break.

"Oh, I'm so happy, mamma," cried little Louise, casting herself weeping into the lap of May who had bent down into a sitting position. Willie threw his arms around her waist and wept. "Mamma, I'll never smoke cigarettes again, and I'll always do as you tell me, and always be a good boy."

Lankey stood some little distance away unobserved by the children. As he saw them so suddenly awaken into happiness from which they were again to be disturbed upon finding that it was not their mother to whom they so fondly clung, the tears streamed down his cheeks. May Thornton wept bitterly, too, as these little ones happily clung on to her in their security.

"Children, children, dear children, I am not your mamma; but your mamma sent me to bring you to her," gently whispered May, caressing them all, and kissing the baby who had been the first to realize that they were deceived. The two larger ones in a tremor and much frightened attempted to draw away, but May, with a mother's instinct, gently held them close. She said softly, "Good children, do not fear nor worry, I'm going to bring you all to your mamma. Surely I am."

"We want our mamma," Willie and Louise now began to cry, though they made no attempt to draw away from the little foster mother who never for a moment ceased caressing and whispering encouragement to them. The baby at first reached out to return to Louise, but it was finally won over by strong caressing from May.

"Who is that man?" Willie suddenly cried as he saw the dark figure of Lankey George. Louise also noticed it, and with a cry of fear they both buried themselves deeper in the arms of May, whom a moment ago they had shunned.

"He is with me, children, to help to bring you to mamma," she said hastily in a soothing tone, and with light strokes upon their cheeks.

As Lankey noticed that he had frightened them, he quickly said: "You are all right, little children; your mamma wants you. Don't be afraid," he ended in good cheer as he drew a step nearer.

Willie was the first to overcome his fright, and now lightly inquired, "Where is papa?"

George and May strongly suspected that their father was incarcerated with their mother, and both simultaneously answered, "Your papa is with your mamma; they want us to fetch you to them."

Their childish surprise and fear quickly vanished. A few more reassuring nods and words made them feel that they were in good hands and soon thereupon they were calm and happy to go to join their parents.

George struck a match and lit a kerosene lamp which stood upon a centre table, and bade May prepare the children to go out. Meanwhile he made certain that the exit was clear. Hurriedly he went out into the hall, where, in the corner, a stairway led to the roof. This was covered with a scuttle, which he quickly removed and returned ready to smuggle the children out of the house.

The children were now eager to go, and were all the while talking about their papa and mamma. May Thornton carried the baby and took Louise by the arm, while George led Willie. For fear that some one would go in and despoil the neat and well-furnished apartment, Lankey locked the door and stuck the key into his pocket.

"Don't make any noise now, youngsters. We want to get away from these bad people to your mamma," whispered May, and they, without a sound, stole up the stairway to the roof. After they crawled through, Lankey placed the scuttle back into its position, and with light steps they hurried over the roofs, reaching the last of the row of six similar houses.

"I know a family in this house who will be all right till their mother comes," lightly whispered George to May, as he bent forward to open the scuttle of that house by which to effect an entrance.

"No, no, we want to go home to our mamma now!" cried Willie, who partly understood it. Louise joined in the demand while the baby hugged its rescuer closer.

With a look at George May said: "We will take them down to my nice little house, where their mamma told us to bring them."

Lankey George understood May, and in like tone responded: "Sure we will." They walked down the couple of flights of stairs and out into the street and hurried towards Hoyt Street, where they halted just long enough to enter a confectionery shop to buy some candy. Then they boarded a Hamilton Avenue car, and in less than twenty minutes reached their destination. Thus, instead of dropping into the apartment of

Lankey's acquaintance with the little ones, they went on towards May's home unnoticed by any one.

Though it was close upon midnight, May Thornton's mother and sisters were happy to be disturbed in so good a cause, and proved as kind and good companions as little May herself. Some food was urged upon the children, as it was understood that they had had nothing since early noon, just before the arrest of the mother.

It was decided that Lankey George should go to the Magistrate Court in the morning and give any aid he could to the children's parents, and inform them that the young ones were in good care. Meanwhile May was to remain with the little ones and make them happy until such a time as they could be restored to each other.

CHAPTER V.

IN THE MAGISTRATE'S COURT.

Lankey George arranged to be in the Court as early as eight o'clock the next morning. The regular Court opening at these petty courts is set for 8.30. He took a seat in the front row in the outer circle, which is spaced off for spectators. Lankey was soon followed by scores of others, who filed into the seats as they entered, and at the time designated for proceedings to begin, the stuffy little court room of Brooklyn swamps was packed.

The spectators were an odd variety, but all were from the poorer class. Youths and the aged parents and relatives and friends of those within the pen, were there, as well as some disinterested ones who, in their idle moments, felt a desire to witness the tragedies and comedies so freely offered.

The walls about the stuffy court were lined with civilian-dressed and uniformed officers, who were detailed for certain purposes. Within the railing were a few regular court lawyers, mostly ravening wolves, who could be had for hire. Agents of the Juvenile System were also on hand, for these are as busy and important in all of our poor man's courts as the judges themselves. A few "Slum Ladies" were also on hand. These social workers aim to aid human progress, though they mistakenly work hand in hand with the Juvenile System.

Mondays are usually heavy calendar days in these lower courts. The offenders brought there have but one day in a week in which to indulge their appetites, and this fast swells the list upon this particular day.

As the dial of the clock showed nine-forty-five the Magistrate appeared, and with dignity seated himself. His honor, the Judge, was a personage of medium height, slimly built and of declining age. He wore a heavy, dark, drooping mustache, and did not look over intelligent, nor well read, one would judge him to be sitting there more for show than for justice.

Several cases were handled in fast routine; the charges were mostly drunkenness and disorderly conduct. Other social offenders of higher crimes were also brought there, but none were held for punishment who were lucky enough to have some influential friend to arrange matters. Where the complaint was not directly backed with power, it was apt to be disregarded.

The O'Neils' case had not yet reached his honor, as these friendless people had no one to hurry it. The influential ones, of whom the Magistrate had previously been informed, were disposed of with merely a customary rebuke.

The first case in which punishment was dealt out was the one preceding that of Mrs. O'Neil. This offender received a sentence of thirty days on "the Island" for failing to pay a board bill to the Juvenile System for his children. The indicted man claimed that this was not due the System, as it had taken and withheld his children without particular cause, and he proclaimed his own ability to board and maintain them at his own home. But justice must yield to superior rule, and the protesting delinquent was detained for punishment.

When Mrs. O'Neil's case appeared she was designated as having been entered as an unknown intoxicated woman. The ordinary habitual "Pen" frequenter hastily responds to the penkeeper's call, but to Mrs. O'Neil the ordeal was new. Besides, she was weak, humiliated and nervous. Her face showed deep worry and anguish. "Here, here, here! ole gal, git a mov' on yo'; the jedge kin't sit her' all day waitin' for ye," roughly declared the doorkeeper as he stepped within the pen, reaching to drag her out.

"O—h," she drew with a piteous cry and staggered. "Why am I so punished? Where is my husband? And give me my little ones," she sobbed.

Another officer rushed to the assistance of the doorman and aided in holding the fainting woman upon her feet. These officers of less intellect and of rough manner are not quick to feel nor to perceive real suffering; their daily contact with brutality, sins and deceit does not refine nor soften their hearts.

"None ov' that shoin' ov' and kids playin', me gal, we'v used ter that. The jedge will lave ye go iv he sees fit," remarked the penkeeper in light sympathy as with his brother officer he dragged her limp form through the door.

That Mrs. O'Neil was not shamming soon dawned upon the officers in whose hands she was. "Sure this is the real thing," whispered the one to the other, as they heavily brought her before the bar and were compelled to clasp their arms around her waist to maintain her in an upright position.

His honor measured her and looked up kindly, realizing that the person before him suffered greatly. He remained silent and mildly gazed at her, permitting her to be relieved by her free flood of tears.

Police officers, clerks and attendants whispered to each other and stepped closer. The spectators in the outer circle arose and craned their necks. All felt that this woman was no habitual social offender, nor was she acquainted with prison and court ordeals. There was a momentary stillness as of the grave, which was only interrupted by the faint spasmodic sounds of her violent emotion.

Lankey George, who knew the O'Neils only from casual description given by the Flanagans, suspected this unhappy woman to be Mrs. O'Neil. Lightly he left his seat and entered within the enclosure where she stood. He was promptly met by a court lawyer, who, in confidence, offered for a five dollar bill to have her acquitted. Disregarding the lawyer's proposition with a glance of scorn, he walked close to one of the officers whose embrace held the tottering woman.

The Magistrate had noticed Lankey, and seemed glad that some one should appear for the woman's relief. Officer O'Sullivan and Jack Stevenson were the complainants. The latter looked at her piteously, but both of them moved nervously. The sergeant, who had feared Stevenson's attitude to the force, had also come to court, and stood a little distance off, constantly sending strong glances to Jack.

The complaint had been drawn up in customary form at the precinct house. It charged an unknown woman with being intoxicated and disorderly. The Magistrate re-read the complaint. Looking first at the officers, he then mildly addressed Mrs. O'Neil without demanding her name: "This complaint charges you with——"

Here he halted, leaned back and combed his hair with his fingers. Sending a reproachful look at the officers, without finishing reading aloud the charges which appeared against her, he said: "You may go home, where you belong, my good woman."

"T-h-a-n-k you," with an audible sob, answered Mrs. O'Neil, who had been somewhat relieved by her tears. Raising herself from the officer's support, she steadied herself against the bar and in faint collected voice demanded: "Where is my husband?" Turning her head she looked around disappointedly as she cried out: "Oh, they have killed him! My husband is murdered! I saw them killing him," she ended hysterically, and fell, grief-stricken, into a sobbing. Lankey George managed to calm her by strongly pleading for the sake of her little children, who were longing and crying for her, she must bear up.

At once there arose a strong commotion within the court-room because of this strong accusation of the arraigned woman, which all knew to be directed against the police officers. The Magistrate looked surprised. Quickly scanning the list of police complaints and finding no one to correspond with her case, he demanded of the officers: "Where is this woman's husband? Why don't you bring him?"

"He's takin' ter the hospital a little while ago, jedge," answered Officer O'Sullivan, before the judge had finished his query. "But sure he'll be all right in a day or two, yer honor."

The Magistrate had not been acquainted with the details of the preceding night at the precinct, nor was it within his jurisdiction to go beyond matters coming before him. There had been no influence here, either way, to bear upon him. He was free to coincide with his own conscience, and naturally he sympathized with the injured woman, and with much kindness said: "I cannot help you now, my good woman; but after he leaves the hospital, which the officers expect he will in a day or so, he will be brought before me, and you may trust to me that I will send him home to you as quick as I can express the words of release. Now, my good woman," he advised, "go home to your children and don't weep any longer; it will not add to your strength."

The Juvenile System's Agent listened to this case. Upon hearing of children at home and the husband in the hospital, he measured up the fairly well-dressed Mrs. O'Neil, and began to take business-like notes. This Humanitarian System cannot afford to step in and care for children where the conditions of home and parents are shown to be too poverty-stricken. The Agent's conclusions regarding the O'Neils were that their system could safely assure guardianship and maintain these children, and that the cost of their support would be easy collectible. Mrs. O'Neil's dejected spirit therefore caused the Juvenile System's agent to be correspondingly joyful.

Tom Ryan, a fellow worker, who had called at the precinct in behalf of O'Neil, with the superintendent of the Planet Mill, had been called to testify to O'Neil's good character and give all the aid they could. Of course, their mission was at an end. They did not know Mrs. O'Neil, though both of them knew Lankey George. They knew George to be a decent fellow, but also knew that he never carried large means about him. As they were about to depart, good-hearted Tom Ryan said, "I think we ought to provide a carriage to take the poor woman home, she looks worn out." Here he fumbled in his pocket and remarked: "I think I have enough——"

"You keep your change," broke in the superintendent. "You work too hard for your couple of dollars. I'll pay and don't say a word." In a second breath he added: "That O'Neil has been with us a short time, but he's one of the best fellows we ever had, and I'll see to it that the firm pays him his wages while he's in the hospital."

The little O'Neil children had awakened as early as seven o'clock on the morning after their arrival at May Thornton's. Mother Thornton had prepared some cocoa and dainty home-made cake which had been liberally streaked with jam. One of the elder Thornton boys, before going to his work, had bought from a toy store around the corner a small set of carpenter's tools for Willie to play with, and May's older sister Katie had provided Louise with a set of kitchen utensils including a set of dishes and a little stove. A large doll which would emit sounds upon touching it brought solace to the baby.

The good food and the toys caught the little ones' interest as soon as they were awake. Though at their first break of sleep they had asked for their parents, the inquiry had died away with confusion of joy.

Before May would be permitted to dress the baby she had to consent to allow it to play a while with the doll. In an amateur, motherly way it fondly put the doll asleep and was loudly delighted where upon squeezing it, it squeaked like a real little baby.

The process of getting into their clothes for the two older ones, too, was slow; though they could dress themselves, they had no time to do so. Willie had to try his saw and hammer and examine his tool chest, while little Louise wanted to set her miniature table and pretend to light the fire in her stove. It was only after much persuasion that they found time to eat their cake and drink their cocoa.

Mother Thornton was greatly affected so suddenly to see these little ones wafted from grief to happiness; she would intermingle tears with laughter as she studied their light spirits. She was a good mother herself, and knew the nature of children, but never before had she had such a chance to study it.

May's older sister was a forelady in the American Manufacturing Company of Brooklyn, and of course had to be at her work, but May stayed at home. She was the real foster mother, and could not remember ever having felt so happy. The temporary care had been shared with May's mother; both would join in amusing the little ones, and now and then take a hand in straightening up the house and preparing the noon-day meal.

As the parlor clock struck ten a messenger knocked upon the kitchen door. It was a message for May from Red Hook Dan, in which he begged her forgiveness and asked her to call and see him at the hospital. He ended his note with the assertion that he begun to realize that May was made of the right "stuff."

Of course, May had no time to play being sentimental with big folks. She always had loved Dan and felt that he loved her, too, but her mind and heart now told her that she could no longer love him, even in his uniform. Upon any other occasion she would have hidden the note from her mother and buried it close to her heart, but without a touch of feeling she now threw it upon the table in front of her mother and, with a faint sigh, remarked: "I'm sorry for poor Dan, but I don't love him any more. I shudder when I think of the cruel look in his eyes as I pleaded for these children, and I fear that he'll never make a good——"

Here she halted. Mother Thornton read her thoughts and was much pleased that she had broken away from Dan, whom she as a mother was better able to judge. She said: "It is no use trying to reform a man if he has not the qualities in him to make a man. No ordinary woman can make him so with a lasting effect. A good woman may improve upon a man who has within him a good conscience and an appreciation of right, but we can never inlay character in man where there is nothing to build upon. Dan used to beat his mother and kick his father; and a man who will beat his mother will beat his wife. Be sure of that, May."

"Don't fear, mother, I'll never marry Dan, even though he should rise to police commissioner," added on May, as she picked up one of the baby's shoes which it had kicked off.

It was nearly eleven o'clock, and, without a moment's intermission, the children had played with their toys from the time they arose. The baby had torn off an arm of her doll and had shredded its little dress; Louise had broken three of her plates, and Willie had broken his saw on Mrs. Thornton's kindling wood. Though they had been awarded much pleasure the first overwhelming joy had now become thinned. Baby began to cling less to her doll and hang more upon May, and the two older ones also showed less interest in their toys.

Though their grief did not bear heavily upon them as they had a parental care which, while not real, naturally could not fail to convey the feeling of trust from a child. A kind word from May or Mrs. Thornton would soon set them at ease again.

"Oh, Mamma! Mamma! Mamma!" suddenly cried Willie, with a loud start, reaching both his arms out. From the window he had perceived a carriage halting in front of the entrance and had recognized the mother who alighted with the help of Lankey.

The joyful words started little Louise from the floor, overturning dishes, which flew scattering about the floor. The baby uttered a few light cries in sympathy and hugged her foster mother still closer.

The scene in this lower hall was deeply pathetic, though blended with joy. Their mother, sad and weak, was touched with joy, and could not stand upon her feet. She rested herself upon the steps. She sadly reflected upon what had befallen her husband as she hugged and in turn was embraced and kissed by the little ones who clung madly to her.

Tears rolled down the cheeks of the trio; from happiness, disappointment, and sorrow poor Mrs. O'Neil's frame shook with emotion; she could not utter a word. Lankey George was overcome, also, and tears trickled down his cheeks. To overcome the effect, he turned and walked down the lower hall and stood a moment at the door leading to the courtyard.

May had brought the baby down to receive its mamma. The sight so affected her that she could not control herself. The young one stretched out its tiny arms, and gave loud cries of joy. Mrs. O'Neil, much overcome and faint, buried her head in the little cluster of lovers and sobbingly caressed them.

"Oh, mamma, come up and see the nice things the lady bought for me," broke out Louise as the first tension of meeting had worn off. "Oh, yes, mamma, and all the things I've got," joined Willie, beginning to explain in detail the various little tools and their uses.

The baby gladly hopped back to her foster mother, and Lankey returned to the group and gently helped Mrs. O'Neil upstairs.

Naturally the poor woman was exhausted; she had not taken a morsel of food for twenty-four hours.

The hard prison floor with the other cruel ordeals, fears, and worries was sufficient to have incapacitated even a stronger woman; but she was brave and made strong effort to control herself. Once within the room, she was placed in a rocking-chair, and was soon cheered by her happy little ones and her kind new friends. But now and again, upon thinking of her husband's plight, she would sink into sad spells which, however, would soon be dispelled by the tumult and light hearts of her little ones. Though, of course, they longed for their papa, they remained measurably contented with their mamma and the good people in whose hands they were.

Mrs. Thornton quickly prepared a cup of tea and toast for Mrs. O'Neil. She feared to offer her anything heavier after so long a fast, but soon after gave her some mutton broth which aided much to strengthen the weak woman.

CHAPTER VI.

THE CRITICAL DILEMMA OF LANKEY GEORGE.

Upon his early rounds the turnkey at the precinct house had been attracted by loud groanings emanating from the direction of O'Neil's cell. It was discovered that the unfortunate man was suffering from a hemorrhage and lay in great agony upon the floor of the cell.

The large measure of whiskey which on the early evening had been poured into him, had temporarily revived and eased him, but the effect of the beating had told upon him after the stimulant had ceased to act. The concrete flooring upon which he rested chilled him and stiffened his limbs, so, at an early hour, in a precarious state, he had been removed to the hospital.

It was quite natural that the acting captain should feel uneasy, particularly so, as upon his return to the station house from court, he was confronted with a special message from headquarters ordering him to bring over a full statement of the facts which bore upon the case of the man now lying critically ill at the hospital.

What the sergeant feared most of all was that it would lead to a general investigation, thus depriving him of his captaincy for the present. He also knew that the general public had long felt disposed to remove the head of this department, and was looking for grounds to work upon. Not only the mayor and the governor were taking a hand in it, but the People's party, a new political organization, was using the inefficiency and brutality of the police department as campaign material for coming election.

Thus, after a brief cogitation while walking up and down, he called his doorman and Officer O'Sullivan into his private room, where he began: "I fear we have to do something to save ourselves. You two officers have always stuck to the department and are good, useful men. This Jack Stevenson I never had much use for; he's one of them proud Yankees better fitted for a Bible class than fer the force; therefore, I've made up my mind to shift the entire blame over upon him, and I've made some erasures upon the blotter and added on a charge against him. Besides," continued he, "I just learned that there has this mornin' been lodged a complaint with the commissioner against Jack Stevenson by the Juvenile System. He's charged with interferin' with the System's agent in performin' his duty, and he not only threw impudence and slurs against the System, but threatened to arrest its agent.

Of course," continued he, "any sane officer should know that this would never do. This System has a chartered and granted right to act as it sees fit, and naturally a patrolman and officer of the law should have known his place and aided the System instead of binderin' it. This charge alone against Jack would get him off the force, and it's our good luck that it should happen at this time, as he now will be afforded no chance at all at his trial before the commissioner."

Thus, while the sergeant and his officers busied themselves plotting against unfortunate Officer Stevenson, Lankey George and the Thorntons were as busy easing the sufferings of poor Mrs. O'Neil. May Thornton had asked permission from her employers to stay away from work for a few days, so she could care for and cheer the stricken woman. Like her husband, Mrs. O'Neil contracted a cold upon the bare cemented flooring of her cell, and a terrible cough had set in which, however, the good care of her benefactors soon broke up.

The first couple of days Lankey took a ride to the park with Willie and Louise, and, upon his return, in company with May Thornton, went in search for different apartments for Mrs. O'Neil, who dreaded to return to her former abode.

In the next block to the Thorntons was found a vacant apartment, and Mrs. O'Neil did not need any urging to take it. Though the neighborhood in which the Thorntons lived was populated with a poor class, comprising many nationalities, there did not exist any clannishness, and a newcomer was permitted to live as he chose. Mrs. O'Neil, moreover, now found a strong friend in the Thorntons, who were among the oldest of settlers and respected by all.

Mrs. O'Neil was naturally too weak to aid in moving her furniture to their new home, but she had a good helper in Lankey, who, upon cleaning out and making ready her new quarters, assisted in making the transfer.

Early the third morning, as Lankey started for the O'Neils' Bond Street apartment, to take up carpets and pack the goods ready for a moving van, upon leaving, he called May Thornton to his side, and whispered that she must keep a good look out for the Juvenile System's agent. "They are on these children's track now. I know their methods. Like a shark follows a ship into mid-ocean, they'll keep up a search for prey."

Lankey George felt himself a very happy man that he could be of assistance to this unfortunate couple. That he had been the means of saving the children from the hands of the System sang like a triumph within his heart. This thought added to his height and spirit. In his late years he had stalked about with downcast face and stooped shoulders, but in this morning's walk he stood erect, throwing his head upward. Now and then he would lightly whistle a tune which he would relieve with a murmur of gratitude that it had been his luck to be present that eventful evening.

Though well known, he had never been popular, but now, since his triumph over the bully, strong Red Hook Dan, the probation officer, he found himself thrust into great popularity. As he walked along the street urchins would cry: "Hallo, Lankey." Corner loafers and gang members would sing out: "Bully for you, George," and factory girls nodded approvingly to him and smiled as they passed.

Lankey George would return the compliments without apparent emotion. He knew they were all tendered to him because of his beating Dan Connors, whom all feared and considered a fighter. George did not rejoice in his victory, but it was the blocking of the Juvenile System which made him happy.

Upon reaching the house in which the O'Neils lived and turning toward the entrance, he was accosted by a guard employed in the Kings Park Hospital, who delivered a message signed by the hospital authorities which stated that his wife had at two o'clock that morning passed away. It bade him call immediately to provide for the body's removal, or she would be interred in Potter's Field.

This sudden blow momentarily staggered Lankey, though he knew of his wife's hopeless condition and felt that death would be a relief to her. In an effort to regain his possession, he supported himself against the guard-rail leading toward the entrance.

Upon delivering his message, the guard departed. Lankey remained distracted, standing as in a trance. This announcement awakened in him his whole life from childhood. He reflected back to the day when he left his home to go out into the world. The first day he met her as a pretty, blooming girl came vividly to his mind. He remembered the first bliss of his married life where his healthy, hopeful, happy wife stood beside him. This brought him remembrance of the one child and then the other and the last that had come into the world to add cheerfulness and happiness. Suddenly he saw, as a phantom, the black hand of the Juvenile System one day carrying away his little ones. The ghastly thought of breaking up his home and having his wife removed to an insane ward came over him. He trembled as he recalled the hardship and longing which he had endured in past years. His mind whirled as he thought of his little children who had been robbed of him and persuaded by the Juvenile System to go to western farms where the last inkling and trace of them disappeared. To Lankey it was all a cruel fate. He now stood alone, bereft of all; helpless and hopeless, he was left to endure till the end should come.

Among his sad reflections, as he there stood, would gleam thoughts of the past few days, where he had aided and relieved the unfortunate O'Neils. He pictured the conditions from which he had saved them. So great was the stress of feeling that to remain upon his feet he had to support himself against the railing.

Thus in hurricanes of thought stood Lankey George, paying no attention to remarks or compliments paid him by neighbors, in whose esteem he so suddenly had arisen. Presently he was disturbed by a hand laid upon his shoulder, and with a light jerk.

"You are Lankey George, are you not?" was demanded. The interrupter was a police officer in civilian attire.

Lankey drew himself quickly together, a second or two stared at the officer as if in doubt of his query. "What, what did you ask me?" he stuttered.

The officer momentarily released his hold and repeated his question. Upon which Lankey, now fully aroused, coolly replied: "Yes, sir, that is what they call me."

"You are under arrest," promptly imposed the officer. "At what I have heard of you, you are rather a dangerous person. I think I better put the clippers on you," he said, as he slipped the handcuffs over George's wrist and bade him walk along.

This arrest, so sudden and unexpected, dealt Lankey George a further stroke. Scarcely able to maintain himself upright, he was dragged to the precinct house, and hauled before the sergeant, who eyed him with his usual accusing glance, void of sympathy.

George had then no thoughts upon anything. To inquire the crime for which he was brought there did not enter his mind. Blank in main, without a murmur, stared at the sergeant, who now said: "You are under arrest for assaulting Probation Officer Dan Connors, who now lies critically ill at the City Hospital."

Lankey was still too overcome to give reply which, however, would have been of no avail. After undergoing the preliminaries of taking down his pedigree, he underwent the ordeal of being searched. The note in his pocket from the hospital authorities refreshed his mind, he began to explain, reaching the sergeant the letter. That judicial person returned it, saying: "I ain't reading nobody's papers," but recommended: "Keep it, and show it to the judge if you like. I can't upon so serious a charge even release you on bail bond. You'll have to stay in jail till your case comes up. I never seen the time yet but that you fellows did not have one excuse nor another." He then motioned an officer to take the prisoner off to a cell, where he was to await arraignment before a magistrate.

It was, however, still early, being only ten minutes past eleven o'clock, but the court of the swamps had closed a few minutes previously, and his honor had left for private haunts. This caused unfortunate George to remain in the precinct cell over night.

It was naturally a long and dreadful day and night. There were no accommodations to encourage either sitting or lying down. He had but the bare cemented flooring of this damp basement cell upon which to rest his body. Through ordeal and strain, tortured in mind and body, he slid to the floor. Soon numb and stiff, he was no longer conscious of aches, but his dulled mind could not keep from pounding, and he longed for death. As he thought of his wife's demise he yearned to lie in peace beside her, but this release was not to be; he had to live and suffer.

Almost in a state of utter collapse, long before court opening, he was brought to the temporary detention room behind the court to await the arrival of the magistrate. It was, however, some little relief to the body, for the room had wooden flooring and a few benches. Among many miserable creatures arraigned for guilt or innocence, his uncomfortable mind strove to consider his situation. He would spasmodically awaken to wonder if he fared worse than half of the world. "As the withering plant dies from lack of sunshine, and the desert suffers from drought, such are man's fortuitous courses in life," mused he. "Yet within it all there is a power of will and strength to endure. What I have suffered will aid another, and my purpose in life shall be to strengthen that of others," thought he. "Every punishment has its rewards. That I saved the O'Neils from perhaps a cruel fate atones to me for more than my sufferings."

Lankey's reflections were interrupted by the "penkeeper," who opened the door and began to empty the locker. A couple of unfortunate women who appeared dead to the world of shame were the first to be taken before the magistrate. They had, like Lankey, lain in a cement padded cell all night, but liquor for which cause they had been brought there, made endurance possible. Sobered up they now apparently were, but they showed neither sign of repentance nor humiliation. That they were old offenders of the law was evident, but whatever caused their downfall was not considered. Society's duties had ended; the stigma was upon them.

A few more prisoners were brought out before Lankey's turn came. Some were returned to the pen for a further hearing, while others received their discharge. Finally it fell upon Lankey George to appear, and the "penkeeper" grabbed him by the arm. This procedure, a classified dignity of magistrate courts to lead prisoners with a secured hold to the bar, could perhaps here have been spared, as the court swarms with civilian and uniformed officers. Any attempt at escape would seem futile. Though George longed for his freedom, he was far too weak to make any effort to secure it.

The magistrate looked over the charge, and explained the seriousness of the case. Lankey, who had neither enjoyed sleep nor rest and looked decidedly unkempt, made no good impression upon the judge, who answered: "I shall remand you to the county jail to await the outcome of Dan Connors' injuries."

The penkeeper prepared to drag Lankey back into the cell.

"Your Honor," pleaded Lankey, collecting himself, "my wife just died, and——"

"Oh, I can't help that," broke off the judge. "You had no business to get into trouble. But I'll fix the bail at fifteen hundred dollars, if that'll do you any good," he ended sarcastically, and motioned the penkeeper to bring out another prisoner.

Of course, Lankey George, a poor man with no real estate, or rich friends, or political backing, could never hope to reach that amount of bail bond. It appeared to him as though society singled out crime according to material, wealth, and position. The poverty branded are cast upon the reef, while the ones affording a bail bond are picked up from the waves and enjoy the freedom of the social craft. Guilty or not, the poverty-ridden must linger in the pit of crime until the day that justice shall proceed and conclude. "The justice within it all is an iniquity measured by the wrongs of society," thought Lankey, as he was led back into the pen to await "Black Maria," the only public transportation utility open in common to the poor.

After Lankey had been assigned to his new prison quarters, realizing the inevitableness of his situation, he begged a guard to attend to the sending off of a message to some up-State relative whom he wished to look after the remains of his wife.

The guard consented to attend it upon a retaining fee of a one-dollar bill, excluding the cost of the message. But what was Lankey's surprise upon searching his pocket and finding but a five-cent piece which was hidden in a corner of his trousers' pocket. Upon leaving the O'Neils, he had two one-dollar bills. Had he been picked by the police? Or was it in the cell, or had he fumbled and lost it during his bewildered spell? He did not know. But all trace of it was gone, and with it his hope.

Lankey George now carried the yoke; he had failed to get his liberty. He was hindered in tendering a last look at his unfortunate wife's remains. He had no way or means to appeal to relatives and the Potter's Field, with no holier ceremonies than such as attend the burying of a dog, was to be the lot of his wife. A hopeless despair engulfed him.

CHAPTER VII.

JACK STEVENSON REDUCED FROM RANKS.

Several days passed. Lankey had no real estate friends to go upon his bail, nor had he politicians or friends to speak for him. His pleadings gained no concessions. The jail-keepers bestowed no other consolation than a shrug of their shoulders. And thus while Lankey George languished in a cell, his unfortunate wife was without ceremony and without followers or mourners, laid away in the city's free burial place.

In the meantime Mrs. O'Neil stayed at the Thorntons. May Thornton felt very uneasy as the second and third day passed and Lankey had not reported. To all their understanding he had intended to prepare for the removal of O'Neil's household goods. Owing to their short acquaintance with him, they naturally indulged in many surmises.

Mrs. O'Neil dreaded much to return to Bond Street, so May Thornton, much disappointed in Lankey, now personally took charge of removing the belongings to their new home.

The third day following Lankey's arrest, as she prepared to go to the O'Neils' Bond Street home, the postman handed her a letter. It was from her old lover, Dan Connors. She was about to throw it into the fire without reading it, but her eyes happened to fall upon a certain line which bore the name of Lankey George. She withdrew the letter and read therein that Lankey was in jail awaiting the outcome of Connors' injuries. The letter also mentioned that the O'Neil children were concealed in her home, but it ended with a plea that if she would forgive him he would not press the charge of assault against Lankey George, nor would he mention the part Lankey had taken in effecting the children's escape from the Juvenile System.

Thus quickly dawned upon May Thornton what had happened to Lankey. The disappointment she had felt toward him promptly flamed to a desire to go to his assistance. She further despised Dan Connors for his arbitrary attempts to regain her affection. This letter, which so clearly unfolded a distinction between law and justice, she secreted, and before proceeding to Bond Street she sought her landlord, who consented to go upon Lankey's bail bond, whereupon he could receive his release until a future trial day.

Overjoyed at his release, that evening and the following day Lankey spent assisting Mrs. O'Neil to adjust her new home. Though he was happy to be helpful, he was sorrowful that he had not been permitted to attend the last offices to his beloved wife. Both Mrs. O'Neil and the Thorntons sympathized strongly with him. Though he did not admit it, they agreed that the cause of present difficulty lay in the fact that he had fought for justice and aided in protecting the helpless O'Neil children from the tentacles of the Juvenile System.

Lankey's trial day had at last been reached; Dan Connors had received his discharge from the hospital and could personally appear against him. The charge preferred against Lankey was assault and interfering against an officer while attending his duty. The System's agent as a witness in his behalf verified that he was called upon by a probation officer to remove children who were abandoned by a pair of drunken parents, and that the prisoner had interfered with the officer.

Lankey had no witnesses to testify in his behalf as to his assertion that the fight had occurred at a private function and was entered in self-defence. The Flanagans and their guests of that night were too friendly toward Dan to go forward and testify to the real facts.

The judge showed some inclination toward taking side with Red Hook Dan, and began his decision: "While this probation officer was on his post and attending his duties, as any regular appointed officer, you were guilty by your act of interfering, and you committed an assault which might have ended with a loss to life, and I will——"

"Your Honor," here broke in Officer Jack Stevenson, stepping forward to the bar, and voluntarily coming to Lankey's aid, "if you will permit me to state a fact, this probation officer had no business in the house where the fight occurred. If you will kindly refer to the precinct station you will find that he was assigned to duties at some other post than that vicinity."

As Officer Jack finished, May Thornton stepped forward nervously, and, without a word, reached the judge the compromising letter which she had received from Dan Connors.

His Honor read the letter, weighed the matter over a moment, and in a changed tone directed to Dan Connors said: "I begin to think you got what you deserve, and you can feel yourself lucky if your police job does not end where it began." Turning to Lankey, he nodded: "You are discharged."

The System's agent, who had appeared in behalf of Dan Connors, had recognized in Jack Stevenson the officer who had interrupted him in his act of carrying away the children, and could barely hold himself from upbraiding him before the judge.

Officer Jack did not know at this time that the System's agent had preferred charges against him, but he did not have to wait long to become so acquainted, for upon his return to the precinct at noon roll call, he was served with a command from the police commissioner to call on a subsequent date to answer to various complaints filed against him.

While Dan Connors felt greatly disappointed with the outcome of his trial, May Thornton was highly pleased, and innocently pressed Lankey's hand which he returned with a thankful look, as both departed for her home in Van Brunt Street.

The trial day of Officer Jack Stevenson was eventually reached, but he was not to enjoy a fate similar to that of Lankey George. The charges preferred against him were serious. While they were garbled and false, they were backed by authority, and the poor officer saw before him the worst experience of his life.

Harry O'Neil, it had been reported, was still in a dangerous state, his sickness had developed into pneumonia, and the entire blame had, by threads of falsehood, been strongly turned against Jack Stevenson. The acting captain and Officer O'Sullivan and the doorman all testified falsely that the injuries were received with kicks and blows from Jack, and that it was only their timely intervention which saved the sick man's life.

Poor Jack Stevenson could offer no defence; his words were strongly overweighed by those of his superiors and his fellow officers, who thus planned to conceal their own outrage. O'Neil, of course, was not present to testify in his behalf.

The next complaint against Officer Jack was assault and interfering with the duties of a Juvenile System's agent. This charge proved as serious and strong as the preceding one. High officials of the System were permitted to be present and forced the complaint. His fellow brother, Officer O'Sullivan, here also testified. He stated that the System only demanded its right, while the agent complained that Officer Jack Stevenson, besides refusing to assist him, actually hindered him in performing his duty, and cuffed and kicked him and used abusive language.

Officer Jack again saw himself in a sad dilemma. He was not, however, permitted to admit that he had interfered in the agent's attempt to force the door, and to explain his conduct. He had simply violated a right of an institution which ruled with a hand of iron.

That poor Jack Stevenson was doomed to fare worse is obvious. The commissioner, much inflamed, arose and commanded Jack to step forward. Removing the shield and cutting off his buttons from the officer's coat, he sternly cried: "You're a disgrace to the force; you should be swung in the stirrups and hung in the gallows! It's the likes of you what puts a blot upon our police force, which has the reputation of bein' the finest in the world." Turning to the System's agent, he continued: "I shall advise you to swear out a warrant for his arrest because of his cowardly way of kickin' you while in your act of rights and duties."

This charge the agent forthwith preferred, being encouraged to do so by high officials of the System. It aided them in showing and maintaining their full power; besides, it should ever be a wholesome lesson to the public to respect their officials.

As poor Jack Stevenson was dishonored and placed under arrest, he bravely replied: "The first charge against me is an infamous lie, and will in time righten itself; as to the second charge, I will say as a free-born man I shall never yield my rights to fight for anyone born under similar statute. I only upheld the Constitution of the United States, which this individual private corporation is daily violating and is permitted to violate. In my ten years of police duty, you have never before had occasion to find an offence against me, and I am indeed proud that you could find no truer cause than the one of infamy against the force, and the other of resisting an injustice against society."

That Officer Jack Stevenson had been dismissed from the force and was now under arrest for assaulting the Juvenile System's agent flew through all boroughs. Evening papers were full of details; some sided with the dismissed officer, while others took an opposite view. Reporters interviewed the unfortunate man in his cell, where he coolly and without complaint explained that all would soon right itself.

May Thornton had been on an errand downtown, and learned from the news bulletin of the trial and dismissal of Officer Jack. She recognized in him the officer who, a couple of days ago, had come to her rescue in having Lankey freed, and she heartily wished that she could return his kindness. Upon reaching home, she sorrowfully recounted the officer's fate, but neither of the Thorntons, nor Mrs. O'Neil believed that Jack Stevenson could have been guilty of brutality.

Scarcely had May finished relating the news when Lankey George hastily opened the door and entered. He had just returned from a visit to the hospital. "I have good news," he exclaimed, as he smiled and threw himself upon a chair. "Harry O'Neil is doing fine; he sat up in bed, and we had quite a chat together. He expects to be out in a——"

"Oh, my! the bulletin said that he was very low with pneumonia," broke in May, as she asked: "Didn't you hear about the police trial?"

"Certainly I did," quickly responded Lankey. "It was a put-up job. Jack Stevenson was a man of no use to the police force, and the Juvenile System had made up their mind to break him for interfering with its agent. Between the police and the System it was thought an opportune moment to get him off the force while Harry O'Neil was sick. It was feared that upon his release from the hospital that testimonies might be brought out involving other officers, and the charge of the Juvenile System alone would then

73

not have been sufficient ground upon which to break him. All these details," he added, "had been overheard and confided to Harry O'Neil by a fellow who lay in the cot next to Red Hook Dan."

While elder Mrs. Thornton and May sat listening in shocked surprise, Mrs. O'Neil sobbed from joy that she might soon expect to have her husband home again. Lankey lighted his pipe, and continued: "Why, Red Hook Dan, with his dislocated shoulder, was in the same ward with Harry. Of course, they had never seen each other, so the one did not know the other. Officer O'Sullivan called twice to see him, and, though Harry recognized in him the officer who kicked him so awful, the officer appeared not to have known him."

Here Lankey was interrupted as Katie Thornton entered, looking greatly dejected. All eyes turned upon her. "What is the matter with you, dear child?" inquired her mother, as she prepared to set the table for the evening meal.

"Oh, the firm is in difficulty, and the factory has closed down," she replied sadly. "They say it will never reopen again," she added, with a sigh.

"Ah, don't worry about that, my Katie; the boys are bringing money enough to the house to keep us all," replied her mother encouragingly, while her sister May in light mood added: "I am going back to my work to-morrow, and I'll keep you in pin money till something else turns up."

It was quite natural that Katie should feel unhappy at the unfortunate turn in her affairs. She had started to work in the American Manufacturing Company at the age of sixteen, and had worked her way to the high position as forelady, and, though she was able and competent, it would not be altogether easy for her to obtain such a satisfactory position.

However, gloom did not hang over the party long. Presently they joined each other at supper, following which they went with Mrs. O'Neil to view her new home. May and Lankey George had taken great pains in helping to set this in order, and the results were surprisingly artistic and comfortable.

CHAPTER VIII.

THE KIDNAPPING OF THE O'NEIL CHILDREN.

The next two weeks carried much of sadness with them. On Monday noon the older of the Thornton boys was brought home from work with his right hand severely lacerated by a machine. The financial depression had reached the firm where May Thornton worked, so she was permitted to work only half time. So, with Katie altogether idle, it left the good Thornton family with but very little income. Food, clothing, and rental had steadily gone up, while wages nominally remained the same. The Thorntons, though commendable people, could never manage to lay money aside. The only one now working steadily was a lad of sixteen, who earned but six dollars per week in a box factory, and this concern, too, for want of work, was laying off hands every day.

Lankey George, who had worked in the coal yard with Flanagan, through Red Hook Dan, had lost his place, and, though he needed work, he felt not particularly uneasy about it. His recent experience had awakened the better spirit which was dormant within him. He had grown to long for something better than jobbing among the lower and underpaid workers. Being originally a carpenter by trade, he was a skilled man with the tools. Up to the time the Juvenile System had broken up his home, he was industrious and had lived comfortably.

Thus, while ill luck suddenly fastened itself upon the O'Neils' friends Mrs. O'Neil was fated to undergo worse ills than she had previously experienced. Although her husband was steadily improving, he was not yet able to leave the hospital. The Planet Mill's superintendent had sent the first week's salary, but thereupon ceased, and the few dollars of her husband's earnings which she had saved dwindled away for rent and needed food and clothing for the little ones.

The saddest stroke that befell the unfortunate woman was at the middle of her third week in her new home. It was on a Monday, little past noon. She had this day sent off her boy, Willie, for school, and had begun to prepare Louise and the baby to make a short visit to their father in the hospital.

It had been noticed that a couple of suspicious persons had been seen hovering about in the vicinity. Of course, Mrs. O'Neil was unknown there, and but for a visit to and from the Thorntons, she had kept entirely to herself. Though she had heard of the Juvenile System's former attempt to kidnap the children, and had been warned of a likely recurrence, her suspicion was not so strong that she felt she had to hold her children under bolts and locks to keep them away from the System.

However, it happened this noon that her landlord was making some repairs in the water inlet to the house, which caused the water to be temporarily shut off. Mrs. O'Neil bade little Louise go to the next block to the Thorntons and fetch a kettle of water. The Juvenile System's agent, by their secret service methods, had recognized the child as their legitimate prey. Though they have the law with them in all their attacks and have been known to raid whole families of children without particular pretext, at this moment they found good cause for procedure. As Louise walked by the agents through the hall, she was accosted by one of them with a rough demand: "Hey, what have you got in that can, kid?"

Louise, in reply, screamed for her mamma, and ran for the door of her home with both the agents closely following. Mrs. O'Neil met the stern intercepters with an inquiry, and at the same time relieving the child of the can. "What have you sent her for in that can?" the agent gruffly asked, as one of them reached for the can. Upon finding it to contain only water, both felt angry and disappointed. A beer kettle in the child's hand was sufficient ground for action, regardless of the contents. Thus, while the System's agent had long ago marked the O'Neil children for their prey, it gave them at least a new ground upon which to apprehend. Amid protestation and pleadings from Mrs. O'Neil, the agents tore away with force the crying and resisting children. The little arms of the baby, encircling its mother's neck, had to yield to unfeeling hands.

The agents boarded a car for the Juvenile System's store room, which is located near the Borough Hall. Poor Mrs. O'Neil, who had suffered so much of late, by this shock was rendered nearly insane. Hysterically crying and screeching, she followed the agents, who held the struggling children and boarded the car.

A few women passengers realized unfortunate Mrs. O'Neil's position, and sympathized with her, but feared to interfere. They knew the System, and dreaded it more than the Black Hand. A couple of men passengers appeared rather disgusted with the scene, and in their slight judgment felt that this woman was no safe person to care for the children, and so accepted that this was the reason that her children had been removed. One laboring man, in blouse and overalls, soiled from work, who sat in the farthest corner, paid the unhappy woman's fare as the conductor persisted in putting her off unless he received her nickel, an item upon which she could gather no thought.

Upon reaching the System's local station, the squawling children were hustled within by the agents, while Mrs. O'Neil was barred from entering with threats of arrest. She was told to appear in the Juvenile Court on the following day, and there to offer any evidence she might wish. Wildly and hysterically she remonstrated, but of course with no avail. The superintendent of the institution finally 'phoned for a police officer who, in a kindly tone, persuaded the unfortunate woman to go home and, in the morning when her children were to be arraigned in court, she could appeal to the judge.

Bewildered and heart-broken, she hurried home. In her haste of departure, she had left her change in the house, and so she was compelled to walk the distance. Utterly exhausted, she reached home, to be met in the doorway by May and Katie Thornton, who had heard of the incident. Helpless as they all were, the best they could do was to console the grief-stricken mother and encourage her with the hope that she would surely get her children again.

It was now past four o'clock. Inconsolable, she staggered up and down her apartment, wringing her hands. Suddenly she screeched out in terror: "Oh, my Willie, where is he? Did they take him, too?" Without further delay, she ran toward the school-house where he was attending, but, alas, the poor woman was too late. The System's agents had drawn from Louise that her brother, Willie, was at school, and forthwith its sleuths had proceeded to the school-house, and upon dismissal had carried the lad along with them.

The agony that Mrs. O'Neil suffered that night cannot be described. She would cry for her husband and for each of their children. Her own incarceration now appeared insignificant. The Thorntons, who had done so much for her and whom she loved, could give no aid to her mind. In her distress she begged to be left alone, so she might cry in peace.

Without sleep and rest, terribly nervous and apprehensive, long before court opening she appeared at the entrance to the juvenile branch. Katie and May Thornton had begged to go along to give any aid they could.

Within this court-room, which deals with juvenile offenders, was shown one of the saddest blots upon human progress. It meant either depravity of children or depravity of parents. It disclosed sad and haggard faces. There were fond and indulgent parents who could not manage and punish their children, but had to ask the judge to discipline them. It showed the lack of a proper fulfilment of parents and also the lack of our organized society to deal with delinquent and careless parents. Most of all, it showed innocent children being punished for parents' crime, and the good children who were seized from worthy parents without cause. But all combined to show a grand industry, a most profitable course for this our private incorporated Juvenile System.

That other mothers suffered a fate similar to Mrs. O'Neil's was evident by the many clean women with sad faces. While perhaps some brought their children to the court to be scolded by the judge, or else had incorrigible youths in the hands of the law, it is apparent that a majority among them were worthy and able to be guardians of their own children, or at least could have been brought to be so, were the laws applied to them instead of to their little ones.

At ten o'clock court began to show signs of activity. The Juvenile System's agent scurried within the railing among the clerks and court habitués, holding whispered conversation with officials, looking up records, taking notes, and writing down accounts. At spaced intervals in an enclosure set apart were placed desks for the sole use of these guardians' agents, where notes, accounts, data and "tap-keeping of youths" were filed away for further reference. A similar lot of lady agents, a specie of slum ladies, showed a like activity. These queer angels are daily demonstrating their methods and peculiar ideas in our juvenile courts. They work for the miserable youths and for the mothers. Their part in our juvenile farce lies in investigating homes, looking into complaints, in interfering and intervening. Their opinion is based upon trivialities and notions and prejudices. They throw much influence upon the action of the court.

One of these women was seen approachng distressed Mrs. O'Neil. She patted her upon the shoulder, whispered good cheer in her ears, and offered her advice. But in the next breath, upon turning her back, it was learned that she whispered strong words of condemnation into the ears of the court and the Juvenile System's agents. She not only betrayed the wretched Mrs. O'Neil, but drew upon her imagination to do so.

As the System's agent, from a little enclosure, brought forward the O'Neil children, the tortured mother experienced something of a convulsion; every limb and muscle contracted and expanded in a spasm. It was a ghastly sight, lasting a couple of seconds. But then she revived and sprang from her seat and, with nervous haste, made toward the judge's seat, in front of which the children were placed. A court officer roughly pushed her back, and bade her to keep her seat till his honor called her. Crazed, Mrs. O'Neil was neither used to court etiquette, nor had thought for her own self. May and Katie Thornton, who sat beside her, tried to calm her, but the sight of her imprisoned children impelled, and in wild anger she rushed by the officer and reached within the enclosure where stood the children.

The scene was most pathetic. Before the court had called her case, she stood begging and pleading to get her children back. A police officer restrained her from laying hands upon the children. The agents of the Juvenile System held a strong grip upon Willie and Louise, who, weeping, struggled to get to their mother. The infant, too, which was held in a matron's arms, cried furiously and scratched and fought to reach its mother.

The judge looked uneasy, though he was accustomed to all sorts of scenes, real or pretended. That Mrs. O'Neil was sincere he did not doubt, but he feared that she was demented. Very often his Honor sternly rebuked the ones overstepping court etiquette, but in his good feeling and judgment for whatever might be the cause, the judge laid aside court rules.

"Now, my good woman, be calm, and I will hear you first," he said, "and you shall not suffer injustice."

"Sure, ye'll be hurtin' yer own case, mum, by losin' yer grit," simultaneously and encouragingly whispered an officer, who stood close by her, but poor Mrs. O'Neil, who had been tried so much of late, could not collect herself. She could only find words to the effect that she was robbed of both her husband and children.

May and Katie Thornton had followed Mrs. O'Neil, but had not been permitted to enter within the railing where stood the demented woman. One of the girls from without the railing began to explain to the judge the unfortunate condition of the woman, and assured him that she was entirely sane, and was only crazed by the tremendous blow of being robbed of her children, and begged in the poor woman's behalf to have the children restored.

Mrs. O'Neil became calmer as her friend spoke, and she forced herself to be strong, hoping every second the judge would deliver her and the children. But of course courts of justice deal with two sides, and the other side being the strongest, had to be heard, and it dealt a blow to Mrs. O'Neil that could not have been more fatal.

"If it pleases your Honor," now out of patience and without show of feeling, broke in the System's agent, "this woman is not the proper custodian for the children. We have proof that this woman and her husband were both locked up for drunkenness and disorderly conduct. Her husband is now in the hospital, and I don't doubt but we can find more against them if it pleases your Honor to have us investigate," ended he, with courteous bow, being much accustomed to the ordeal.

The judge looked uncertain. The young and respectable appearing Thornton's story had appealed to him; he would have liked to return the children to the mother; but, though he was a judge, he must, to a great extent, bend himself to the wishes and demands of the powerful Juvenile System, whose influence could both make and break him. He could not safely release them except upon stronger proof of her fitness and ability properly to guard and maintain them. As he sat speculating a moment or two with Mrs.

O'Neil's eyes resting pleadingly upon him, a tall, clerical-looking person stepped behind the judge's chair and whispered a few words.

The intruder was a Presbyterian minister called Headstrong. He was a regular court runner and debauched religion with all his bunco courses and perfidious acts of false mercy. Being a staunch supporter of the Juvenile System, he also worked hand in hand with any movement that tried to infringe upon nature's course and starved the soul of man.

That his words were not in the unfortunate woman and miserable children's behalf was soon clear. The judge also showed it as he forthwith and without further uncertainty, though with a strain of sympathy, said: "From all appearances the Juvenile System acted within its right. There appears proof that the System was appealed to to take care of the children, and, besides, you, my good woman, are not fully rational and able to care for them in your present state, so——"

At this point Mrs. O'Neil, who understood the reverse decision, dropped upon her knees, piteously imploring and crying for the judge to change his decision; but her plea was of no avail. Nervously and uneasily he moved about, but he dared not to change the verdict.

"Your Honor," again said one of the Thornton girls with her hand stretched forward appealingly, "the baby is still nursing upon its mother's breast, and it may mean——"

"Oh, don't worry about that, Miss," sharply and with a victorious grin broke in the System's agent, "we have special prepared food for infants."

The harrowing final scene, where the children were dragged away by the victorious agent, and the mother lugged out of court by attending court officers, cannot be described. That Mrs. O'Neil did not entirely succumb was due to her physical strength, but never a moment did the Thornton girls fail to ease her anguish.

CHAPTER IX.

MRS. O'NEIL'S VISIT AT ONE OF THE SYSTEM'S HOMES.

Our "shake-up" or "shifting-about police system" leaves the officers with their families regularly on the move, and prepared to obey a political order for the good of the force. This gypsy system had been an advantage to Jack Stevenson. In his ten years on the force he had been shifted twenty-four times to various localities, and in all parts of the boroughs. It had made him popular. All good citizens soon recognized in him a respectable and trustworthy officer; he was looked upon as an exemplary man, and it had been predicted that one of his character would not wear out his uniform upon the police force. His sudden dismissal from the force had doubled the public's interest in him.

The opposing political parties had began to make campaign material out of Jack's abrupt dismissal from the force without sufficient ground. While the department was clogged with discredited and doubtful characters, there at least had never been proven anything against Jack Stevenson. The sick man, Harry O'Neil, had not appeared against him, and should the Juvenile System, a private directorate, run the police force as it does our special session judges and its courts, then the time would soon come when it would claim guardianship over the entire metropolis. In this and like manner ran the general public's opinion, and a few newspapers pictured Jack Stevenson as a martyr. In some journals he was lauded as a hero for his fearlessness in casting himself against the powerful Juvenile System.

The old political party, who owns and controls the police system, and whose protégé the Juvenile System is, soon realized their error and made overtures through Jack's friends that he should apply for re-instatement on the force upon technical grounds. He had assurance that simple formalities would re-install him. By this course the politicians anticipated closing the matter.

However, Jack Stevenson was able and intelligent, and felt that he could make his livelihood within other limits, and so declined it. He planned that he would right himself and clear his name and then punish those who had brought about his downfall. This little friction in Jack's life stirred his ambition; he took up social affairs vigorously and in these he received encouragement and support from all boroughs.

The People's Independent Party was well formed, and every district had its organized quarters. Its head-quarters was in the Borough of Manhattan, and Jack Stevenson was made chairman. He was also a leader of his own home district, and affairs were soon satisfactory to him.

Jack's ten years on the police force had furnished him ample experience. By one or two speeches he proved himself eloquent and forceful; this added to his popularity. He gained respect and it brought him a tremendous following. Had he desired to run independently as mayor, he would have received unanimous support. But at present his wishes were to reach the assembly only, and thereto he laid his plans.

His first thoughts, upon reaching the assembly, were to introduce and influence the passage of a bill to wipe out of existence all the private juvenile institutions or systems, which Jack looked upon as the most dangerous foes to future generations. He had long recognized them as a breeder of crime. "The course of committing spirited and neglected children to strict, unnatural courses of development, must either stunt or corrupt them," he always argued. He not only planned to destroy the powerful juvenile institutions, but he also aimed at entirely abolishing the children's courts and establishing some means whereby the parent branch should be held responsible for their own progeny up to its mature state.

He held the opinion that courts are mature stages, and that children who are immature should be regulated only through natural phases of parenthood, this being the only right channel of influence. It is not a court's duty to systematize a child; its duty should lie in systematizing and compelling parents to do their best duty.

Upon one of his electioneering trips in South Brooklyn for the coming election, he had heard of the outrageous capture of the O'Neil children by the Juvenile System. While such methods were common, in this instance, at least, where he knew there was no reason for stepping in as guardian, and a proper investigation would have ended in the System's defeat. It made Jack's blood boil, and forthwith he planned to effect an inquiry into the methods of the institution and its treatment of the children. He felt, too, that the outcome of an investigation would be an aid in furthering his bill aimed at abolishing the institution.

Of course, Jack was not acquainted with the O'Neils, nor had he held further association with them than being thrown in touch with them at the precinct house. But long before this unfortunate occurrence he had singled out the Juvenile System as a brutal parody upon benevolence, and more than once had he been eager for a chance to check its ravages upon the social body.

After two months' lingering, Harry O'Neil had been discharged from the hospital as cured. But it was a sad home into which he entered. His children were gone, and his true, strong wife had grown aged and broken in spirit. Her dark-brown hair had turned gray, and her smooth features were furrowed from suffering. The eyes that always sparkled, now shone as a dim light hid away in deep hollows.

The O'Neils' savings through this hardship had entirely been used. The Thorntons, with only May on half time and the youngest lad with a few dollars a week, had scarcely enough for themselves, but Lankey George had been fortunate. He had taken up his trade, and obtained a position as foreman with a building concern, and regularly he supplied May Thornton with sufficient money to carry on the O'Neils' household. Lankey had become a strong friend of the O'Neils, but sought always to aid them through the Thorntons, so as to avoid the embarrassment of the gratitude of the unhappy couple.

Harry had been home from the hospital now nearly two weeks, but was hardly strong enough to undertake hard work. He felt, however, that he must do something, as he had not been accustomed to live upon charity. His old place in the Planet Mills had been filled, but Lankey had spoken for him at a near-by lumber yard, where his firm bought building material, so his prospects were good for the future when he became ready for work.

One morning, as he was going to his new job, the postman brought Harry O'Neil a letter from the Juve-

nile System. It bore the signature of the superintendent, and read:

"MR. HARRY O'NEIL,

"DEAR SIR: You are herewith informed that Justice
Bilking of the Court of Special Sessions has directed
that you shall pay toward the support of your children
in the Juvenile System the sum of $16.50. A failure
to make this payment on your part will be reported to
the court for such action as it may deem proper to
take.   Respectfully,

"H. CLYDE PRESTAGE, Supt."

Harry begged leave to remain away from work to
attend to the matter. He called at the Brooklyn branch
of the Juvenile System, and declared his willingness
to pay the demand, providing his children were returned to him. The clerk in charge curtly informed
him that the Juvenile System was not open for any
proposition, and to avoid further inconvenience he had
better pay the demanded amount. Harry O'Neil remonstrated and begged to see some higher authority.

The superintendent was conveniently at hand, and
replied with sarcasm: "You would like to get your
children, eh? You think your $16.50 will make our
institution rich? Why didn't you provide a proper
home for them? Your wife is a drunkard, and I have
evidence that she runs with other——"

The superintendent did not finish his last sentence.
Harry had understood him. The accusation of drunkenness struck him as vile, but when he touched upon
his wife's fidelity O'Neil, inflamed with fury, reached
over the railing and demanded: "Another word out of
your foul lips and I shall get in there and tear you to
pieces."

The strong words and threatening combat drew
other assistance from within an adjoining room. The

superintendent, a moral coward, a "brow-beater" of weak women and children, in whose contact he was mostly thrown, felt that Harry would attack him, and stepped behind his assistant and edged his way into an adjoining office. The assistant saw in O'Neil a man who could not be trifled with, and in a meditating tone, replied: "I'm sorry, my good man; but this is but a branch of the Juvenile System; the main office is over in Manhattan. We cannot release anyone unless by approval of the board of directors."

Mr. O'Neil answered: "Well, your branch seems to have taken it upon itself to kidnap my children——"

"It's no use arguing, my friend. This is the rule of the System; if you wish you may go to the main office," broke in the assistant lightly. Not caring to inflame the man further, he bowed and left for an inner room.

Harry concluded that it was useless to proceed farther here, and prepared for the head-quarters of the Juvenile System in Manhattan. As he entered the spacious office he was met by a young man who inquired his mission. Though treated politely, he was firmly made to understand that there laid no remedy at present; it was a matter of the special committee to decide upon children's release, at whose option they were bound to the age of twenty-one.

Heart-broken, O'Neil went home to his longing wife. While he was always open and confided everything to her, he felt it here his duty to deceive her. Patting her sunken cheeks, he cheerfully said: "Don't worry, my Nell, we'll soon have the little ones back."

The Juvenile System condescendingly grants a day of grace to the unfortunate mothers and children. It is termed visiting day, and occurs at a stated time at the last of the month. The institution is open for visitors from one o'clock, noon, until five P. M. All

inmates on that afternoon are permitted to throw off
their rough blue jeans working costumes for a better
attire, so as to look neat and attractive, and thus imbue
a feeling of extreme care and attention among relatives and strangers who may call. The windows,
floors, and panels of the hall, library, and reception
room for that afternoon have been carefully cleaned
and scrubbed, so the abode resembles a saintly retreat.

While Harry would have loved to visit his little
ones, he feared to lose his job, as they were pretty
busy and he had then been there less than a week.
Therefore, he applied for a special permit for a Sunday visit, which he heard was now and then granted.
It was decided that Mrs. O'Neil should go. May
Thornton wished to accompany her, but it was her
day at work, and Katie could not leave the home, as
her injured brother needed constant attention. The
elder Mrs. Thornton at this time was down with a
severe attack of rheumatism.

Though Mrs. O'Neil was robbed of the joy of having her children constantly with her, she was momentarily happy to be permitted to see them. She bought
them candies, fruits, and little delicacies. Her broken
heart was light as she left the car near the institution
and entered the corridor, where she hoped to meet
and embrace them.

"Oh, you are Mrs. O'Neil? Glad to meet you; so
you are to visit your little Louise and the baby?" said
the matron, in a pretended kindness, motioning her to
take a seat till little Louise came downstairs. "The
baby, I am sorry, you cannot see to-day; we sent it to
the hospital ward at Randalls Island; we couldn't have
it here, you know. But it's in good hands; the city is
taking care of it," continued the matron encouragingly.

A shudder went through the mother. Her little speck of happiness had gone; she was bewildered. Why did they send away her baby to the hospital ward? Was it sick or dying? Why was her little Louise not here to meet her? Where was Willie? These and other questions surged through her troubled mind. The shock nearly dazed her anew. She caught the arms of her chair to support herself and tried to speak, but her tongue seemed paralyzed.

The matron, noticing Mrs. O'Neil's agitation, went on cheerfully: "Your children are all right. Your Louise is a good, pretty child, and is getting the very best of care. The Juvenile System is an institution which every mother should be proud of."

Mrs. O'Neil suddenly gained her faculties and demanded impatiently: "Is baby ill? Why don't Louise and Willie come?"

"Why, now, my good woman, the baby is not ill, but don't you know we can't be bothered with such tiny little ones. Louise is dressing herself. But your boy is not here; he's up on the farm at Hastings Hill among the bigger lads," said the matron, in the same forced tone.

At this moment Louise came down the stairway. She noticed her mother, and both flew to embrace each other. Poor Mrs. O'Neil dropped on her knees and hugged her child around the waist, while the child threw her tiny arms around her mother's neck. Both kissed each other wildly. "I knew you was downstairs, but I had to make the teacher's bed, clean the windows, and help other girls to scrub the matron's room before I was permitted——"

The matron never allows the hardships imposed upon the little ones to be laid open to parents or visitors, and so in feigned kindness she interrupted little

Louise by saying: "You are so happy to see your mother, poor child, that you imagine what you really would do."

As Louise entered the visiting room, her eyes and thoughts fell upon her mother, and she had not noticed the matron. Though she was only a recently arrived inmate in the institution, she had already learned that she must hold her tongue regarding her duties and the System's course. Like other children of the institution, she had reason to fear the matron.

While the matron wore an air of pretended kindness, her presence chilled Louise. The poor child trembled as she tried to whisper and talk to her mother, frequently stealing glances at her guardian.

Mrs. O'Neil appreciated the situation, but was helpless in assisting her child. This forced embarrassment at last culminated in the girl breaking out in a spell of piteous crying. She buried her little head into her mother's breast and sobbed convulsively. She uttered no word, but in spasms of sobs clung faster and faster to her mother, who sat straining herself to withhold her own sorrow, begging the little one to be brave.

Matrons of such institutions are not required to have a too sensitive nature, for fear that their better inclination would revolt. Yet in this instance she was sensibly affected. She arose and walked over and kindly stroked the child whose little body convulsively shook with her smothered sobs. "Be brave, my little child; don't fear me. I assure you I shall be really good to you so long as you are with me."

That this bidding came from the matron's heart was manifest; she wiped a tear from her eyes, and left the room, saying: "My dear little girl, tell your mother all; I shall not punish you."

Other visitors, relatives, or friends now came. Several of the inmates had reached the reception room. Many touching and pathetic scenes were witnessed through the meeting of parents and children. Little ones who had been in the institution but a short time spoke openly and freely, but those who had stayed there for some while whispered and in their weighing words would keep their eyes roving about in the direction where the matron or attendants sat with complacent smiles and watching demeanor.

Mrs. O'Neil remained there to the end of the visiting hour. The matron who had entertained her then appeared and bade her good-bye. She said encouragingly: "Do not worry for your child, so long I am here with her." In a low tone she added earnestly, as she pressed her hand: "I feel that you are one of the good many wronged mothers. You should have the custody of your own children. I am working here for hire, and wish to God I could find other employment and not be forced to play sympathy here and give a wolf's tender."

The visit to the institution had not invoked a better spirit in the unfortunate mother. She worried about the baby and about Willie, whom she had not seen, and little Louise's tale about the institution which she had been permitted to learn in full depressed her that she could hardly breathe. The child complained of the work exacted from the tiny children. As Mrs. O'Neil understood it, it was a place of detention for little underfed slaves. All the neatness, cleanness, and polished interior represented hours of child slavery. Aroused from their childish morning slumber, it was sewing, mending, polishing, sweeping, cleaning, scouring, scrubbing, washing, bed-making, dish-washing, pantry and kitchen work and general labor from the early hour till tired knees, arms, and backs found refuge in their lightly covered cots. The only real rest afforded them was at their few hours of schooling, where the poor grade of teachers sat yawning and eager to be rid of them. The little inmates had to toil and the institution was kept in proud condition on the drain of their youthful bodies.

Perhaps, with all, had the little ones been properly fed and nourished, their young faces would not have been blotted with scars of premature age. Louise had complained of their daily routine of food, which consisted of oatmeal and molasses, dry bread, with a cup of thin milk, bean soup and pickles and some thick stew without a morsel of meat in it. A heavy plum pudding was the only extra allowance, and this was dealt out each Sunday. But once the child had the taste of fish, a morsel left from one of the teacher's plate and given her in appreciation of extra service she had tendered.

Butter was as scarce as fish and meats. Eggs they never saw nor fruits nor delicacies, unless parents brought them on visiting days. None of them, while there, ever enjoyed as good a meal as is afforded even among the poorest of the poor.

These deplorable conditions preyed greatly upon the poor woman's mind. She feared that her boy fared similarly and was overworked and underfed. And what would become of her infant? She hoped it fared better, as it was in the city's hands. While not receiving home care and food, it was at least under no private money-making scheme, like that of the Juvenile System.

That night she complained to her husband. She did not weep, nor could she weep; but she was singularly depressed. She felt so heavy-hearted and so tired and weak that she scarcely could move about. While she had managed to cook Harry's supper, she could not walk about to clear the table. Hopelessly worn out, and as one longing for eternal rest, in despair she threw herself upon her bed.

CHAPTER X.

LANKEY'S ARRAIGNMENT OF THE SYSTEM.

The next few days followed uneventfully. It was a Saturday noon and half holiday. Harry had just received his first full week's pay. Though he had been at work two full weeks, it was a custom of the firm to hold back one week's salary. As he opened his envelope which contained fifteen dollars he said to himself: "I think I had better pay the Juvenile System half of its demand and the remaining eight dollars and twenty-five cents next week, or else I fear my little ones will suffer for my show of disobedience." He had noticed a sign displayed in the office of the Juvenile System to the effect that the office kept open every day as late as eight P. M., and he decided, after changing his working attire, to prepare thither.

As he reached the entrance to his home he was accosted by a man dressed in a blue serge suit, who stood leaning against the sill of the show window of the store floor. "Are you Harry O'Neil?" he inquired, stepping toward him.

O'Neil's troubles of late had made him somewhat nervous. He had suffered much, and learned to look upon guilt, innocence, and justice as mere courses of fate; so momentarily he looked uneasy, stared, and made no reply.

"There is no use denying it," quickly applied the stranger, and handed him a paper. "I'm a court officer; this is a summons for you to obey."

Harry gave a sigh of relief as the detailed officer executed his mission and left. "Any more trouble to come my way?" he remarked, as he opened the paper and read: "The Court of Special Session. The People, complainant vs. Harry O'Neil, defendant."

He pondered while he continued to read. It ordered him to appear in court on a certain day under threats of certain penalty for his failure to obey. "The People vs. Harry O'Neil," he murmured. He could not grasp the idea, as he had committed no crime in which the people or the public could find cause to prosecute. But then again he realized by his last experiences that justice was crimsoned with guilt, and that innocence was no adequate shield for protection.

Suddenly it occurred to him that he had received a letter a few days previously from the Juvenile System under threats of prosecution for his failure to pay their demand. He drew the letter from an inside pocket and re-read it. True enough, it mentioned the Court of Special Session, and also one of the special judges' name was attached. "But why, then," thought he, "does it not say the Juvenile System against Harry O'Neil, instead of the People?"

Harry was no scholar, but he possessed sound intelligence. He figured that there must be some radical wrong with our laws and courts where it permits a private corporation like the Juvenile System to cloak themselves as the People and prosecute for selfish ends in the People's or Public's name. He deposited the papers in his pocket and decided, instead of going to the office of the Juvenile System, as he had planned, to wait and have a talk with his friend Lankey George, who had some knowledge beyond his in the matter of law.

Lankey, who was a steady visitor at the O'Neils,

was sitting at the kitchen table and reading the morning news as Harry entered. It was half holiday, too, upon Lankey's job. He knew that Mrs. O'Neil was sick in bed and unable to provide her husband's dinner, so he had hurried there in time and brought with him meat and vegetables for a good meal which his good friend, May Thornton, was now preparing.

Katie Thornton had obtained another position in which she was to start the following Monday, so her sister May concluded as her firm was not overbusy, to stay away from work and remain daily in attendance upon Mrs. O'Neil, who was constantly in bed, helpless, and too weak to provide meals for herself and husband. It was a great sacrifice on May's part, but she had learned to love Mrs. O'Neil for her good qualities, and greatly sympathized with her in her afflictions.

Lankey George was studying May Thornton. Though young, she was a woman in all respects, and very much to his liking. They had been together a great deal of late and entertained much of the same feeling toward each other. While George was a good deal older, he was very much of a man, and looked young for his age. He had greatly improved in personal care and habits since he had met May, and very often she chided him for any laxness she detected.

Harry O'Neil could not thank May enough; his wife had always pictured her as a true angel, and he learned to know it himself. Much of the assistance was derived from Lankey, however, who did it without thought of reward. But Harry now bore a brotherly feeling toward George, and would not have done less if positions were reversed.

May had prepared some broth for Mrs. O'Neil, which she partook of sparingly, and, while the men-folks sat a⁺ their noon meal in the kitchen, she dished something out for herself, and sat in the bedroom within view of the sick woman and ate her dinner.

"It is a great time they are having along the canal at the coal pockets," began Lankey, putting down his paper. "The yard I worked in is burnt down by the strikers, and my old fellow-worker, Flanagan, is in the hospital with a fractured skull. The poor fellow was taken for a scab as he came out of the yard with some clothes, and a strike sympathizer hit him with a brick."

"Those strikes are not happy occurrences," replied Harry. "One reduced me down to where I am to-day. I sympathize greatly with the men who strike for more pay, when they need it, for they are ground down to the lowest ebb of living. And I also greatly sympathize with the scabs who are forced, by their own wants, to take hold of something. Many scabs are good men, it is but their temporary position what makes them scabs; they are as anxious as the strikers to get as much wages as they can, and would themselves be ready to strike if they dared to. It is their stomachs, their needs, my friend," ended he sadly, thinking of his late and former position with a family to provide for and the wolf at the door.

"That is so," agreed Lankey. "In my judgment, where all is controlled by trust and monopolism, and no real supply and demand counts, there should be means of public arbitration to regulate compensation of the producing element, the laborers, in order that they can exist."

"You are upon the right issue, George," said Harry, "methods and means to properly live and exist is as much of a public concern as is the general health itself, and should be regulated on basis of cost of living and supply and demand of labor. Were hours and wages regulated by a public commission, the saintly trust people would then be at liberty to swell their price, as the money value on labor would be in conformity, and follow suit."

"Yes, that would be chips for money, and money for chips, and enough of it to play the game through," jokingly remarked Lankey. "The whole of life throughout is exchanging products. When the public is compelled to pay the trusts' demands, the trusts should be compelled to pay the public's demand."

"Yes, it's a poor rule that won't work both ways," responded Harry. "At present it works only one way, and that is the trusts' end of it. Not until the public takes hold of it at the other end will starvation, hunger and strikes be avoided. Strikes, idleness, and starvation naturally follow ill causes."

"You are quite a philosopher," complimented George laughingly, "but while we speak of it, tell me about the strike which affected you."

"Oh, yes, that was the Rapid Transit. It was a Wall Street deal, but it was said that some millionaires sold short, went short, or whatever we call it, and got cornered and bought out the labor leaders to force a strike so the stock would decline sufficiently to let them out even."

"Did the stock drop?"

"I suppose it did. At all events, there was a great tie-up. You remember the militia were out and the people ran riot. In my judgment there was no cause for strike at the time, but it was a case of being misled by leaders."

"Just so, as I said a while ago," recalled Lankey. "Had there been a public arbitration or commission, I suppose things would not have run that way. The road would have run until matters could have been looked into. Truly, it would do away with much flim-flamming from all sides."

"Yes, and it would do away with all labor unions and labor leaders; the maintenance of either is expensive, and they effect nothing but grievance and discontent. A regular established public board of arbitration could compel and arrange things to correspond with conditions of things. Well, ah, but what's the use of talking?" he said abruptly, with an expression of disgust upon his face.

Lankey George reached for the paper and, after a moment, remarked: "I see that Roundsman O'Sullivan received a——" Here he halted a moment, reflecting, though without changing the position of his paper. It had just occurred to him that this O'Sullivan was former Patrolman O'Sullivan, who had gained his promotion to roundsman principally at Harry's cost, and he did not care to recall those sad experiences to his friend.

Harry had not caught the officer's name, nor did he expect any cause for repression, so he blandly asked: "What did you say the roundsman received?"

"He acted so brutally with his night-stick in dealing with strikers and sympathizers that a gang assailed him. He was kicked and beaten so he is not expected to live."

"I am sorry for the poor fellow," cried Harry, "though I do not approve of police officers taking an active hand in such matters one way or another, beyond protecting the innocent public. Who knows but that those uniformed officers might themselves either have been among the scabs or among the strikers if circumstances had not favored them better?"

"You are talking good sense," said Lankey. He

would have said more, but just then May entered. Their eyes met, and he thought of something else.

The meal having been finished, May wanted to clear the table and wash up. "Say, child," said Lankey, "I'm not born to do a woman's work, nor do I like a man who does it unless on stated occasion; but I think you are entitled to a little rest while Harry and I do our own cleaning up. I have cooked and washed dishes many a time when I found it part of my duty, and I can do it again, and I am sure my friend can do it, too. If you'll let us look out for this end of the house a little while I will feel you do me a favor," he ended smilingly, and lightly pushed her away.

This was much to Harry's liking; household duties were to him not altogether new. Though he would prefer a hard day's physical labor to a woman's monotonous work, he had, like good men among the poor class where servants are not within reach, given a hand now and then to relieve his wife, whose cares with the children at times overburdened her. Both of these strong men thereupon began to clear the table and wash their dishes and put them in place, as though it were their customary work. Upon the end of their task May had returned from the sick room and naturally complimented them.

Both men now lit their pipes and re-seated themselves at the table. Harry drew the court summons from his pocket and handed it to George, asking him the meaning of it. At the same time he handed him the letter he had received from the Juvenile System a few days previously.

"Why, of course this complaint," quickly replied Lankey, "is the Juvenile System against you, and not the People, as it reads. I'm not a lawyer, but I dare say upon common reason that they have no more right to use the claim of the people than any other private concern that may sue you. To be sure," he continued, "the courts and judges commit children to the institution, but private as it is in its tenor, where neither books nor accounts are open for public inspection, I doubt much that any higher court would find the term legal. Nay, I doubt if the true interpretation was put to the Constitution of the United States, if it would not be found that the commitment by the judges and all the System's courses are illegal. It is as though the Juvenile System rules and regulates our courts and judges (which it does, however) and take proceedings above the statutes and it makes a dishcloth out of the Constitution of the land."

"Well, what would you advise me to do?"

"Why, Harry, if you pay the Juvenile System's demand they profit by it and will continue to hold the children in order to have you to draw on, and again you take your chance. The court may impose a sentence upon you at from one to three months in the workhouse. The Juvenile System people have everything to gain and nothing to lose. It reaches out for the children to have a full house of young ones. Of course, it is rather a show-card for them to have a big stall of youngsters. Philanthropists and the charitably inclined donate out of good faith in their wish to provide good homes for the little ones. Were the institution empty, the contributions would cease; naturally it is part of the System's scheme to have their hopper full to show off with, and they generally attack and reach out for the better poor so they can levy on both sides. While the donors give to the institution's support, the System, with aid of courts and judges, impose board money upon the parents of the unfortunate children. It leaves, as you see, a surplus from both sides, which is ample for the directors and officers of the institution to live on like lords and grand dukes among the swells at Newport and Tuxedo or to travel abroad and mix among London's aristocrats."

"My observation has been that the System never reaches out for the real poor where there is absolutely no chance to collect board money. If such are thrust upon them, they manage to serf them out to far western farms and in turn draw upon these for donations. Another note which has come before me is that stupid, incorrigible, backward, crippled, or deformed children, or anyone the least lacking physically or mentally, this Juvenile System manages to shove over upon the community or public charity. Furthermore, any who, through ill treatment in the Juvenile System, where frequently children decline physically or mentally or otherwise, and thus become a burden to the System, are sent to Randalls Island wards or public supporting quarters.

"The Juvenile institution's greediness is in all instances linked with shame. The practices in some are, besides, inhuman and indecent," continued he. "It is a fact that girls with luxurious growths of pretty hair have suffered the injury of being sheared and their pretty locks have been disposed of by the System's officials to the highest bidder among the dealers in human hair. The System's revenue upon that score is said to be tremendous, but can only be guessed at. The records of the Randalls Island wards, the System's handy agent, where the shearing is done, could probably disclose how many crops of marketable hair is trimmed and turned over to the Juvenile officers.

"The System wants all the benefit there is in it. It means much to have a strong, clean stock of children. These little serfs with their own labor practically work the home farm at Hastings Hill, New York, and support the institution and themselves. Thus all money reaching the institution from private donors and forced from children's parents is practically clean profit. Besides, our State government pays into the System's treasury fifty thousand dollars per year. It is a huge shame," he went on, in bitter anger, "that a people of our day can be so imposed upon. It uses; nay, rules, our public courts, judges, hospitals, and wards. It exacts money from the public treasury; it draws money from poor parents; it deceives and defrauds the generously inclined out of handsome sums of money; but, worst of all, it half feeds and overworks these little immature children so that upon their release they are like withered flowers, all nature and spirit is crushed out of them, criminally tainted, worthless and useless; they die a burden to themselves and to society," ended he, wiping away a dew of perspiration which had found its way through his sincere and passionate argument. He would probably have said more, but just then May brought a letter and laid it in front of Mr. O'Neil.

May again withdrew, though only after having exchanged a few happy glances with George. That they were fast growing into a deep affection for each other was easily discerned. Harry opened the letter while Lankey, like a boy of twenty, rested his cheeks between his two flat hands with the elbows resting upon his knees.

"It's a pass from the Juvenile System allowing me to visit my Willie to-morrow," happily exclaimed Harry, looking at his friend's peculiar position, though without taking particular notice.

"What—what—what did you say?" quickly said Lankey, straightening himself and smiling, though whether he smiled from a dear reflection of May Thornton, or from finding himself in so awkward a position, he did not disclose. However, Harry repeated his words.

May again entered the room where they sat, as Mrs. O'Neil was sleeping quietly. She took out from a closet a sewing basket, and, seating herself at the table, began to mend a gown which Mrs. O'Neil had torn. Harry told her of the pass and of his desire to go and visit the boy in the morning, as long as she was so kind as to stay with his sick wife.

"I love Mrs. O'Neil as a sister, and would give my life to save her. I shall not leave the house until she is able to be up and about. I promised her that, and I'll keep my word," said May earnestly.

"I'll take a trip with you up to Hastings Hills, Harry," said Lankey.

"And I'll have a nice supper ready for you both when you return home," chimed in May.

"Well, you and May can have a talk by yourselves while I go out to the stores and buy something for the little fellow to make him happy with upon our visit," said O'Neil, leaving the room.

The little chat that May and Lankey had we can reasonably imagine was a happy one, and to their liking. Both were flushed and red-checked and looked as happy as young spooners when Harry presently returned. After enjoying tea together and having some more discussion, Lankey went home. O'Neil took up his night quarters in a spare bedroom, while May joined Mrs. O'Neil.

CHAPTER XI.

A VISIT TO HASTINGS FARM.

Sunday was beautifully bright, and it added cheer to Harry O'Neil in his proposed visit. Though his sick wife could not share with him the joy of the journey to her boy, she at least showed animation at his going. For the first time since she took to her bed she sat in an upright position, though weak and scant of breath, she spoke a good deal before he departed. Her talk consisted of longing expressions and hopes of future reunion, and as Harry kissed her good-by it was as though her soul and heart accompanied him. She fell back upon the pillow, exhausted at her effort, but her face was full of expression, and there was a cheerful and hopeful cast in her eyes.

Harry went about with a happy, light heart. The flicker of life and hope within his wife had added a fortune in joy to him, and the prospect of seeing his boy gave life a roseate hue. Despite his weight of suffering, it was a happy day, and what would it not be for his poor boy, he fondly pictured. Tucking his bundle of precious little gifts under his arm, he and Lankey set out for the Hastings farms.

"I'm so happy, dear May, for that supper you promised us upon our return," smilingly remarked George, as the girl bade them good-by.

"You cannot anticipate it more than I do." She went to the front window and watched the pair till they turned the corner.

Lankey also had bought some fruit and candies for the boy and also a dozen two-cent stamps. Harry did not quite see the necessity of bringing stamps along. He thought at least if writing was permitted that the inmates would receive free postage from the institution, as long as they had no chance to earn it.

"Ah, yes, earn it," said Lankey, with some little force. "They earn it, all right. There are boys there who work as much as a man, but get only one cent a day."

"One cent a day? You are jesting," exclaimed Harry, in a doubtful tone.

"Why, it's like this. Boys in the institution are put to work and must work. The lads may be kept there until they are twenty-one years of age, and the law prescribes that even a prisoner must get a certain compensation for his work. To be within the law, the System had adopted a minimum scale of one cent per day, though some earn and are worth as much as three dollars per day. As to writing being permitted, it is to the extent that letters have to pass the censorship of the institution. Never a letter goes in or out of the institution that is not opened and read by the censors. If matters therein from either side is not satisfactory to the System, the letter is destroyed."

"Why, I can hardly believe it!" cried Harry, in surprise and disgust. "It would be a federal offence to withhold or open mail. These inmates are not murderers. Even if the institution could be looked upon as a lawful guardian, laws do not give it the right to open and withhold mail."

"Well, they do it, nevertheless," was all Lankey answered.

Each bought a paper and boarded the train, and for some little while both sat scanning the news. Suddenly Lankey brought Harry's attention to a paragraph, which read: "Candidate for the Assembly, Jack Stevenson, the former police officer, whose dismissal from the force was laid to the Juvenile System, has driven the first nail into the coffin. The governor has appointed a commission to look into the treatment of the unfortunate inmates of the Juvenile System, and also its methods of acquiring custody of the children."

Three columns were devoted to explaining various accusations and complaints. The article spoke decidedly against the Juvenile System, and expressed the warmest approval of Jack's action, with wishes of all success in his efforts to bring to light the facts.

O'Neil was joyous to hear it, and read the matter through twice. Lankey George, too, felt pleased, and he would have given much to have been assured of Jack Stevenson's success in ending the System's practice. Lankey had not forgotten Jack's kind turn in his difficulty, and there was perhaps no man he wished stronger success. But he was skeptical of any success in "showing up" or retarding the System's practice and progress. He remembered several attempts upon the part of reformers and investigators, but the backing and influence of the Juvenile institution upon every turn was able to vindicate it. The commissions were wined and dined and shown other favors by the rich directors of the System, and these attentions on all occasions secured a general good report. Lankey's observation had been that after every investigation the System had so riveted its armor, as to be able to defy both the public and the Constitution. It would take nothing less from a Martinique calamity to right conditions and wipe out the Juvenile System.

Lankey, however, did not wish to discourage his friend, nor could he lend himself to give false hopes. Carelessly he said: "If Jack Stevenson carries out what others have failed in, he has more than earned what he will get—the gratitude of tens of thousands—for no better man than Jack ever trod within the Assembly chamber."

"But he's only a candidate," reminded Harry.

"Oh, that's so; I forgot," corrected Lankey; "but whatever failure or success he may ·meet with hereafter, the general feeling is now that he will be elected."

"He was the officer who was on trial for beating me, was he not?"

"Yes, but I believe he was the innocent one," responded Lankey, with warmth.

"It's a pity that I was not there. I swear that I could pick the brute among——" Here he abruptly halted. His features changed with surprise. He had turned a page of his paper and recognized Jack Stevenson's picture. "Oh, why," he cried, gathering himself, "that man saved my life! Another officer jumped on top of my breast, and this man pulled him off with a warning to act humanly, but after that all was blank to me."

"Too bad, too bad; but he'll be vindicated yet," sadly noted Lankey.

"It will be a happy day of my life if I can aid him," nodded Harry.

At this point of their conversation they had reached the end of their journey by rail. They had yet a great distance of ground to cover by foot, as the so-termed Juvenile Village was located in the centre of the great stretch of farm land, and lay farther on. The extreme outer parts were obscure wilderness, hilly and overgrown with underbrush. The System had shrewdly selected a model place, in that it required more than a youngster's skill to find a straight road in order to escape. Nervy and venturesome boys, who have attempted this, have nearly always been apprehended before reaching the outer limits.

A handsome, broad, well-tended automobile track ran to the main village, but this was too far and too roundabout for pedestrians, its use being designed for the rich directors and officials, and wealthy contributors and public men of standing. Visitors, approaching thus, were apt to wonder at the coziness and comfort which the children of the underworld were deriving gratis.

Of course, poor parents had no money for automobile hire. Weak mothers, who were the most frequent visitors, took any or all courses through rough ground, brush, and underwood, with an occasional rest here and there till, tired and footsore, they reached the sanctum of their children's destiny. Harry and George followed this same unrelied track. They had, however, the advantage that the sun shone clear, which stood for them as a compass; it saved them many a turn which a dark and sultry day would have caused.

The monotony was interrupted only now and then by the sight of a tired, sickly mother with a child or two by her side, resting upon a rock or fallen log. These were upon the same mission as Harry and George, but had not the same physical advantages.

After a few more turns Harry and his companion finally caught sight of the distant cottages, a place of child serfdom. The distant prospect was most beautiful with lines of handsomely built cottages, modest and neat in architecture, independently arranged. Each was surrounded with pretty little lawns and flower beds, and had well-tended pathways leading to both entrances. The houses on either side had a front view. The shingles of the roof and the portals and exterior walls and woodwork showed no lack of paint. The windows were shaded and curtained. In fact, the sight bespoke neatness and excellent care, and apparently was a fit place to house a king's son.

Harry's heart leaped with joy as they neared the cottages. He was happy at the thought of meeting his son and the appearance of the home banished his fears of his boy's well being. Had his dear wife only been along to see the condition under which their boy was kept, it would at least, to some extent, have relieved her mind. But he was glad that he would have some good news to take home.

Neither spoke as they walked in the direction of the cottages. Lankey guessed his friend's thoughts, but did not care to shake his views, for fear of depressing his spirit upon meeting his boy.

The cottages were arranged and known by numbers, and were some fifty rods apart from one another. The one in which Willie O'Neil was assigned with nineteen other boys, was known as No. 40. Upon inquiry the cottage was pointed out. The two visitors turned into the neat path towards the entrance and pressed the electric button. Harry hugged his bundle tight as he heard sounds at the door. His heart, beating with hope that it was his boy whom he longed to embrace.

The door was opened by a boy. It was not Willie, but a lad about a year or so younger. They were ushered within and invited to take a seat in the sitting room till the matron came. The interior of this pretty cottage corresponded with the exterior. The reception or sitting room in which they sat was remarkable for neatness and taste; the flooring was inlaid parquet, the walls laid in hardwood panels halfway to the ceiling, the remaining half was covered with heavy furred burlap. The room was furnished with light rockers and easy chairs. In the centre was placed a Japanese pedestal upon which stood a beautiful winged palm-leaf tree. At the end of the sitting room, which ran oblong, were two pretty panelled sliding doors which stood open to afford visitors a view of the cleanness and tidiness with which they were arranged.

On the left, as they entered, was a larger one, this being the children's dining room. It held a half dozen tables, with four chairs to each, arranged at suitable intervals and giving ample space for comfort. The furniture was hardwood, and there were handsomely polished tables. All had pretty white damask, newly laundered coverings; on each was placed a silver caster. The ceiling was bluish white, the walls were panelled three-quarters up to the ceiling. The window panes and woodwork were free from specks of dust and the hardwood flooring was polished and reflected as though it were a mirror. Everything showed scrupulous cleanliness, and could not help commanding approval at a glance.

The other room upon the left, the boys' library, was somewhat smaller. In the centre stood a large, oblong table covered with writing material and illustrated pamphlets. A bookcase, which contained forty or fifty books, was placed against the wall between two windows. All within, too, looked as span and clean as though it knew no occupants, yet distributed about the room were sixteen or eighteen boys. An observer could not at first thought fail to be impressed with the extreme care and neatness which must affect the minds of the young who came within its influence.

One wing of the floor above was occupied by the matron, and the other as a sleeping apartment for the detained boys, and this was connected with a broad staircase railed with turned baluster. The newel-post in the lower end of the stairway, which was directly in front of the sitting room, was handsomely carved. On its top arose a heavy electric bulb which was rested upon a crown.

The whole gave an impression that it could not be a detaining place for bad or wild boys; it seemed more like that of a sunny retreat for little angels. Harry

O'Neil looked at it all with amazement, and momentarily he forgot his mission. As he recovered he thought that it was not possible that his boy could be put in so fine a place. He looked about at all the youngsters who wore neat blue uniforms with brass buttons and behaved like gentlemen. "This must be some one of the director's home, and these neat chaps must be visitors or relatives of the better class," he mused.

Lankey remarked his perplexity, and said: "The whole thing is a game; but I shan't tell you just yet."

Harry did not have to wait long before learning something. While they were sitting awaiting the matron to present to her the permit to visit, one of the youngsters in his slippers which he wore, upon his tiptoes, walked to where they sat and in a whisper asked if they were to visit any one in their cottage.

"Willie O'Neil is in this cottage, is he not?" quickly queried Harry.

"Yes, but—but—he—is——" he stuttered, looking around. "Well, you better see the matron. If I was to speak a word without permission I'd be clipped into the drill squad over in the fifth ward on a sixty days' turn." He spoke, in a suppressed tone, and furtively watched the stairway in which direction the matron was expected to appear.

Harry's heart sunk as he wondered what it could mean. His son's absence; this little boy's fearful and guarded manner, and his mention of punishment, drill squad, and the fifth ward. These thoughts flashed upon him with his eyes meeting this extremely neat home with apparently nothing wanting to give the appearance of true benevolence. What could he think?

Awakening from his first blow, he was determined that he would learn more of the inside conditions. To give no show of fear for his boy's safety and the conditions under which he now lived, in a pretended carelessness, he said: "You boys have pretty nice times here, and a neat and tidy home."

"Gee, mister, if you only knew!" whispered the boy. "We are put in our good clothes on Sunday to show off for some o' them big guys what come in automobiles and other visitors. But we cannot go outside the place nor stir from the room. Instead of going outside to play, we must sit and read the old books over and over again. It makes a feller sick," he ended, in disgust, as he threw another look at the stairway.

In a whisper, he proceeded: "Dem fine floors, stairs, walls, and windows, and all that junk o' brass we must scrub clean and polish all the time and every day, so our knees and hands blister and our backs ache like anything. It's all well for you folks coming up ter see it, to cut up 'bout a nice home and a clean shack, but we boys have to do it," he said reproachfully, having mistaken Harry's view. "We can't even walk, but must sit for fear of serapin' the floor. If we talk the matron scolds us and reports us to the 'Super.' And that means a spell in the drill squad in the fifth ward," he continued expressively, as he pointed out through the windows toward a large brick building.

Harry was about to ask further information about the fifth ward and the drill squad, but was hindered as the lad resumed: "You see them fine table cloths? If a feller should happen to spill a drop of bean soup on it, it's good-by to him. And the stuff we get to eat is so rank that we can't eat it, and then we don't get much of anything but the same mince every day."

"Sure, mister, what we get we work hard for," he continued; "some of us what works always in the cottages are chased out of our bunks every morning at four o'clock and have to begin to set the tables and then go way up on the road to the bake house and kitchen and fetch the grub for us and the matron. Then we have to clean and scrub and set tables again and again for grub, and then clean, wash, and scrub, and again——"

"Don't you go to school?" broke in Harry.

"Gee, school? A couple Misses what don't know nothing about nothing sit and read a book and then we go to sleep, but that is only about three hours a day sometimes. The rest of the time we work, either in the cottages making beds, house-cleaning, or over in the bake shop and kitchen, or in the tailor shop or shoe shop, or in the garden or cutting grass, hoeing potatoes or other work in the field. When it rains them fellers what work outside are sent in and clean pig-pens or other work. Gee whiz! we have to work here, all right," he came, with a shake of his head. "If I was working like that in the city I'd make lots of money, you bet," he ended, with a nod of assurance.

"How old are you?" asked Harry.

"I'm thirteen years, but lots of smaller boys work as hard as I do, and there's big fellers, too, as big as you, mister. They mostly work on the farms, and don't get nothing for it."

"It's all work and no play with you boys," remarked Lankey sadly.

"You're right, mister, but nobody believes it. Them old guys coming up in their automobiles and fine carriages think we do nothin' but eat and sleep and go to school, and they praise the matrons and the 'Super' for all the work they don't do nothing of. And then they come oncet in a while and speak down in the hall near the ferry, and tell us about how lucky we are. The minister in the church tells us to pray for our good home and thank the good people giving it to us. Gee whiz! it's tough, ain't it?" he ended, shrugging his shoulders.

"How long are you here for?" asked Harry.

"Search me, boss," replied the lad; "we're all here for so long as they can keep us, I guess. If our parents don't send no money and clothes to the institution, they try to tell us that there is some rich farmers out West who wants to adopt us and give us a good home with plenty of fruit, candy, and good clothes. But no Westloe for me; this is tough enough."

"What do you mean by Westloe?" asked Harry.

"Three of the bugs what runs this business sits in the room up in the office buildin' one day each month and have some of us lads, what they think will go west on farms, up and see them. They tell us our parents are drunkards and bad, and we ought to go out West. That is what we call Westloe."

"Won't you tell us about the fifth ward and the drill squad?"

"Gee! that's a hole," exclaimed he; "we are sent there for doin' nothin'. I was there once for pickin' an apple and eatin' it when I worked on the farm, and one time we had a drill practice for paradin' on the anniversary day. My old man happened to come up ter see me; he had no visitin' permit, as they don't grant them always, but he walked over near the paraders. I spied him and turned my head just a little bit like this"—here the lad turned his head in a one-eighth position from a straight point. "Gee! the Monitor hit me awful hard. After the parade day I got sixty days in the fifth ward, but got off thirty days for good drill." Here he halted a moment, and then continued: "Fifth ward is a ranker, you bet! There's always a dozen or more there. It's on the loft over the powerhouse. We drill all day from six

116

o'clock mornin' to dark; no chairs, no bench, nothing to sit on, and nothing to lay on exceptin' the floor and we get a half quilt to sleep on sometimes when it's real, real cold"—he indicated with a shudder—"and only water and dry bread all the time. Beatin' and kickin' fer ours if we get tired. Sometimes we have to stand with both arms outstretched for fifteen minutes, so it gets black before our eyes. It hurted me onet so in my back and on the left side of my breast that I dropped and the blood runned out of my nose like anything. For fear of a beatin', I asked permission to go to the toilet, where I rested a few minutes; then the Monitor came and slapped me a good one and made me run round the floor for a long, long while. Gee!"

"Are visitors allowed in your fifth ward?" asked Lankey.

"You bet no! Not even the fine ladies and big guys what come up ter see the place. They are shown about by the matron and 'Super,' and only around inside here, and in our bedroom, which looks real fine. And then as they stand and look at the cottages and the fine little gardens, they smile to each other, and say something what we don't hear nothing of. Then go away."

"When is the anniversary day?"

"Next month; but it ain't for nobody but the fine people and their family and big judges. We are walkin' up and down for them like sholdiers, and make motions with hands up and down like real sholdiers what's in the army," he answered. "But it ain't for our parents and anybody what ain't invited," he said, in a warning tone.

"Can you tell me something about Willie O'Neil?" asked Harry finally.

Again he cast a glance at the stairway, and in the

same cautious tone continued: "Gee! don't tell anything what I told you to nobody; or it'll be all up
with me."

Harry assured him of their silence and bade him to
go on.

"Willie and another lad what the matron calls
'Piggy,' 'cause he can always eat, and cries 'cause he
can't get enough," began he, "were sent to the ferry
for mail for the office. Some one had broken open a
chew-gum box and taken som't of it out. Piggy was
seen chewing gum and he got the blame, though he
said he didn't, and Willie was sent sixty days in the
drill squad in fifth ward, 'cause he wouldn't say Piggy
took it. I wouldn't have squealed anyhow. Would
you?" he asked, and then he went on: "We never get
much of anything nice anyhow, even if our parents
bring us sompt'in' and our matron don't like us.
Sometimes she keeps it for us and when we want it
she sells it to us for the few pennies——"

The lad abruptly broke off. Steps were heard upon
the upper landing. Lightly, and as quick as a cat, he
bounded from the visiting room into the library, picked
up a book, and pretended he was quietly studying.
The other lads, who, in their free spell of oversight,
had been tiptoeing about and whispering to each other,
likewise quickly sought seats. Whether reading or
not, none ever dared to gaze aside from his book while
the matron was there.

"Well, well, how do you do? Pleasant day, isn't
it?" said the matron in a most affable manner, with
smiles and a bow to Harry and Lankey, who, in return, responded: "Well, I suppose you are up to see
your boys? Have you with you your visiting permits?" she inquired, before their bow had ended.

As Harry handed her the permit she pleasantly

bade them be seated, and, as she unfolded the permit, she made a slight motion with the hand, and said: "Don't you think this is a pleasant home for the boys? Why, why, Willie O'Neil? You are Mr. O'Neil, I suppose? Glad to see you," she followed up, as she noted the name, and slightly tinged her tone with sadness: "But I am very sorry, for I feaɪ you cannot see the boy to-day—he———"

She halted a moment, and with more ease said: "He is put away over in another building with some other boys for an infraction upon our rules. We don't punish children, but we simply make them understand that they must obey, and have at times to put them aside to shame themselves. You understand?"

Harry O'Neil had by the little lad's tale been prepared for the worst, and the shock did not unnerve him. On the contrary, he could barely compose himself from anger. He finally demanded: "The visiting permit states I can see my son this day. I must see him, and I demand to be shown him."

"No, the visiting permit says you may, but not necessarily that you can," responded the matron. "If you wish, however, you can go to the office building, where you can see the superintendent, or some one else. I can do nothing further for you."

It took but a few minutes for them to reach the office building. The superintendent happened to be present, and he met them with measured curtness. He was used to meeting similar disappointed and grieved parents, and made it a rule to be short. "I cannot help it; the matter does not lay with me. The boy is punished for insubordination———"

"For not telling a———" broke in Harry hastily; but stopped short as he suddenly remembered that the little informant in the cottage had requested him not to tell of their talk.

"What? For not telling a what, did you say?" flurried the superintendent.

"For not telling me not to waste my time and money to come all the way up here to suffer a disappointment," with a flash, replied O'Neil.

The superintendent appeared satisfied, and said: "Well, we can't help these things; you wrote for a permit, and the clerk sent it; we have no special method to compare applications for visits and infractions children. You must take your chances on that, my friend," he ended, shrugging his shoulders.

Much discouraged, Harry now pleaded: "Is there no way I can see my boy to-day? His mother is in bed and very sick, and will feel disappointed. And I have brought him some little things that would please him, so it will be a great joy, both for him and me, to meet just for a greeting and good cheer. His mother——"

"It's no use arguing; our rule forbids it. When children are under discipline no one can see them. Parents in this particular instance play no rôle. Our System is by court and law appointed the child's guardian. If you have any clothing or matters to give him, you can leave it with the matron at his cottage. Upon the end of his discipline, it will be handed to him." This speech was delivered abruptly; and, with a bow, he said: "Good-by, gentlemen." Whereupon he returned to an inner room in the office building and closed the door.

Lankey had not spoken a word throughout. "It's no use knocking your head against a stone wall, Harry," he said, touching upon the shoulders his friend, who stood dumb and paralyzed.

But still wishing to leave the remembrances for his lad, at such a time as he would be free, they returned to the cottage where he delivered his package to the matron, begging her to give it to Willie as soon as the rule permitted.

It was still early. Broken-hearted and disgusted, and cursing the System and its rules, Harry staggered homeward. The disappointment, anger, and impressions received had momentarily weakened him, so he was forced to grasp Lankey's arm for support.

Beautiful nature, which had so enlivened Harry upon his morning start, had not suffered with him. The sun shone just as brilliantly. The sparrows and humming-birds and other feathered things of joy flew from branch to branch, hopping and chirping. Chipmunks and squirrels played hide-and-seek on the branches and boughs.

It was as though kindness and beauty and love were expressed in all creation. But within Harry was a gnawing, unsatisfied sense of longing and a baffled hope. His hopes were scattered; upon his return home he was to crush out the last glow of life held within his wife. He had nothing to convey her but sad tales of miserable torture which must befall her son. Worst of all, he had not been permitted to hear or see him; if, indeed, he was still among the living.

Physically strong and powerful as Harry was, he could not stand upon his feet, so deadening was his despair. Without speaking, he pointed to Lankey to take a seat, and, exhausted, sank upon a log. His friend read his thoughts and knew his feeling. Laying his arm upon Harry's shoulder, he said: "Dear friend, I feel for you; I know what you would say if you could speak. Your mind is in a tumult; but calm yourself; you have yet not foundered upon the reef."

"Thank you, good friend; it is perhaps a weakness not becoming a man, but I cannot help it," answered Harry, a bit relieved. "I love my home, I love my children, and I love my wife. But she will never survive the shock of to-day, and I shall have lost all. I stand with a shattered past and a broken future."

"Ah, it's far from being a weakness; nor is it a coward's trait to fight the battle you have fought, but whatever be your sorrows of the past, they will aid you in the future," said Lankey. "I suffered the loss of my children as you did. Their lives were lost to me upon far western farms. My poor wife was bereft of her mind. She was not strong enough to carry the load, and so I lost my home and all that was dear to me. Though it left me a broken pathway and scars in life, it has added to my heart's depth and soul's capacities. The pleasure I have in being with you in this, your trouble, more than rewards me for all my sorrows."

"Good friend, George, I will bear it all with a brave heart," answered Harry, much encouraged. "Life is but a short span, a tick of eternity. Shall dawn of yonder shores meet me, I shall feel that my life has not been wasted," he said, as he arose, followed by Lankey.

These little thoughts which had eliminated from the pair, much inspired and refreshed them. It dispelled the deep sadness which had settled over Harry, and relieved his friend Lankey, who shared the pains with him.

CHAPTER XII.

RED HOOK DAN CONNORS' LETTER.

As Harry expected, Mrs. O'Neil suffered a relapse upon his return from the Juvenile Farm on Hastings Hills, for she had strongly cherished hopes of news of her boy.

Time passed, but little May Thornton stood patiently by her. The poor woman felt a cheer with

The Little Sufferers

May beside her, and for hours they would sit and lightly discourse, but their talk would always drift back to her lost children. May felt hopeful that the children would soon be restored to her, and never ceased to assure the lamenting mother that the day was not far off, bidding her have courage and patience.

In her prayers May never failed to plead for the children's return, and she laid awake till many a midnight racking her little head with thoughts of means by which she could get the little ones returned. Sometimes she would plan to disguise herself as a Sister of Charity and carry them away. As such she knew she would be permitted access and freedom anywhere, and in particular in homes of the System, which caters to anything that can aid its false benevolence. Another time she planned to obtain a position as servant in the home of the System, and thus find means to get away with the little ones. Once she urged her oldest brother, a strong favorite among his associates, to join in politics and use his influence among leaders and high politicians to intercede for the release of the O'Neil children.

Naturally she confided all her plans to Lankey George. Their love had grown so they had reached to an understanding that they were to marry as soon as the O'Neil home had been restored. Though Lankey did not discourage her various plans, he put no faith therein. The children were at different stations, and a plot to recapture them must be carried out simultaneously. May's hope of obtaining a position as servant in the System's home was not at all probable. George urged as reason that the Juvenile System, which has its lockers full of little slaves for each of which it draws pay and can at any time reach its fangs for more, would hire no one on pay, not even for free board.

The plan that her older brother should take a hand in local politics and make a mark around the primaries and polls appealed to George. "Politicians and the Juvenile System reciprocate; if you control many votes, you can make a demand upon your district leader."

One morning May Thornton received a note from Red Hook Dan Connors. It began with a slight reproach for not acting in his favor in court upon the day Lankey George was on trial for having beaten him, but he wrote that he had forgiven all and would be glad, if for nothing else, for friendship's sake, to see and speak to her. Owing to the outcome of that trial, he further wrote that he had not attained his position upon the police force. His police job as probation officer had ended, but through strong influence he had obtained a position as agent with the Juvenile System, and for her sake would help to get the O'Neil children restored to the family.

His letter was not couched in the terms of passionate love, as had been his former writing. On the contrary, it ran with a distant respect, and was in a language more intelligent than she knew Dan to be able to write. It ended with deep wishes to her and the whole Thornton family, and with a kind request to meet him at the Flanagans' home on the following afternoon at two o'clock, where they would lay plans and devise the best means for the release of the children.

May read the letter three or four times; she studied it, and asked herself if it could be true. The style of the letter was manifestly not his, though she recognized the handwriting. She had passionately loved and trusted Dan at one time, but now she despised and mistrusted him. She pondered a long while on how to treat the letter. "If he proposes to renew our friendship, that can never be," she murmured to herself, and her thoughts turned to Lankey George, to whom her deepest feelings turned.

Could Dan have suddenly become so much a better man as the letter would indicate? Would he aid the O'Neils without making any demand upon her? These and other questions she asked herself, as she hid the letter away. She did not wish to lay a false hope for her sick friend, but decided to consult first with her mother and afterward with George. The matter pressed her so much that she could not wait till evening when Harry returned. So, after attending the present wants of her sick friend, she prepared herself to go home.

Mrs. Thornton looked the letter over carefully and shook her head, warning May that it was some trick. "He may love you, but if the quality does not lie buried alongside his heart, it's a dangerous love for you to enter into."

"Oh, don't fear, mother; I'll never marry Dan Connors, even though he was the president of the Juvenile System itself," protested May. "I think too much of George for that. But what I wanted to know is, do you think he is sincere when he offers to aid me in getting the children back?"

"Certainly Dan Connors is sincere. He will get the children for you; but his action is not impelled by love for the suffering little ones or their parents. You are the price he will demand."

"I'll die before I marry him," May exclaimed firmly. "But oh, I must help that poor woman; she will die if——"

"Don't worry, May; there will be other means by which to get the children," interrupted Mrs. Thornton comfortingly. "I wouldn't take any stock in that letter; just forget it and burn it; anyway, I fail to see how, while others fail, he could get the children."

"That's so, mother," returned May, relieved. "Dan always talked and promised too much. I won't mind a word he writes; but truly I would do mostly anything, could I help poor Mrs. O'Neil and the children." She arose, threw the letter into the stove, and returned to Mrs. O'Neil.

This afternoon was the regular visiting day at the institution. Mr. O'Neil, whose work would not permit him to lay off, generally took advantage of the Sunday special permits, and would visit in turn one or the other of the children.

Visits are economic factors to the Juvenile System, as relatives and parents and friends on such days never fail to bring along supplies of underwear and other miscellanies which will cover or fill the body of the inmates. While Mrs. O'Neil was not strong enough to join her, May prepared to go alone, and of course took with her a package of gifts.

Little Louise was naturally glad for everything, but while the matron absented herself, she had a chance to whisper into May's ear, bidding her not to bring any more clothes. "Dem children what is sent out west on big farms get all our good things what people bring with them, and we get nothing but these old things which is so cold." Here she turned up her outer gingham wrapper and showed threadworn muslin underwear two sizes too small. The child had lots of other tales of complaints which all ran in the same tone. The burden of it was that it was a wretched life, with neither home nor love, pleasure nor joy, feeling nor sympathy. It was work, and nothing to gratify nor satisfy; nothing to humor one; withal, it was a longing and a pleading to be taken home.

May Thornton stood helpless; she could give no help. She loved the child as a little sister, and it saddened her much to hear and think of the little girl's plight. She would, however, mildly interpret conditions to the sick mother, for fear of aggravating her ills.

That night after supper Harry O'Neil attended a meeting of the Lumber-handlers' Union. He left May alone with Lankey and the sick woman. George was her steady visitor, and she naturally divided her time with him during the evening hours.

"Say, May," suddenly asked Lankey, as they had sat together, "do you know your old sweetheart, Dan Connors, is employed by the Juvenile System?"

As Lankey so suddenly made this inquiry, May reflected upon the letter she had got. It brought a rush of blood to her cheeks. George noticed it, and remarked: "What is the matter, child, your face is getting as red as a brick wall?"

Lankey's remark did not aid her any; she stuttered a moment, tried to speak, but couldn't. She felt guilty that she had not told him of Dan's letter.

"What's the matter, dear? I love you as God loves the truth, and would shorten my life to bring you happiness; but I want no tinkering of hearts. If your heart beats for Dan Connors let it beat his way only. I will bravely surrender and aid you both to become happy," said Lankey, as May was endeavoring to command words.

"Well, I know I should, but—but I——" she stuttered, and made a further effort to calm herself.

"You know you should what?" broke in Lankey, sincerely touched and not grasping her meaning. "But you have not been fair to me by concealing it. That you love him is neither a shame nor a blame; but you should have——"

"George! George! Dear George, please let me explain! While perhaps I am wrong by not having told you, you are doing me a great injustice by——" exclaimed the girl; but she again was interrupted as the door suddenly opened and May's sister, Katie, entered. She held in her hand a letter which, upon noticing Lankey, she made a slight attempt to conceal. That George and May were emotionally stirred she did not suspect, for in her presence both had forced calmness upon themselves. Lankey spoke to her as usual. After exchanging a few words of general observation and of current news, Katie excused herself to Lankey, and asked her sister for a moment's private conversation. The girls drew into an adjoining room.

Quick of perception, Lankey noticed that Katie had attempted to conceal the message she carried. He also remarked an air of unusual secrecy about her, and for some few moments he speculated upon it. May's action a moment since had roused suspicion. He felt jealous and feared that she was not true to him. Why did she deceive him? Could she not have told him that she loved Dan best? Such thoughts agitated his mind, and he reproached himself that a man of his age should think of marrying again. Had he not had trouble enough? "Oh, it's just as well that it should happen as it did. The poor little girl is not bad; she just hasn't learned to know her heart. God give her luck and spare her to happiness," he sighed, feeling a bit relieved that he could view the situation so sensibly.

May and her sister remained but a few seconds within the adjoining room. As they re-entered, May carried in her hand the letter which her sister had brought. Lankey quickly collected himself and tried to appear unconcerned. "Sit down and let us have a chat," he bade Katie, forcing a smile.

The Little Sufferers

May could read Lankey; there was something about him which did not speak content. She felt that his mind had not been satisfied, and was anxious to explain what she was interrupted in saying at the time of her sister's entrance. Gazing perplexedly at him, she seated herself on the opposite side of the table. Katie begged to be excused, as a girl friend was waiting for her at her home, and departed.

As Lankey's eyes met the gaze of May, which was beautifully true, though sad, he blushed and felt much ashamed. He had been too hasty in judging her guilty, and he longed to offer her an apology. He was about to speak, when May said: "Have whatever thought of me you like, but I must explain——"

"Ah! when I look upon you, dear, that is all the explanation I require; I feel like a silly boy that I could have distrusted you."

"Nevertheless, I must explain," she said.

Then she told of her former lover's letter, dwelling upon its contents. She stated her mother's views and her own conclusion, and that she had destroyed it as absurd. As she finished she smilingly handed George the letter which she still held in her hand, saying: "This, too, is from Dan Connors. I want you to open it and read it for me."

This request did not affect him happily. He knew enough, and trusted her implicitly, and hated himself that thoughts to the contrary could have entered his head. "I shall not read it, my child; read it yourself," he answered, returning the letter.

"Oh, you read it, please," she exclaimed persistently, handing the letter back; "you read so much better than I."

Reluctantly he consented, but begged leave first to explain how Dan Connors' name had come into his life that very evening. To this she consented; whereupon

Lankey unfolded an evening's paper and read aloud: "Laws and the Juvenile System's rules prevent parents from getting their children. The System's agent, Dan Connors, yesterday locked up in the Juvenile System's room two well-dressed babies, one not a year and a half old, and the other three years old. The children were taken into custody within a few rods of their home, because their nurse was found slightly under the influence of liquor. Daniel Murry, a well-to-do broker, the children's father, and their frantic mother, accompanied by a lawyer, drove in their automobile to the office of the Juvenile System. The anxious parents were told they could neither get their children, nor see them until the court and the System had decided upon the matter. They learned, moreover, that the System was, till further notice, their lawful guardian. Furthermore, the Juvenile System refused to allow the frantic mother to see the unhappy children.

"Mr. Murry, with his counsellor, scoured town and tried to get judges to order their release; but it was learned that they did not have such jurisdiction."

The paper further commented: "Such incidents are not infrequent in any good family. While wife-beaters, assaulters, and all grades of criminals can immediately be released from jail upon bail bond by any district judge, innocent children or infants who need their mother's immediate care must remain in jail. Does not such a remarkable and astounding condition show the immensity and authority of the private Juvenile System and the limited power of our social system?"

"Awful! Awful!" repeated May, "that such cruelty can exist in a great, good country. Let us now see what Dan has to say." She nodded to Lankey, upon which he opened the letter and read:

"DEAR MAY: I waited for you at the Flanagans' house as my former letter stated. Knowing of the interest you take in the O'Neil family, I feel that had you received the letter you would have come. You surely cannot fear that an old friend will do an injury to you. For the next few days I will be away in the country, delivering some little children to their farming destination, but will return two weeks from to-day. So, if you have the matter at heart, please meet me at same hour and place two weeks hence. With kind wishes to your family and self, very sincerely yours, DAN CONNORS."

The letter was thus postscripted:

"The nature of the matter requires absolute secrecy, and for that reason I beg you to meet me entirely alone."

The letter was intelligently written, and it showed nothing to lead her to suspect danger to her nor any proposition of a reunion. Lankey considered it a moment and advised her to go.

"Well, but if he—he——" here she stopped for words to go on.

Lankey understood her, and added: "If he proposes to reopen a union, let it rest with your heart. Dan has political influence, and, as agent for the System, he is in a position to do a great deal toward having the children released. When I look upon my good friend Harry and the unhappy woman in her bed within, and think of the unfortunate children who are doomed to far Western farms to forget their parents and probably die immaturely from labor and drudgery, my blood curdles. It reflects upon my life of misery and all who are gone and have suffered with me."

"I will go," she said, with a spirited look; "I will plead with him upon bended knees. I have learned to love them all as they were my own. But I'll never marry him," she added, with determination.

"He would not be cur enough to insist upon that; but our duties lie in helping each other. Life is but short, and your earthly acts are your heavenly abodes. You could not offer your life for a better cause than to give it to save a family of five who, in my judgment, are otherwise doomed to dissolution and final destruction," said he gravely.

"Oh, I will! But, no, I can't! I—I love you," she cried, and buried her head in her hands.

Lankey, greatly touched, continued gravely: "Don't borrow any worry, dear child! I hardly believe it will come to such a demand as that. You are the cornerstone of my life; the only speck of hope I now have. Your loss to me would rip my heart asunder, but my soul, my spirit of heaven, would brighten, were I to aid in securing others happiness, to save others from a doom that not only staggers the body, but kills the soul."

"But—but—would you that I be sacrificed? I would, I would, but——" painfully exclaimed the poor girl, as she broke off, sobbing deeply.

"I would not have you sacrificed, dear May. Life to me will be withered without you, and God forbid that it should come to where you should be sacrificed. It would be an immense blow to all our hopes, but our duties must be considered. My atonement would rest with my soul's proclamation; it bids me suffer myself for others."

"But, oh, how could I make such a sacrifice?" expostulated May.

"You shall not suffer yourself, unless you are persuaded by your own spirit of thought. I shall not ask you to sacrifice yourself, but if fate so bids I must, with my life and hopes buried within you, stand aside and permit its course. The loss of you would be a lasting blow, from which I could not recover. It would be a sacrifice for us both. Within the depth of our souls, inextinguishable lights would gleam, and there would always point the better way. Though the suffering be for others, the reward would be our own. But it has not yet come to that, and I pray for our souls' relief that it will not come. Let us not despair," he ended cheerfully, stroking her gently on the cheek.

"No, what you say is so. While it would be my life's glory to help the unfortunate O'Neils, I hope it can be accomplished without yielding our own happiness," returned May, looking up cheerfully.

They remained sitting and lightly touched upon little details in relieving the O'Neils, and presently shifted over upon their own future hopes. At length they were disturbed, as Harry O'Neil entered. After having cast a glance at his sick wife, who was peacefully sleeping, he took a seat at the table beside them. He described the tremendous parade and demonstration which Jack Stevenson, candidate for the Assembly, had received. The People's Independent Party were thronging through all boroughs and proceeding with bands of music and illuminations with lanterns, torches and banners with inscriptions. They lauded Jack as a proper candidate. Upon the canvas of one wagon was printed in large letters: "The Cruelty of the Juvenile System must end. The obsolete method of punishing children for parents' neglect must, to save the generation, receive its death-knell." The other wagon's transparency bore the inscription: "Take police out of politics. Let us have a force to protect our interests and not blunderers and brutes to act for politicians and their parties."

Harry was happy, and May felt cheered with hope as O'Neil related Jack Stevenson's strong progress on his attempt to overthrow the System, for this meant the ultimate release of the little ones.

Lankey tried to show buoyancy though he did not feel it. He had for years watched and studied the various attempts, by a few individual reformers, to take away the tremendous power of the Juvenile System and lift the yoke which is now carried by many innocent youths and good parents. But his hopes had been blasted, as every attempt had met with failure and the System had fattened and now towered above all as a guardian angel and a benevolence to abused childhood. In order to add courage to his girl's hopes and that of his friend Harry, Lankey remarked: "The people will some day awaken to the fact and shove away the blinds which now shield the unchristian charity of the System."

"In the morning," now said Harry, as they arose and parted for the night, "I have to be at the Special Session Court in answer to the complaint of the Juvenile System, or rather the People as complainants, in which name it reads."

CHAPTER XIII.

HARRY O'NEIL DISAPPOINTED.

At ten o'clock sharp, as the summons read, Harry O'Neil stalked inside the Special Session court-room of Brooklyn Swamps. He took a seat within the crowded enclosure. The chairs and benches were crowded with all classes of criminals, new and old offenders. Their crimes attributed to them ranged from receiving of stolen goods, highway robbery, assault and battery, up to that of delinquency in payments to the Juvenile System. All of them were at present free; either out upon bail bond or upon summons.

In conjunction with its public duties, this people's court is a tributary to the private Juvenile System. The court exacts, collects, and coerces for it. Naturally with these extra duties it is a busy forum, and it requires three judges.

Upon matters of irregularities in payments into the Juvenile System, the dignitaries are relieved from the burden of adjusting guilt or innocence. There is no question of that kind. Towering above them is the System's superintendent. He renders the verdict; upon him hangs the decision. The descending judges simply consent and deliver the verdict of the System.

As the case of the People against Harry O'Neil was called, the System's superintendent appeared. He was stern, and he read the court his order which the judge again conveyed. Interpreted, the command was: "You pay or you go to jail. I will give you to the twenty-ninth."

Harry had brought money with him. He concluded not to take advantage of the grace of time, and proposed to make an immediate settlement. He was referred to the System's local branch office to pay his judgment, and he forthwith repaired there. He soon reached the System's handsome building. As he entered the office he gaped with wonderment. Though only a local branch, it was wholly alive with activity. It had the appearance of a banking system. Spaces were railed off and glass partitioned. A line of unfortunates, mostly women; some well-clothed, and others in rags, stood awaiting to take their turn in depositing their money with the receiving clerk. Each depositor held a pass-book in hand, and, upon reaching the window, the book with money was handed in above the counter. The clerk within counted the bills or change and receipted the book with a stamp, whereupon he again returned it.

All these depositors' pass-books bore credit vouchers only. There was a receiving window, but none for withdrawing money. Once passed over the counter, it is saved from withdrawal; it becomes a part of the System's hoardings and of no concern to the depositors or to the public.

Harry O'Neil as yet had no pass-book, but was credited by the clerk with the amount he paid. It was stamped into a brand-new book and handed him, with instructions to call regularly. He left the institution with the rank and file of the socially mulcted, and soon reached his home. The day was gone, which added to his fine, meant one day's loss in pay.

Harry O'Neil, however, showed no sign of despondency; he was a brave man, and had partly become accustomed to abide fate's working. He cherished the hope that things would soon come his way, but did not lie idle to await that deliverance.

Harry had worked himself into favor with his firm, who now offered to aid him in getting his children released. It was a little after nine o'clock this following morning that Harry, light at heart, set out with one of his employers, the head of the firm. He kissed his wife good-by. The sick woman was hopeful of success as her husband, and thought she felt strong enough to sit up.

There were none among them there who looked for a more speedy relief than May Thornton. In fact, she had never abandoned the hope of getting the children released, for these last couple of days, since her receipt of Dan Connors' second letter, she had however, been a very unhappy girl. She had promised the bereaved mother that she should have her children, though it be the cost of her own life. The piteous clamoring of little Louise had been silenced by the promise that she could surely depend on her soon to have her released. In her evening prayers she had implored God to suggest means by which she could bring about the release of the little ones. And now her prayers had been heard; she could fulfil her promise. But alas, was it at the cost of her own happiness, her own life? In order to establish their release, would she have to marry Dan Connors? This would indeed be a sacrifice of herself. It would mean a living death, a continued torture to soul and body.

May would carry herself bravely in front of her sick friend and Harry. George felt as touched as the poor girl. He loved her, and would have fought and risked his life for her, but he was not selfish enough to bid her to stay by him if her duties called her elsewhere. He knew that a man in Dan Connors' position, and with a varied political influence, would be the one most likely to effect the children's release. Past records and experience had convinced George that openly to fight the Juvenile System, as Jack Stevenson was now doing, and cause them to be subject to investigating commissions, would aggravate the System. In the end it would clinch them more, hand in hand, with the political machines.

"The Juvenile System cannot afford to weaken nor relent, no matter upon how strong a public demonstration; it would be an acknowledgment of the System's wrong course. To attack it is like fighting fire with kerosene. The only remedy for its not becoming more powerful is to leave it devour what it has, but save what it has not yet secured. Watch your little ones as a shepherd watches his flock," was Lankey's logic.

George, however, would never for a moment discourage May. He would say: "Bear it up, child. Nothing is really so bad as it looks. What enfeebles us most is that we are always looking for worse to come. Our minds are too apt to go to extremes upon either side. It is likewise so with our hopes and happiness, upon realizing them, they often show but very faint."

Elder Mrs. Thornton would worry with May; and, though she would encourage and hope for the best, she felt anxious over the outcome. She knew what it meant, should her daughter marry Red Hook Dan, and she also felt that May's mind was so strongly set upon helping the O'Neils, that her happiness depended thereupon.

All this day, while Harry and his employer were scurrying about, appealing to various heads of weight and power in the Juvenile System, Mrs. O'Neil and May were doing but very little else than speaking of the joy it would bring them, were they to obtain the children's release. May had heard that many rich business people or men of power very often got children released for their parents, by either having the judge speak for them to the System, or else speaking through friends who were large donators, or else directors or associate members of the Juvenile System. It was natural they would fasten some hope upon this day's understanding, as Harry O'Neil's firm were, besides rich and reputable business people, known as generous contributors to most institutions which appealed to them for aid. It might reasonably be expected that the Juvenile System also derived some benefit from Harry's firm, as the System's course was to beg for funds from any known individual or firm which were charitably inclined.

The parlor clock struck seven. May long since had supper ready and the table prepared, but Harry had not as yet appeared. "Probably they will bring the children along with them," hopefully ventured Mrs. O'Neil. She felt so improved and cheerful that she begged May to give her another cup of tea. They agreed that Harry's long absence meant good news.

They had left early in the morning for the sole purpose of having the children released, and Harry's employer was not likely to spend a whole day without attaining results. Both of them would listen at every footstep to catch the first tiding of the children's return.

As the dial of the clock showed seven-thirty, Lankey George entered and joined the women in the sick room. He was happy to see Mrs. O'Neil so much improved, and he also noted May's good spirit. As he seated himself, he lightly inquired if there were any good news.

"Don't you think Harry is detained so as to bring the children with him, since he stays so long? He said when he left that he would be back about three or four o'clock," said Mrs. O'Neil buoyantly.

"You know that Mr. O'Neil would not stay away so long unless something kept him," added on May, in a similar tone.

Lankey had been much tried of late in showing a false spirit. It pained him to hold out rash hopes, and it also hurt him as much to give them his discouraging ideas. In his opinion, had Harry returned early, it would indicate a good result; but the longer the time the less hope he held out. It meant too much scouring about to fulfil the object. Had they to go too much out of the way, and through many different channels, he feared that the chances diminished.

Of course Lankey had to offer some kind of opinion, as both of the faces looked at him for a reply. "Well, to me it seems an ill omen to stay so long, but again it takes time to produce anything good. Let us hope for the best, and not be discouraged."

Barely had he expressed himself before footsteps from the hall were heard. Mrs. O'Neil and May listened with their breath in suspense, but only the steps of one were heard; it was Harry which all recognized. Their spirits immediately sank within them; it was the first step of their disappointment. Mrs. O'Neil, who was about to drink her tea, without taking it, let the cup sink back upon the saucer.

Harry, covered with mud, entered, looking much tired and worn. He tried to assume a pleasant look, but his dejected spirit could not be hidden. His wife and May measured him with disappointment. Mrs. O'Neil tried to be heroic, and lay back upon the pillow smiling to her husband, for whom she felt as strongly as for herself, and she said: "Let us not worry, dear, but live in hope." But the poor woman deceived to encourage her husband, who looked crestfallen. She was worrying herself, and it gave a sting to her long declining hopes.

"Yes, that is so, my Nelly," returned Harry, in forced cheerfulness. "If we but have patience and courage, things will come out right."

May was as unhappy as any of them. She had brought her mind to look upon it as a duty to save the O'Neils at any cost, and she loved the family enough to do so. The only hope she now bore was that Dan Connors would release them. But what would it cost? She could not think; she leaned back in her chair and gazed blankly about.

Lankey noticed it; he felt for the three, and he feared the worst. Others' joy would mean his and May's sorrow; but now it was all sorrow and no happiness. Could he and May but purchase their happiness, their own sorrow would be somewhat tinged with joy.

A few moments of silence followed, which George broke by saying: "A black sky does not always bring rain; let us await and look for the clear patch back of it."

Lankey George grew to be much of a philosopher as

he became older. He was well read in his younger days, and had in humble life of late years continued to read. His manifold sad experiences in life, combined with his good qualities and knowledge, had made him broad and deep. His words and influence greatly prevailed upon his friends, who always felt a relief in his presence.

"George and I will go out in the kitchen and take a bit to eat," said Harry, rising. He was too disappointed and heartsick to eat anything, but was anxious to explain to George this day's experience, which he cared not to do in his wife's presence for fear of aggravating her ills.

May followed to take the things out of the oven where she had placed them. "To get my children and save my wife, my only hope now lies in Jack Stevenson's success," began Harry, after seating himself.

May, who overheard it, said nothing. She cast a glance at Lankey, which he met squarely, though both hearts were heavy. Neither Harry nor his wife suspected that May's heart could be the means of, or stood in readiness to break for the healing of theirs. Had the good O'Neils been aware of her intention, neither of them would have consented, as they both had learned to love her as one of their own.

After having supplied himself with some little food, Harry again said: "At seven-thirty to-morrow night there is to be the biggest demonstration at Cooper Union which has ever been held in the city. Jack Stevenson is going to speak upon the Juvenile System's course, and he invites a debate thereon. He bids every mother and father come and listen, and every citizen to meet with him and decide if the Juvenile System's charter and rights are not entirely un-American."

"That man Jack Stevenson, if for nothing else than

his courage, has earned the right to be mayor of the best town in the States," remarked Lankey, a little sceptically, as he lightly thumped his fingers on the edge of the table.

"You don't seem to have much expectation of his success; don't you think it will work to a good effect?" searchingly said Harry. "I hope you will come along to hear him, anyway."

"I certainly will go to hear him," answered Lankey. "I love to hear a good man, particularly if he speaks from the heart, which I feel Stevenson does. As to the effect, it is at least an agitation. No brook was ever so clear but a stirring would throw something upon its surface. Churn up the Juvenile System, and the stench will awaken Satan; but then, my friend, the rest of the world are not angels," he ended cautiously.

"You never commit yourself, George," lightly laughed Harry. "If I did not know you so well, I would take you for a pessimist. But whatever be the result from Jack Stevenson's crusade, I shall forever remember him with thanks."

"Yes, I am pessimistic when I deal with hell and fire. The brimstone of the Juvenile System had burned into the heart of society. It is crowned with wreaths of shame, and will remain a master foe until the curse which made it will crush and swallow it," returned Lankey savagely. "But then let us not despair, friend. The remnant of heaven is the happy glow within us, and I feel the joy of heaven that I bore my sufferings as I did. At the end of it all I shall feel I was the victor."

Harry was carried away from his purpose of explaining his day's journey by his friend's utterances, and remained sitting a moment, as if to take up the thread. Lankey aided him by asking: "Did you meet with reverse results all along the line?"

"That is just what I wanted to tell you!" cried Harry. "Yesterday you know I was at court, and afterward in the Juvenile System's clearing house, as you call it, and squared my accounts. I explained to you last night of the sumptuous office and their clean up-to-date banking system, but I meant to ask you what the System's purpose is in having around the walls in its outer room so many and various pictures of ragged and cadaverous-looking little children? Each picture had a clipping with printed matter thereon, and a number pasted upon it."

"If you read the clippings you would notice that it explains of cases where the System had been called upon. These are but extremely low cases which the System generally steer clear of; a few are selected which they hold out merely as a business card, so as to have it appear that the System is caring for the real homeless and neglected, and thus awaken donors' sympathy. These miserable scrapings from the slums are, however, soon disposed of by the System; they are either merchandised out west to do farm labor, or else shoved over upon the city training schools. Of course, if they are good, healthy workers, they are retained, for the System keeps no one to eat his head off. As to the numbers by which each picture is identified, this is a convenient method of their own to keep track and trace their stock. Every picture in the rogues' gallery also carries its number; so do carcasses in slaughter-houses, and every merchant numbers his goods. Don't you see?"

As George finished Harry began: "Well, I was very much disappointed and my boss felt as disgusted as I. Our first visit was to see the session judges. We saw Bilkings, Clemmons, Amus, and a couple of others in this borough and Manhattan. All of these judiciaries sit upon Juvenile cases, and are known to be friendly with the System. While they perhaps have no power to direct the System upon any course, they at least are so close that a word of recommendation would be considered. These judges scanned us over and they would probe to find out if we carried any letter or held strong affiliations with any of the established political parties. My boss, interceding for me, had no individual standing upon any political score, which fact they soon grasped, and each of them ventured the contention that the children were better off in the Juvenile System.

"One judge, whose name was O'Keen, or some name like it," he continued, "was extremely frank and more courteous than any of the others. He shook his head gravely and explained to us that the Juvenile System grants no release to children, except upon its own desire. Judges are helpless to act or to interfere. When once a child is committed, unless a judge has a good standing with the Juvenile System, his recommendations have no weight at all. He was powerless to aid us, but he advised us to go to the branch and lay our pleas before the superintendent.

"Thereupon we proceeded to the local branch of the System. We dropped into a seat, awaiting the superintendent, who, with his assistant, was busy negotiating a deal with a man named Miller who was anxious to have his seventeen-year-old son released, as he was very poor and had a sick wife and could not afford to continue payments. As I understood it, Miller owed the System thirty-six dollars. It would not deliver the youth up unless the full amount was paid, or they were given some security that the money would be paid, and meanwhile the amount, or ratio, per week accumulated. The superintendent and Miller, after some dickering, finally came to terms of settlement. The System was to receive one-third cash upon the delivery of the goods—the lad I meant"—he corrected himself—"and the System was to draw fifty cents per week out of the young man's wages from a promised job until the balance was paid."

"That is a clean game of legalized ransoming," exclaimed Lankey. "While upon its exterior it seems to be but a petty scheme, it is monstrous in gross results, and it strikes at the hearts of the poor mothers."

"Well, I'd be glad to pay nearly any amount for my children, and I would break a bank to get the money," said Harry reflectively.

"Yes, many a parent," responded Lankey, "when idle for want of work, in order to meet the System's demand, is forced to defraud his landlord, grocer, and butcher. Nay, I have heard of instances where mothers sell their honor to get a few dollars to hand over to the System for fear of arrest in failure to comply. However small the amount appears which the System requires, it is not always so easy for a poor family to meet the demand, besides caring for their own immediate needs. While it no doubt cost something, were parents to keep them, it would but be nominal, as rents, fuel, and care remain the same. There can be nothing so preposterous," continued he, "as that poor working parents should be compelled to pay a monthly bondage for their children. When children reach sixteen or seventeen and up, they should rather be a help than a burden. But of course it is by this course that the Juvenile System thrives; besides tolling the parents of these young people for board and clothing, it enslaves them on its farms."

"The System's method of holding children is clean up-to-date, as their little serfs are held out as bait for innocent donors, and, through its systems of courts, it blackmails the parents. It is a clear gain at either turn."

Both men now remained still for a few moments whereupon Lankey again began: "As to the lad seventeen years old you spoke about which the System saw fit to release upon moneyed terms, it is probable that some influence had been brought to bear upon it. However, the superintendent's persistency in securing himself and getting what he craved, notwithstanding the man's pleading of poverty, is a further evidence that the Juvenile System is not run upon a charity basis."

"Well, as I said," replied Harry, "upon the close of the deal between the superintendent and the father, we were motioned by the clerk to step near. The superintendent remained standing in the background, viewing us out of the corner of his eyes. He listened attentively, but said nothing. 'I am Mr. X.,' began my boss, and handed his card through an opening in the glass partition. 'I came to see what can be done about this man's children. He is very respectable, and an able man, and his home——'

" 'Well, you needn't mind about all that; that is for the System to decide. Have you got a letter from any of the judges?' broke off the clerk.

" 'We have been to several of the judges,' answered my boss, 'but it appears that they have no control in the matter.'

" 'Nor have they,' the clerk again broke in. 'It lies entirely with our committee at Hastings Hill whether it feels disposed to release the children or not. I am sorry we can do nothing for you here this time,' he ended abruptly, and began his work.

"The clerk's demeanor discouraged further presentment of our case. Disgusted, we proceeded to Hastings Hill. My boss hired a carriage at the railroad terminal, which took us up the hill to the Juvenile

Village, which you know lies in the centre of the farm.

"Happy, and in anticipation of seeing my boy, I alighted from the carriage at the office building and ran to his cottage. The matron in charge met us with a stern rebuke for calling without a permit.

"'It is only on regular visiting days and by special Sunday permits that parents are received. Children cannot be disturbed in their duties,' she remarked, and recommended us to go to the office upon any other business.

"However, the superintendent was not then in. While awaiting him, we walked around the grounds. But truly, George, if you ever read any fairy tales of dwarf lands you would think the writer had copied it from the Juvenile System. The grounds thereabout were swarmed with these little half-grown youngsters. All were clothed in overalls and jumpers, soiled and dirty from labor. It was a hurry and hustling everywhere. In the shoe-shop, tailor-shop, upon the fields, gardens, and all around the System's territory these little mites were each at their post. They all appeared alike, excepting some looked more tired than others. Although it all had the atmosphere of reality, it appeared like a colony of matured dwarfs.

"I was anxious that my boy should notice me, that we might greet each other, but their strict discipline has taught them to watch their work and stay at it. And in their gait, to and fro, look straight ahead. However, after waiting three quarters of an hour, the superintendent of this famous spot met us.

"'What can I do for you?' he asked, in a measured politeness.

"We began to explain our mission, but had scarcely spoken the sentence out as he half turned and said:

'Oh, you are on the wrong track. I'm not tending to that part of the business. You will have to go to the main office down in Manhattan, where the committee sits upon all official matters.'

"Angered and disappointed, we re-entered our waiting carriage and drove back to the train, reaching the main office just before the closing hour. The committee was still in session, but busy. A clerk bade us to take a seat till we were called. The door into the committee room stood ajar, and this enabled us to overhear and follow the proceedings.

"It appeared that a friendly interceder and a father, who had a son in the institution, were calling upon a similar mission as ours. How old the lad was which the System held in captivity can be guessed at, as he was committed past his fifteenth year, and as the conversation ran he had now been in the System's charge for two years. The interceder spoke nothing for a long while. The father was heard complaining: 'I am working for small wages and need all my earnings to keep up my home; every dollar is a great deal to me. That boy I supported for more than fifteen years, up to two years ago, when he was committed to the institution, and now when he reaches an age when he could be of some help to me and earn some little——'

" 'Ah, you want your boy out so he can go to work for you?' sneeringly snapped one of the sitting committee men.

" 'Not exactly, sir,' retorted the pleading father, 'but it at least relieves me of caring for him any longer. I have other little ones to look after, and that lad is big enough to earn his own support.'

"Here a voice which I learned came from his friendly interceder was heard. He said: 'Yes, I guess he earns his support where he is. I have looked thoroughly into the matters, and I find this man's son was

148

committed and held under Penal Code 675. It is no criminal offence, but simply a charge of disorderly conduct, for which a grown or mature person receives at most but a punishment of a three months' servitude at any public institution. This boy has now served two years with his release apparently far off, and you maintain that you have a right to call on his parents to contribute for his——'

"'Here, here! Whom are you who dare to speak thus? For your imprudence I will now hold the lad until he is twenty-one,' interrupted a stern, loud voice, evidently one of the committee members.

"'Oh, very well. I shall proceed to have the lad out upon *habeas corpus*,' returned the interceder. 'As a matter of fact, the boy's commitment was based on no actual offence of being disorderly. It was a technical charge preferred by the boy's mother, to break him of the habit of running about with other boys. She asked the sitting judge at the Juvenile Court to send him away for a couple of weeks. As to whom I am,' continued he, 'I am a reporter for *The Knocker*, and I thank you for having given me material for an excellent story.'

"'Well, well! Here, my dear sir,' in a much modified tone, came from the same committee man, 'let us not become so hasty and lose our heads. Your explanation of the boy's commitment which you say was adopted to keep the boy away from bad company entirely alters my position in the matter. Under the circumstances I don't see how we could hold the boy. I cannot release the boy at once, but two weeks from to-day, which falls on the nineteenth, his father may call for him at Hastings Hill,' he ended, with affability, and thanked the reporter for having called."

At this point of Harry O'Neil's narrative Lankey George broke in: "The delay of two weeks in releasing the lad was the committee man's clever thought. On the seventeenth, don't you know, is the System's anniversary day. Every inmate is needed to make a show and impress the rich invited guests."

"The System's people in this instance, however, met their Waterloo," remarked Harry.

"An elephant will trumpet and tremble for fear upon seeing a mouse," returned Lankey. "The giant Juvenile System could not suffer the least attacks upon it by any measly writers. It is not the fear of effect, but the vision of being gazed at from all sides which makes the System tremble."

"However," said O'Neil, "we were not so fortunate as the ones preceding us. We were roughly motioned into the committee room, where the three members sat. They all looked a bit flurried and a bit mild, but soon became stern. 'Well, what do you want?' was demanded by the committee's spokesman.

"My boss, a man of personality and a fluent speaker, after introducing himself, informed them of my desire, and offered the System to vouch for the children's safety and good care. He also explained my wife's serious illness, and added that if the children were not returned it would mean their mother's death.

"'Well,' dryly replied the spokesman, 'the children are there too short a time to be on the home list. The best we can do for you is to send an attendant down to see their mother once. Anyway, she is not fit to take care of them if she is as sick as you say.'

"'Oh, God!' said I. 'Had she the children, the mother would be cured and herself again in less than a week.'

"'You are a good prophet, my man. We sit here and hear so many excuses it nearly tires us to listen,' answered the spokesman, looking at his watch, as with his associates he arose and prepared to leave. 'I don't see how we can consider the matter at present. You will have to excuse us, the time has drawn out so late,' wherewith the trio passed us and left the building. They entered a waiting automobile and sped away.

"How I felt I need not explain; and my boss—well, you know it all," abruptly ended Harry, with disgust upon his face.

"I'm sorry for you, friend," sympathized Lankey. "While your firm is one of high standing in the business world and regarded well, I never look for much influence from such sources when dealing with tardy and shady problems. Why, a vagranted, repeating voter from any of the Bowery or Pell Street lodging houses would have had more weight and influence in this and like instances," cried Lankey, as he bade them good night.

CHAPTER XIV.

JACK STEVENSON UPON THE JUVENILE QUESTION.

May Thornton daily read the paper for Mrs. O'Neil. She greatly revived her sick friend this morning, as she showed her a page which spoke of Assembly Candidate Jack Stevenson's contemplated meeting for that evening at Cooper Union, where he promised publicly to lay open the flaws of society's dealing with the children, and agitate an upheaval against the formidable Juvenile System.

"God bless that man! He's fighting for a grand cause, for every child he returns to its mother he earns a heaven. For truly, dear May, a mother's love for her children has no comparison," said Mrs. O'Neil, and she added longingly: "If I only felt a little bit stronger I would go over; I should love to hear him."

"Harry and Lankey are going; I should love to go, too, but——" and May halted reflectively.

"But you don't like to leave me alone?" added on Mrs. O'Neil. "How can I live to repay you, dear May, for what you have done for me? A sister, nay, a mother, could not have watched more faithful over me than you have. In my bereavement you have shone as a star of hope; you are illuminating my wretched life. I should love to live to see that you would at least be rewarded for your tender care." Raising herself into a sitting position, she said to May, as she reached out her hand: "You must go to hear Jack Stevenson to-night, I beg you. I feel very strong and well and can easily get along alone."

"Indeed, if I go," quickly said May, "mother and my little sister will be here and keep you company. Katie is——" here she halted.

"Katie is going out with her company?" surmisingly said the sick woman, smiling gently. "You began to tell me the other night as the men folks came and interrupted us. He is a policeman you said?"

"Yes, and he is doing duty in Jack Stevenson's home district. Quite a coincidence, isn't it?" answered May. "He knows Jack well, and thinks he's a fine fellow, but he dare not show his good feeling toward him because of the animosity which the Department holds against him. For the least little thing these policemen do which does not suit certain politicians, they are transferred, and are given double post, or they lay in fear of some plot to fine or break them. He told Katie all about it."

"But you will promise me to go to-night then?" asked Mrs. O'Neil, as May finished. "We'll have lots of things to talk about to-morrow. Oh, I so long to hear it; I know his plan must be good and will help us mothers. But," she added, "if it is not convenient for your mother, I really feel well enough to remain alone."

"Don't speak that way," mildly reproached May. "You know that mother loves to spend a little while with you, she——"

"All right, dear, thank you," broke in Mrs. O'Neil. "I know she does, and I feel so happy when any of you are around me, that I cannot explain it. God was kind to me that he sent me in my affliction such good people as you all are. It is truly as Lankey says, 'There never was a night so dark but light could be made to reflect,'" she ended.

As Mrs. O'Neil mentioned Lankey's name May's face flushed. Though they often spoke of George, she at that moment fancied something of the joy it would afford her to be with him for the entire evening. Though O'Neil was to go along, his company never interfered with their talk and thoughts. Generally he would, when in their presence, appear too absorbed to regard them. However, May was fully awake to what her friend said, and with a bow of acknowledgment replied: "Yes, truly, that is so." But then a dark cloud drew over her face, she sadly reflected upon Red Hook Dan's letters. What would be to lighten her burden? Was she ultimately to give herself to effect the release of the little ones and restore the health of her friend?

But May did not remain in sad thoughts long, for her friend was in too good spirit for her to feel depressed. The night's promised event quickened hopes that Jack Stevenson would, by his forceful attack, break the Juvenile System and release the children and thus scattered the last of her depressing thoughts.

May busied herself with everything, as was her custom; she was never idle, if not engaged in housecleaning, cooking, or ironing, she would sit beside Mrs.

O'Neil and mend, sew, or knit. Nevertheless, this day seemed to drag out longer than usual. George was to be there at six o'clock, and join them at supper, after which they were to go to the meeting. Every fifteen minutes she would stir restlessly. At last when it reached five minutes of six, George entered, with Harry following ten minutes later.

After ending their meal, May set her little sister to work, cleaning the table and washing the dishes, while she herself prepared to join Lankey and Harry, who were both in readiness. The trio reached the meeting hall an hour before the appointed time. That they were not too early showed itself, as half the hall was then filled, and they were followed by streams of listeners. Half an hour before the time announced, there was barely standing room.

The assembly was of a greatly mixed variety; it had neither political nor religious aspect; there seemed no one class nor nationality. On the seats beside an ill-clothed, careworn mother, would sit a finely dressed lady or maiden with comfortable expression; beside a gentleman with gold-rimmed spectacles would crowd a dusky laborer or mechanic. It was a joining of old and young, rich and poor, happy and gloomy, to hear Jack Stevenson, who had of late sprung into prominence for his bravery in his single-handed attack upon the Juvenile System, which was by this civilized nation looked upon as an empire within a kingdom.

The audience did not have to wait long; Jack appeared ten minutes ahead of time. The hall rang with applause as he took his place upon the platform. Beside him were a couple of his friends and perhaps a dozen jurists and other eminent men of talent whom the Juvenile System had hired to step up and defend any attack which might be directed against it.

Jack Stevenson easily looked their superior. His

clean-cut, stalwart and healthy appearance was easily noted. He had a soul and heart, and feared not to expound the truth. His opponents, though richly dressed and wearing the tender of gentlemen, were haggard. They stood beside him as a Judas to defend the System; they were to sell their blood and crucify children on the cross of shame. Jack Stevenson was cheered and lauded with praises; he had won the victory before he had begun.

While not a college graduate, Jack was well educated, and was intelligent, forceful, and convincing. He had a natural gift of words. He had of late been thrown much before the public and had delivered many addresses, which fact aided him to impress masters of mind, and gave effect to his every word.

He introduced himself, not with any political flourish, nor as a candidate, not to force himself upon a public, but simply as an American, as a citizen who had a right to be heard upon a topic of burning importance.

"Ladies and gentlemen," he began, as he drew near the outer edge of the stage, "did it ever dawn upon you that the childhood of to-day is a nation's future? The bane of the young is the course of the old. Childhood and youth are a nation's wealth and strength; as it is reared, it becomes effective. Let me say, that if we cannot improve thereupon, we cannot build thereon.

"Take a glimpse inside of the panels of our Juvenile or Children's Courts," he continued, "and you are gazing upon a wholesale depraved system, a hampering of youthful growth. You will see many good little ones of able and thrifty parents brought there for no crime whatever, and you will see a cesspool of misguided little ones stagnated through parental neglect, who are flowing through society and to pollute the rest of the world. These unfortunate little ones, immature in mind, innocent of their own plight and conditions, are for causes, or no causes, made to face stern mature courses of courts and justices which grown society had established to deal with mature conditions only. This young growth is ripped away from nature's bosom of true parental care and planted out in artificial nurseries, kindred asylums, and institutions, which thrive and wax fat from profits wrenched from the marrow of these little ones.

"A Juvenile Court and Institution is by no means a good start in life; it not alone casts a shadow upon a child's future, but it reflects upon its parents and it reflects upon the child's future father and motherhood. Children's courts and institutions are sinful because they do not consent to correct evil where the evil lies. A child's guilt lies only in the extent of its parental grant. Whether this grant be hereditary or due to too much liberty, these little ones cannot be held responsible beyond their own understanding and teachings as to right and wrong.

"Children's courts are crimsoned with guilt for its lack of good and fundamentally true purposes. They are the elementary course which aid and abet the seizing of innocent little children and turning them over upon to be guarded and cared for, or rather ruptured in mind and body, by juvenile corporations, cloaked under names of benevolent juvenile institutions——"

"Sir! Sir! Sir! I protest," interrupted a venerable appearing judge, who had been called to defend the System. "On behalf of our good government, which ordains laws and saw fit to establish such courts which stand for the principles which it represents, I hereby, as a citizen respecting such laws, ask you to

rescind your statement and express yourself with more
regard for our worthy State and its laws."

His Honor bowed pompously as he reseated himself. The hall was a tumult of loud hisses and whistling, and with this sentiment of encouragement Jack
Stevenson proceeded. With a bow toward his Honor,
he began:

"Thank you, sir, I have nothing to withdraw, but I
shall be as regardful of rights and as moderate as
circumstances will permit, but I shall not hide facts,
nor shield wrong. That the best of governments can
be in error is evident by the fact that we people are
constantly learning and changing our thoughts and
making laws to suit. What I have said is but mild
toward what I contemplate saying." He paused to
look toward his large audience, who madly applauded
him as he threw this bomb. The defenders of the
System shifted nervously about. "The land with its
trade-mark of freedom and liberty, with a constitutional grant, tolerates a private institution to go into
homes and abduct children, imprison, punish, exact
ransoms, drudge them and chattel them about the country to slave for farmers. This is as much an avowed
fact, as it is a fact that our juvenile courts and session judges aid, abide, and approve thereof."

The twelve or more gentlemen who had appeared
to defend the Juvenile Course and System winced and
moved uneasily upon their chairs, but remained seated.
Jack Stevenson continued: "Among others we have
one—a private incorporated company with a consoli-
dated board of directors—which acts and works upon
self-made laws. It handles youngsters from all around
the States as though they were herds of cattle or common merchandise. This private incorporated Juvenile
System which lives and exists under our State laws

has apparently more right and power than is vested in any really public institution. Wonderful, is it not? But it is nevertheless a truth. (Great applause and hissing.) This private System," resumed he, "draws from the State fifty thousand dollars annually; it has a chartered right to enter homes of the poor and, without warrant or any established course, seize the children from this miserable class and through mechanism of courts and justice, under threats of arrest and punishment, blackmail parents for payment for the keeping of their children.

"These little ones are half fed, half clothed, half schooled, and are worked from their tiny age up to their final release. They neither see freedom, real sunshine, nor receive a caressing nod; no word of love or encouragement ever reaches them. It is all true," he added dramatically. "Were I to lay it all before you, it would read like a tale of Siberian cruelty.

"Now while this System draws from the tax-payers fifty thousand dollars annually, and has the use of our courts, judges, police, hospitals, and other allied public properties, no system of accounting has ever been offered or given out. In fact, it could not be forced from the governing body. 'It is none of the public's business,' is the System's answer. Now, in addition, this System extorts from parents, grafts upon the sympathy of individual donors, and sweats the little ones to the drain of their marrows."

"Will you permit me?" said a speaker from the group, stepping forward. "Our friend, Mr. Stevenson, is inconsistent and unfair; he is talking under a spell of prejudice against the Juvenile System. Some of you are, perhaps, well aware of that he was dismissed from the police force some while ago for some indiscreet act or failure to live up to his duties. One of the System's agents appeared against him for just causes, and his dismissal from the force he lays to the Juvenile System, and now he seeks revenge by circulating false rumors."

That this speaker was not as generally approved as Jack instantly was apparent. Not a single sound of applause was heard, but only continued groans and hissing. He was about to reseat himself when Jack Stevenson challenged his statement. "If any one is inconsistent and unfair, it seems rather to be laid to you, as you are becoming personal. Though I beg to say that you were very modest in arraigning me, were it not more of good form for you to disprove my statements with some facts to the contrary?"

Upon this the former speaker again moved forward. "I will disprove it, sir," he began hotly. "The Juvenile System has been in existence for fifty-three years; this fact alone adds honor to its title. A patriot, a noble veteran of American wars, who bears pure old English aristocratic blood, established it. Of excellent character, honorable of purposes as he was, he would never have lent himself to a scheme where the slightest thread of dishonor and injustice were ever likely to be shown in effect. To show you some of the System's splendid doings, I will read you a recent abstract of work done," he added, and drew a typewritten slip from an inner pocket, and read: "One branch of the Juvenile System in their four months' work, comparing with ten years ago, shows there is an increase of 180 per cent. in the number of investigations, and an increase of 1,600 per cent. in the item of prosecution upon the juvenile cases, with a 300 per cent. increase in the number of children indefinitely detained," ended he, satisfied, re-seating himself.

"Thank you, I shall discuss your last statement first," responded Jack Stevenson. "Your own proof of facts is that the community must be simmering in juvenile filth, and grows lower in sin at a tremendous rate. Your abstracts of facts also admit or otherwise accuse the weakness and lack of our government system that cannot compute its own statements upon so vital a matter as childhood, the corner-stone of the nation. Does it not show, sir," directed Jack, "that there is need of reform where a private money-grabbing corporation can lay claims and exercise itself as a clinic to perfect a coming generation? While we speak of it, let me state," said Jack, "there is alone in some single division of these children courts brought before judges yearly six thousand children, all ranging from infancy to sixteen. Upon both of these shown facts, does it not prove that courts and institutions to deal with children are no proper social remedies?"

"Let me again say," he continued, after a second pause, "our children's courts are unnatural institution schools for our youths. A reprimand there tendered does, at best, but imbue fear, and truly a child cannot blossom upon fear; its impulsive mind and unruly spirit cannot be corrected by a mild nor severe judge. The force of character and bidding must be forced upon children by natural care, which must lay within their very homes. A children's court should be within a child's own home; the parent should be encouraged and required by society to aid and correct. The delinquencies should be brought upon the parents who are the natural and true guardians. Our juvenile courts are but truly an imposition upon the child's right.

"So, likewise, is a juvenile institution. A system for a child to be brought up and reared in should be within the home of its parents. There he was designed to receive instructions and refreshments, to nourish both body and soul. Its parents are the only ones who can fully develop the child. It is their duty and their care, and they should be the ones to suffer and be punished upon shirking responsibilities which they have taken upon themselves. Let me impress upon you," he continued, "a child brought into life has a natural right to be taught and reared until it reaches a state of physical and mental independence when it is able to satisfy its own wants as existence demands.

"Courts and institutions are but exterior social attributes and incidents of mature's dealings, an immature soul cannot be brought close thereto. Pampered institutions, as the Juvenile System and likewise the Catholic Protectory, which act as guardians of these unfortunate children, and which are depraved in themselves, can add nothing to better their conditions. While the bodies of these little juvenile victims are but half nourished, the soul part of the child is entirely starved. They are reared under conditions that cannot show real humanity, real warmth and love. Such miserable children, as they grow older, become dwarfed in body and spirit.

"The natural training of all growths, whether it be plant, vegetable or human life, must be in the manner designed by the Creator; artificial application stunts all. The system of training and rearing must be of natural blend, or else the entire impulse of growth will wither and fail to unfold."

After halting a moment he continued: "Touching back upon our Honored Judge's remark that this particular Juvenile System or Society has existed fifty-three years, and was planned with the noblest of spirit and started by a God-sent of man, adds nothing to its present methods, which are faulty and false. Whatever the original purpose of this private organization was, I shall not question, but the Tammany order and also the Mafia of Italy were originally formed for good purposes, but now both of these have degenerated, and are the black hands of society, each after its own peculiar effective manner. The one makes and has the law and uses it to extort, and the other——"

"Here, here!" broke off a speaker threateningly as he jumped from his seat. "Do you liken the Juvenile System to the dreaded Mafia order of Italy? By your intimation you are not only insulting the courts, and our honored judges who in their duties deal with the system, but you betray the fate of our government, who grants it to exist."

This little incident provoked a turmoil in the audience. Men arose to their feet, stamped, clapped, whistled, hooted and shouted. Mingled with this was an uproar of laughter, and, as Jack began again, he was tendered a fresh ovation of cheers.

"There is no need of taking offence at my statements," he resumed, as the excitement abated and the offended speaker reseated himself. "If I likened the Tammany and the Juvenile System to the black hand, I should perhaps have added that their hands are gloved. We don't see them. No other apology can I extend you. In some respects I should apologize to the two organizations. I named——"

Now arose another from among their midst, a defender of the System. He held in his hand some enlarged pictures of the Juvenile Village. They were pretty, handsome cottages, which showed extremely neatly laid out surroundings. He began to explain the beauty of it all, of the physical and natural advantages to the city youths, the superior facilities for training of youths taken away from the slums. He did not, however, dwell upon conditions under which these beautiful surroundings were maintained, nor the cost of the youthful strength exacted to keep up appearances. He did not reveal the fact that it was a moneyed system of the strictest order, too raw in discipline, too severe for a young and growing child who needs kindness and living guidance. He also omitted to state the effect it had upon an incarcerated child. Truly it was but a picture of a grim bird in a handsomely gilded cage. The speaker, however, was not sincere; he could not arouse effect, he merely warbled and made a motion and shortly reseated himself.

"What this gentleman showed you was a soulless heaven. As to its design, it may well be likened to a negro plantation system of old, remodeled upon up-to-date ideas and standards of our new benevolent slave masters and industrial syndicates. These grind the souls of the poor and defenceless as much in these days as in the days of old. Only, as I said, the modes are different. The System has built handsome cottages, but the souls herded within are as lifeless, hopeless wrecks. It has finely carved cupboards, but nothing therein to strengthen their worn bodies. It has etiquette and schools, but nothing to strengthen the mind. It is exterior display and interior cruelty. It is a farce, and will remain so as long as it is based upon money consideration. While in public institutions there is much lacking, they nevertheless show a less taint of dishonesty, and can be tolerated if need be."

"My experience as a judge is," volunteered a person with snow-white hair, who looked kind and sympathetic, "that in so large communities as the one in which we live, that we need both courts and institutions to correct the evils of youth where parents are neither able nor willing. The separate children's courts are an advantage over the old method of bring-

ing the little ones before the magistrate courts. While
I agree that juvenile crime is not decreasing, I believe
in treating it with kindness and consideration, which
can be done only by having an individual branch to
apply to and deal with this class."

He seated himself, looking as if he had scored a
point. Jack Stevenson quickly arose and replied:

"Your Honor is right in saying that we need
courts and institutions to correct the evils. But the
evils of the young are the examples and doings of the
old, and it is there the punishment should be laid.
When parents are neither able nor willing, as you
said, they should be made to care. It is not a court's
duty to systematize a child, but to systematize its parents. Where the parental system is proper, a child
must naturally follow in the right course. A social
system is not a propagator of youth, but a propagator
of principles. It is a mature's position, and must
deal only with those past their majority. Until a
minor child has reached the System's growth, it remains part and parcel of its maker. It does not require wealth to produce good children, poverty-
stricken homes can bring as good results if there is
no barrier for children to founder upon. A mere mention of Lincoln's name proves this.

"Mischievousness and wildness in a youth is not
necessarily a criminal nature, it leads thereto only if
permitted to develop upon stronger lines. Youngsters, if permitted to shift about and rear themselves
upon the street, for lack of true parental care, naturally must degenerate and go astray. But to gather
them in an asylum to finish their growth under cruel
artificial surroundings is a cruel remedy, if it will at
best remedy it.

"As to the idea of kindness which his Honor a moment ago touched upon, I wish to state that, to bring

a spirited boy before a judge to be patted on the cheeks with encouragement, and told that he is a pretty good boy, will not make him so. It is true we can gain more by a system of kindness than by one of cruelty, but it is as true that no result can follow a cause where there is neither system nor method to build from. And again," he continued, "a judge at best can but inspire fear. Upon fear we cannot retrieve good feeling and regards. Whether the judge's tenor was mild or hard, it would only affect the lad externally. Would he not obey, and could he not respect his parents without the aid of courts, it would add no influence to his better inner self to go into court for admonition. Would he yield to the judge's demand it would then, at all events, but be in a spirit of contempt for his parents' inability to exert compulsion.

"A boy who must be brought to court for a reprimand cannot be a pretty good boy. Such a coaxing from an exterior source will have no effect upon a self-willed youngster; it only sours his spirit. He sees his upbraiding parent ridiculed, and he feels that the fault lies with them.

"Your Honor reflected upon the separate children's court system as being an advantage over the old system of magistrate's courts," Jack said, directing his attention to the former speaker. "I will say that, though it may appear humiliating to drag unruly youngsters to a court where drunkards and disorderly characters are brought, it is worth remarking that these unruly youngsters grow, thrive and associate daily among that class, and have become so accustomed to the lower order of life that they cannot be humiliated by remaining a few minutes before a judge who sits before a class of their own associates and familiars.

"It is a fact that since the advent of children's courts juvenile crime or mischief has increased. We believe it lies in the fact that mischievous youngsters look upon these juvenile courts somewhat as a stage drama. Many brought before that court of whom we have knowledge consider themselves heroes; at all events they hold less fear for this mild form of punishment than for that in magistrate courts, where stronger examples are shown.

"While both parents and children formerly showed a fear, or at least respect, for a regular magistrate court, the juvenile courts have to them no meaning other than that of kindergarten. The neglectful parents who, by their own disposition and example, are unable to control their children find it very often convenient to hand their unruly offspring to this little petty system, and have the judge scold them. The parents in most cases are not serious; they do not want their children punished. It is natural that there can be no lasting effect where neither seriousness nor principle exist.

"However, neither magistrate nor children's courts, nor asylums, nor institutions can correct or assume natural guardianship, nor mould the mind of a child whose true parents still live. This is because an immature mind cannot understand the cause of the institution's existence, beyond being a dispenser of punishment. These miserable youths will lack the confidence and will awaken to the fact that there is neither real love nor feeling to be found there. They will awaken to realize that it is coarser obligations which bind them. Truly such children have less to cling to than the ones entirely orphaned."

"Aye, yes, how about orphaned children?" asked a loud voice from among the audience.

"Orphaned children," replied Jack, "may, through

kindred Asylums or Institutions, grow up and reach the better estate of man by reason of their feeling of helplessness; their sole lone position in the world. Their little moulding self is set to reflect, they know they must lean against the external world. The coarser obligations of Society smile upon them less hard. Their own little self does not feel its bereaved position laid to them as a punishment for their errors, nor as a reflection upon the depravity of their parents. In their unfortunate position they learn to appreciate any kindness. Their speck of soul, their natural love for their parents whom they have not learned to disrespect, stirs them and keeps aglow their better sentiments. Aye, their inspiration and hope for meeting their departed parents at a future day encourages them on; thus they can grow good despite all disadvantages.

"Again, remove a youth from his parents, place him in an Institution. This child will feel himself a martyr, punished for some cause it really cannot grasp. The child's spirit immediately becomes inflamed; natural instinct conveys to him that he has a right to be where his parents are. Restraint invokes hatred, not only against Society, but against parents who the child, by a certain grain of reason, feels to be the cause of his unhappy plight.

"Thus we may conclude that children removed or committed through parental cause to Institutions find nothing therein to inspire their minds. Though they look forward some day to receive their freedom, and to meet their parents, it is with a feeling blended with reproach. Their cruel detention, their youthful restraint, upon their rightful freedom and liberty add nothing inspiring to their minds; they learn to despise that which they felt they should have loved. These juvenile youngsters who grow up with no examples before them, while not really bad when committed, will soon become so, or at best will not improve.

"Now then, let us reverse positions and we will establish the remedy. Reprove the parent instead of the child; not only would the father and mother assume their responsibilities, but this method would install a deeper fear within the child. The most stubborn and incorrigible child has still a speck of good nature. No boy is so strongly unruly that he would not awaken, were his parents to suffer punishment for him. It would take away that bragging pose of being a hero. It would break his colt's nature. He would feel that he martyrs his parents; it would strengthen his love and respect for them. Verily, study a child's nature and you will find within it lies a rule that says: inflict a punishment upon another and it has a strong and more lasting effect upon his mind than were he to suffer it himself.

"However, can it be more preposterous that a human race with seeds of endowments should bear so reprehensible children that their infant state and young pliable minds cannot be controlled and taught righteousness by their own makers? And that in order to sustain a right growth external forces and courses have to be subterfuged to? Is it not a mortal sin that a child in its teens should be hauled before the Courts of Justice, while the parents are complacently permitted to root in evil and in fact thus encouraged in it? Does it seem intelligent that a mere infant should be immured in an Institution, deprived of its freedom, while the parents, the whole cause, are allowed to saunter at large, free to enjoy nature and to continue their work of corruption?

"Furthermore, should a parent's obligation to parentdom but consist in bringing children into the world and throw in upon Social Institutions to be provided by public funds? Should not the burden imposed by themselves be carried by themselves? Truly, the Courts and Institutions which now blight the lives of youths should be invoked to punish the guilty ones, which is to be found in the parent branch. The disciplinary training schools and parochial Institutions should be clinics for delinquent parents, and there would be less disgrace brought upon an innocent human mind, and Society would grow better for it."

"Permit me to remind you," interrupted a System's sympathizer, and stepped forward. He was clean shaven and lean, and wore a Prince Albert, and looked in all pious. "While I do not wish to reflect upon the working of our great good government system or upon the working of any of its Institutions, I, though, however, wish to say that there is none among our private Christian Endeavor institutions which treat their charges so cruelly and neglectingly as is prevalent and proven in and among the city's disciplinary and training schools."

He reseated himself, and it was noticed that several sympathizers pressed his hands. All of them appeared extremely pleased.

"Ah, my friend," quickly flanked Jack, "I am glad you brought this question forward. The burden of real bad, incorrigible and untrained children, and the ones mostly in need of sympathy and care, your Christion Endeavor System does not bother with. Your adopted are of a class of children who, in most instances, are in no need of strict discipline, and should have remained in their own homes in care of their own parents, who are all able and could be made to care and rear them themselves. Another fact is that these private benevolent systems pick their own charges and select their own stock of youngsters. The ill and the scum of society they shove or throw over upon the public as unredeemable, or perhaps as unprofitable, whichever way we choose to look upon it. And still another fact is," continued he, "that nearly all of these unfortunate inmates now imprisoned in our public, disciplinary, and training quarters have, upon one time or another, or rather, suffered their first incarceration in some one of the various private systems. Aye, a primary course from which they graduated a medium to influence and inflame their ills——"

"Sir! Sir! I bid you guard your utterings," broke off a little individual, as he sprang to his feet and in a threatening manner shook his fist at Jack Stevenson. "Are you insinuating that our good charitable, Christian institutions are perfecters of crime?" He was too excited to speak further, his words clogged in his mouth, and exhaustingly he threw himself back upon his seat.

This little incident created a tremendous stir among the listening circle. A thunderous shouting, hooting, stamping, clapping, and whistling rung through the hall, so that the building vibrated. Jack stood cool and looked piteously at the infuriated little capacity who sat wriggled up in the corner.

"I am not insinuating," responded Jack, in slight defiance, as the turmoil had subsided. "I am accusing, and a thorough investigation will verify my complaint. What is further, there would be proved as strong ill treatment of inmates within the walls of those private benevolent institutions as has ever been laid bare among the ones entirely run by the public.

"Now in all fairness, let me ask you gentlemen," he addressed the entire group of System's sympathizers, who apparently sat as beaten. "Does it seem sane, does it seem true, that a government as ours, framed upon strict co-allied public principles, should be unable, unworthy, and incompetent of treating, caring for and correcting its own factious portion of society; attend its own neglected subjects? And, in order to fulfil human obligations and social duties, our standard form of government must throw into private cares, private dungeons, this miserable, neglected portion of our commonwealth? Is it not a vital shame that private courses, individual modes and systems can step in and take precedence over our government institutions and plank down rules, punish, lead, and affect part of the society? Where is the Constitution? Where are the rights of the remainder of society? Where is self-government?"

As Jack received no answer but weird looks, he continued: "Inabilities and failures by our adopted form of government to control and regulate its own functions and care for its own burdens, enforce its own examples, such a public system should be met with dissolution. Should it not? Our form of government must, after your view, be a weakling shame. Patriots as you desire to shine, you are by your acts and courses proclaiming monarchial sovereignty and individual rule, against which our forefathers put their lives down.

"In concluding my talk, I will state, this free, human-loving country, it is estimated, has one hundred and fifty thousand of these little neglected children stowed together within solitary brick walls of cruel, heartless institutions, who, through unnatural training and lack of true care, are blossoming into imbeciles and surging society with bad growth, implanting into our newer race a grade of moral, physical, and mental defected. I wish strongly to recommend this proposition: If we cannot presently lead ourselves to compel a proper parental system to care for their own progenies, let us not ruin these youths, but seek to have them distributed throughout the country in proper and individual homes, where they at least, to some extent, will derive part of that which nature designed them," added he, bowing, and thanked the audience.

The applauding and cheering was tremendous, while the various speakers who had come to defend the Juvenile System hurriedly sneaked off with their hats nearly covering their eyes. Jack Stevenson remained standing, as a hero, in the fight against the System of courts and institutions. As he proceeded to leave the platform, he was borne on the shoulders of strong, approving men. Weeping and crying mothers surrounded him with thanks, and pleaded that he should help them to have their little ones released.

Harry O'Neil and May Thornton both wept with joy, and hoped that he had not failed to deal a final blow to the System which caused them so deep a worry. Lankey George approved of all of Jack's speech, and would have loved to press his hand; but the crowd which surrounded Jack hindered any of the trio from coming within reaching distance of the much-honored and beloved speaker. But, glad in heart and satisfied in mind, the three left the hall.

CHAPTER XV.

A LIGHT-HEARTED DINNER PARTY.

Sunshine now lit up the O'Neils' household. Mrs. O'Neil, though weak and colorless, was much improved. She began to sit up a greater part of the day, and would faintly walk around the room and sit in the kitchen with May, while she was at work.

Jack Stevenson's successful progress in his campaign against the Juvenile System imbued her with such strong hopes of the release of her little ones, that in her thoughts she would plan a reception for their home-coming. May Thornton felt similarly hopeful, and had decided not to meet Dan Connors on the day he appointed, and, as the time passed, the appointment had slipped her mind. She no longer gave it a thought, but longed for election day, when Jack Stevenson would be elected to the Assembly and hurry through his bill to abolish the System.

Harry O'Neil felt as happy as either of them; he worried no longer for his wife, who showed continual improvement, and he had as much faith in Jack Stevenson's success as did his wife and May. They bought two or three papers daily and read accounts of the strong progress the People's Party were making throughout all boroughs. Jack Stevenson was through it all a Lincoln of the day. He was fighting to free the white little human slaves, who suffered and endured more than the negroes of old, and he sought to establish a proper and good remedy, whereby conditions could be righted and the nation buttressed with a healthy growth of youths. Of course, some of the dailies which were controlled by other political factions and who were friendly with the Juvenile System, severely criticised and belittled Jack Stevenson, and pictured him as ambitious for his own political purposes. One or two issues went so far as to say that, if elected and seated, he would vote for shelving his own bill affecting the Juvenile System. Papers which were antagonistic to the hopes of the O'Neils, it is natural that they did not read. Harry might hurriedly scan them, but he took no stock in their attitude.

Lankey George was not too over-buoyant, and never spoke much on Jack's coming success. "The sun has its spots," he always said, when things shone too bright, but he sincerely hoped for the best. He felt that Jack was true and sincere, but he would not discount his victory. Lankey's study of politics had taught him that it was not the public or people who ruled and regulated things, but political machines, run by the unscrupulous few. Should the People's Independent Party carry all the boroughs, it could not expect to do so upon fair methods.

A week hence would be settled the political outcome of Jack's efforts. Both of the good women looked forward to election day with a bridal longing, and every public tongue had Jack elected, consequently to all exterior view there could be no failure. Every day passed happily, merrily, and full of hope; on the evenings the Thorntons would call and spend a few hours in Mrs. O'Neil's and May's company, and over their cups of tea they would renew their discourse which always ran in the same strain.

The Sunday before election all the O'Neils' rooms were lighted to their fullest degree. Mrs. O'Neil had this day herself helped May to cook a dainty afternoon dinner. Mrs. Thornton and both of May's sisters had joined them at the table, and, with Harry and Lankey, they made quite a light-hearted dinner party. Over the table Harry and Lankey began to discuss Jack Stevenson's meeting, and passed remarks upon the various speakers and speeches.

"Jack certainly gave it to some of those judges; he made them turn black in spots. They had to pull hard and still they could not draw their load," remarked Harry, with such glee that he nearly swallowed the chicken leg which he was picking.

"You nearly caught it," responded Lankey merrily. "A mule and a beer pump are both made to draw, and so are those poor judges. The politicians hang on them, so does the Juvenile System, and also their conscience or feelings of right draw upon them. It is consequently not to be wondered at that they should turn black in spots. Most of our judges are no doubt learned men, at least more so than the average layman," he continued, in a more serious tone, "but economic conditions they never study; theirs is but cool theory. They have book learning to the extent of a writer's pen, and system of dead laws without measurement of circumstances and conditions. They cannot understand practical conditions, as all matters come before them in blended form. You cannot tell a saw by its buzz, nor can you understand the system of the poor unless you have seen the inside of their homes and their everyday conditions. Let these judges take a stroll about the vicinity of the poor, and view the parents sitting sipping their beer at nights and roll tipsy into bed while their children run about the streets until midnight or frolic in hallways and alleys. Naturally these youngsters must go wrong, nor can it be expected that these children can respect their parents. Such offspring grow up wild as an ungardened plant. It is as Jack says: Punish and teach the parents to do their duties, and there would be less bad children, and there would be no need of children's courts nor kindred Juvenile Institutions."

Here Lankey lit his pipe, and took up the conversation: "Juvenile depravity is so common that it is looked upon as a social necessity. Many of our philosophers on the bench give sanction to the idea that child depravity and vice are categorically one, and as baser qualities of man both must have space and room to thrive and to a certain extent be tolerated. It's another way of saying that wild oats are to be expected. In their opinion neither parent nor child is responsible. Their philosophy is, that angelic existence would be mythical, were all the world shorn of devils. Aye, some of our most learned go so far in reasoning that they look upon hell as the primary course to heaven, and the deviltry of man as angelic irrigation and as essential to mankind, as is a steam valve to a boiler." Here he added laughingly: "Of course, we are not all philosophers, and, therefore, must think slowly." Lankey moved his chair closer to his friend, and, in a light tone, mixed with seriousness and mirth, he went on: "While our system of courts and institutions take it upon themselves to maternalize and regulate infantile and immature growth, why not as naturally enter upon a plan of propagating youth? Planting and raising are relatively one issue, and remain paralleled until it has been perfected to a complete state of development.

"However," added he, after a moment's pause, "this method of our children's court to fine-comb the children and let the parents continue to heed vermin, does not end the spread of the disease."

"By the way, while our republican form of government grants so unlimited rights to a private corporation under which it may act as keepers, guardians, teachers, and also to correct and punish our young folks," suddenly broke in Harry, "why should not as just and proper that grant apply to the grown folks?

"Truly, this half-shingling a house makes a rudely cover. As the Juvenile System has a tackle upon one-half of Society, it would be in conformity to hand over the remainder. All public schools, almshouses, reformatories, prisons, and kindred State institutions might, as socially proper, be run by a private chartered clique.

"We enjoy but a partial government by the people. A semi-public——"

"A semi-feudal system," broke off Lankey. "And

176

it will remain so, so long as one or a body can acquire laws to rule, punish, and infract upon a whole people as now it does. Indeed, our government should be broad enough to handle all matters pertaining and affecting its own people, regardless of age, stage, and conditions in life. Let me say," continued he, "in a country as this, which proclaims religious freedom, we have altogether too much religious hysterics. We are certainly not far removed from the dark ages, the old friars' state, where the monks and cloisters laid the rules and yoked the people, so long as we permit any religious sect of humanitarians disguised to lay edicts for the general people to go by.

"Search into the methods of any of our benevolent lauded systems," resumed he, "whether such are termed Children's Aid Society, Prevention of Cruelty to Animals, Catholic Protectories, Vice-Crusaders, or various linked others of moral tenders. All are laden with graft and shame. Vandals of our constitutional grant. But it is as Jack says, 'Their hands are gloved,'" ended he.

Here he was interrupted by Mrs. O'Neil, who said:

"Mrs. Thornton was just telling me she read that a learned man wrote that a mother's love and feeling for her children is but simple animal nature, like that of the coarser herd. A hen will scratch for her brood of chicks; an eagle will claw for hers, and a tigress will fight for her cubs, as will a wretched mother fight for hers. I think that man was insulting. Don't you?" she ended inquiringly.

"Well, yes, I think he was rather mean, if he ended there," answered Lankey. "While there exists the same acute fondness in both animals and humans, we can but compare it as sunlight and twilight. The lower orders will discard their offspring upon the arrival of a new brood; the cord of connection here breaks. The human or motherly love is supplanted with a more lasting intelligence and sense of duty. A mother will live on and cling to hers by her own feeling of responsibility and love. Her reflective mind and her memories are the connecting thread of continued attraction. A woman's love for her husband can be as deep as a bottomless ocean, but her love for her child is as an endless chasm in the universe."

. "Well, now I think I love my husband as much as I do my children," entered Mrs. O'Neil, sending a look from her eyes to her husband which spoke the truth.

"There is no end to a woman's love in either sphere, but it affects differently; she might die for either. Her love for her husband is acquired; it is linked with sense and reason, and can be broken by the same cord; a mother's love for her child is natural, it is her flame of soul and self, there is no cord to break, for it is an integral part of her."

"We can love others, besides our husband and children," remarked Mrs. O'Neil, sending a loving glance toward her true friend, May, which was ardently returned.

Lankey George understood her meaning, and fondly stared at May as he said: "She is like a sunbeam, she radiates from the centre of her heart."

May thanked them, and blushed; but said nothing, whereupon her sister, Katie, in a teasing tone, responded: "Ah, George, don't flatter her too much, you may later find flaws you didn't look for."

All of them laughed, and George mildly assented to the possibility which he thought quite unlikely. "Very true," he went on, "every star has its measured depth. But, nevertheless, dear May, a girl like you can travel with any girl and eclipse the best of men."

"There is no mistake about that," here entered Harry; "women as a rule are too over-fond of their children. I love my little ones, but could always see their faults."

"Here you spoke wisely," responded George. "To sit as a judge before your own children is what is lacking with many a parent, regardless of social standing. It is safe to remark that any parents idolizing their children will some day suffer scorn. As much as a child needs parental love, a bosom to cling to, and a heart and ear to confide into, again as much it needs a firm, deep example and a ruling of seriousness to direct him. Upon growing to manhood or womanhood, children never betray strong love and respect for a parent whom they never learned to obey. A brilliant boy, brought up under strict influence and strong example, carries with him to the grave the memory of his mother and father.

"The majority of parents with juvenile offenders," continued George, "never impress upon their little ones' minds the real seriousness of their doings. Mischief is only looked upon as harmless pranks, both by mothers and fathers, and no stronger reprimand or explanation or warning is given than a light remark of, 'You better look out!' This vague admonition so customary and in the tone it is spoken, has no other significance to the little mind than a warning of 'Not to be caught,' and, of course, they ply their deviltry in the spirit of ascertaining how far they can go and elude detection and apprehension. In their career, they are led in upon a stronger line and become habitual or chronic offenders. It is obvious that the parents are entirely to blame; they do not add the right interpretation, nor show symptoms of seriousness. That responsibility should undoubtedly be enforced upon the parents' mind, if by no other means than by punishing them. They should realize the consequences of their immature's acts."

"While we talk about it, the word love is a great word, isn't it?" remarked Katie.

"Ah, love is the broadest of all words; it can neither be measured nor adjusted. While the word is that of man, the action is cosmic," answered Lankey. "The very word of hatred is blended with love; every impulse and action, if cherished by our own feeling, is grounded in love. Whether our desires for gratifications be for the good or the better to ourselves or others, they are lovers' actions."

"I don't follow," said Mrs. Thornton. "We can only love with our hearts."

"It is not the physical heart which stipulates warmth and love, but it is from the deeper thought cells of man where it bounds. It is a peculiar action, and is grooved deeper than all combined senses," returned Lankey.

"Yes, surely love is a deep feeling," adjoined Mrs. O'Neil.

"Aye, truly. It is an ideal fixture of one's own self," responded Lankey. "A loveless person is in himself a pity. He lacks the virtues of true existence. He is as a wickless lamp, and his life must be like an outburned ember.

"Love is the radiating centre of all creation; it is a wisdom's system. We, endowed, are grains of this system. The Creator, the aspiring cause, is beautiful and lovable, and the true source of will and wants. Thus love is a cosmic abode, and we humans are part and parcel thereof," ended he.

"Why, a cat or a dog or any animal is a part of creation," broached Katie.

"To be sure. But the lower order is not endowed with higher receptive qualities. Nothing in creation can stretch beyond its receptive mind. Gratifications, wants, wills, and ambitions of the lower life are narrow. Their gift of love, the higher trend of wisdom, is not divinely sanctioned them, and they cannot aspire beyond their receptivity."

"Say, George, you have so finely defined a mother's love for her husband and children and all other kinds of love, now let us have your definition, or rather your experience, on lover's love," broke in Katie Thornton, with a laugh. "This will interest me more."

"There are as many ways to look at it as there is to describe the orbs. The definition must correspond with one's own imagination," evasively answered Lankey.

"Oh, no, that's no explanation, George; you must do better," quickly returned Katie. Mrs. O'Neil supported her in this demand.

"Perhaps not, but it leaves one to guess at his own position. As for me, I would prefer to outline the solar system."

"No, no, George; a man who could conquer a heart such as May's must be a little out of the common, and be able to depict a lover's dream," affirmed Mrs. O'Neil.

"Very well, then," replied Lankey, in mock seriousness. He looked at May, who sat leisurely picking at the fringe of the table cloth. The others of the company stared at him, longing to reach his conclusion. "Lovers' love is strong emotions which can be stilled only by the gain of one's desire. It is as varied as the seasons, and it requires a sieve to sift it down to the real qualities. An attack of heart spasms we have all doubtless had at one time or another," he ventured. "The quantity and quality of such emotional affliction can be measured only by one's own gauge. The earlier attacks, or primary state of love, are more or less of a hysteric form, which grows and diminishes upon its own impulses.

"Lovers' love differs from platonic and other forms of friendship and love in this, that it is grounded in a passionate fondness which lies in sex differences.

"A man's love for a woman can be as burning as a woman's love for a man, and the sting can have the same effect, yet the quantity and quality is as different as sheep's wool. Man's love for woman, upon reaching attainment, simmers down to a strong attachment, while a woman's love for a man burns on and never lacks the sentiment which it first bore. Common sense and duties should be unbreakable bonds upon both sides."

As Lankey finished, they all merrily clapped their hands. "I must write that down, and have it before me as a recipe," said Katie, as their merriment subsided.

"Ah, nay, as a recipe it is invaluable," reminded Lankey, looking at Katie. "Lovers' love is not made to order. The cavities of the heart cannot be filled by a hollow hand, and, though, as I said before, it has no direct lines to be gauged by, it must have an impulsive touch to flame from, and upon which it can grow and live on by a nourishing care and feeling."

"Then, as I understand you, a man's love is not as strong and durable as a woman's?"

"Woman is more faithful," explained Lankey. "While both are linked and thrive on respect and feeling, a man can love and divide his feeling, but a woman can love only the one she feels she loves. And, again, a woman's love can turn to hatred. The one she at one time loved and pictured in her heart, she can learn to despise so that his existence is a pain to her. Let me note, though," said he, "the first cause, the bond, must have been broken by man, by the one she loved; for verily man's fidelity and a cherished tender will cement a woman's love so that it can with-stand all batterings."

During this last speech May sat somewhat buried in thought; she reflected upon her old love with Dan Con-nors, whom she now both feared and despised. Lankey George felt much relieved, as the women folks again took up discussing their own. For a while they dwelt upon Katie, who was preparing her trousseau; she had kept company but a short while, though she and her policeman loved each other enough to hurry along the nuptials. Her betrothed was drawing fourteen hundred per year, and had a promotion in view, and thus saw easily his way clear of maintaining a home. He was a country lad, and all his folks lived far off in a Western state. Boarding house life tired him, and he had planned to marry at an early date. Of course, Mother Thornton found no objection, though she always held the opinion that a longer acquaintance would strengthen their understanding of each other.

While they laid plans and exchanged views, Harry began lightly to complain: "If that lad of mine shall remain a long while in the Juvenile System, I fear my hopes for his higher schooling are gone. Willie was rather inclined to study. In my younger days, I was eager for schooling, and I have often wished that I had reached higher in all branches. I had planned that none of mine should ever lack the chances to learn all that could be stored in them, but——"

"Don't worry, Harry, though he should be detained in the Juvenile System to twenty-one, if he has the grain within him, with a little encouragement, he can reach up. Gladstone learned languages at the age of eighty. We can learn at any age if we plan to do so. He will, of course, be at a disadvantage if at the same time he has to take to physical labor for self-mainte-nance."

"Speaking of it," responded Harry, "a professor in one of our universities recently expounded that learning and teaching above ordinary algebra and letter-writing, is a waste of brain tissues for the common man."

"I am no evangelist on higher studies excepting upon its right lines," replied Lankey, "though I will say, every new issue opens a channel of thought, every new thought is a grain of wisdom, and wisdom is the radiating centre of creation, and of the force of the universe. But," he added, "many a gifted man studies himself into jail, or at least earns it for the advantages he took of his learning. And again many a man with no brains to learn, ruins his natural trend by a useless waste. But all should learn to follow and make the most of the times."

"The professor I spoke of before I reckon need have no fear that the world will become over-stocked with learned men. The average boy would rather play truant. Though I think as you that all should learn up to certain lines."

"The best of children from the best of parents will 'play hookey,' if they are not guarded," here remarked Lankey. "Schooling is a tiresome routine of mature's requirements for these little immature ones. A grown person will become restless and tired upon long and irksome occupation, particularly where study is required; so what can be expected from youngsters in their earliest time of sprouting and with the lightest of minds? It is natural at that age, that the necessity of learning and the higher knowledge shall not have reached them. Teaching and knowledge are too remote for the little ones to see into. While it is handicraft, and of use to the grown, it is for the little folks nothing but a useless drudgery, or rather a torture. We all like to shirk where there is no charm, what, then, may be expected from a less settled mind?"

"That's so," agreed Harry, as he permitted Lankey to go on.

"While truancy can lead on to crime for the simple reason that youngsters will run about without supervision in their hours of schooling, it is functionally no crime, nor does it imply moral inadequacies nor lack of better thoughts within their little minds. Of course, to carry on an intelligent system of society, schooling and teaching becomes necessary. While most children do not crave for it, we all, nevertheless, approve of it upon our maturity, and we all look upon it as an advantage, and it should be compulsory upon a parent to see that his child partakes of the advantage."

"Well, I understand that parents are now and then hauled to court for their negligence of holding their children thereto."

"True; but it's very seldom," replied Lankey. "We never heard that a parent received a sterner rebuke from a judge than a cast of pity for being bothered with such bad children, or maybe a word of warning. The courts customarily arraign the children; such truants are, to some extent, scolded and warned by the judges, but upon their release their parents will fondly explain that their boys are not worse than others. The effect is a re-occurrence. A further course is the Juvenile Institution, where the associates and mingling with others as bad as they are, with the effect that they receive no learning at all.

"These methods of hauling the little ones to court for their shirking of school duties is no encouragement to the youths, for the reason I stated some while ago: it invokes a hatred against the school authorities, for such little ones feel they are to attend school only to please their teachers."

"While we dwell upon it," asked Harry, "do you believe in corporal punishment administered to school children?"

"Under a government system where there is no touch of seriousness applied to neglectful parents, I believe in some method of punishing the little ones. It is essential that a child must obey some one in order to continue with such tiresome routines as schooling. If parents are permitted to disregard their duties, the teacher stands piteously helpless if he cannot impose the duties upon the children."

"As moulders of young minds and builders of ethics," resumed Lankey, after a short pause, "disciplinary training schools or juvenile institutions are without exception failures. The environments are such that these detained ones cannot grow and become morally adequate. As vile growth and ungardened plants, these are heaped into unfertilized soil. It *is* natural that, if not entirely bad when committed, they will become so upon mixing and blending with other ills. Nay, corral from a hundred to a thousand raw youngsters into one institution, with no other care than cool, unfeeling attention and strict coarse rules. What must not be the result? Their devilish spirit must grow rampant where they, in their frisky nature, see nothing good to copy from and nothing worthy to mould from.

"Our disciplinary and juvenile institutions are an elementary course, criminal in effect. The advanced class or higher branch is at the Elmira Reformatory, and the final course is at our State's prison, Sing-Sing. Our criminal courts can verify it all in detail. And, ah, the immoralities practised by these unfortunate youths within walls of institutions are so shocking and sad that it puts a blot upon indecency. The parenthood is the primary cause of these evils. Society is equally, a cause by neglecting to effect a truer condition," he ended.

"Say, Harry," now interrupted Mrs. O'Neil, "May and I have planned to attend church next Sunday if I improve as much as I have these last few days. I think you and Lankey ought to be ashamed of yourselves that you never go there," she mildly reproached.

Mrs. Thornton and May agreed with this censure. Katie, who always felt in humor of chiding, attacked Lankey: "You can bet if you were my fellow, you would have to go."

Harry agreed to his neglect of Sunday duties, whereto Lankey but dryly answered: "It is not the height of the church spire which leads nearest heaven; the floor strewn with sand within the humblest cottage is just as near."

"You are terrible," mildly reproached Katie. May smiled, but said nothing, whereas Mrs. Thornton remarked sadly: "Folks nowadays seem to drift away from church; but, indeed, I feel it a blessing to go. Father Rex, of our Holy Church, is a good and saintly man, his sermons give me great comfort. Truly he inspires the feeling that he can save me. A high priest and holy as he is, I really think he can."

"No man, be he ever so good, can link his name with heaven and assure safe passage there," replied Lankey. "I have faith in Father Rex as being a good moral man; but many a humble forester, whose altar and Christly edifice is simply nature's green woods, adorned with arching blue skies above, are nearer the gateway of heaven than he in his robes with his censer."

"Oh, George!" protested all the women folks. "Father Rex is at the head of the Brotherhood of Good Angels, and he does much work in relieving the hungry and poor. Those woodsmen are but half Christian," added Katie.

"A half moon shines on full faces," responded Lankey. "Woodsmen or uncouth men of hills and forests will help a stranger, console the sorrowed, and feed the hungry with as deep, aye, deeper, spirit and heart than will our full-crested evangelists, who hover within costly buildings walled with memorial windows."

"Oh, no, Lankey, we cannot agree with you on that," they all said, shaking their heads. "If Father Rex and all those of high and churchly rank were not more saintly or holy than we others, they could not preach for us and advise us."

"It is not the feathers that make the ostrich big," retorted Lankey. "The powerful ecclesiastics are towering high above us common mortals and strutting about in saintly plumes. Pluck them, and you will find their bodies are but of the mortal clay, and their spirits as much linked to the worldly as those of beggars or woodchoppers, who toil for a living."

"You don't believe in rites and religious ceremony of any kind? Indeed, I'm sorry for you," lightly reproached Katie.

"Warmth of devotion to each other is the only unction of man. Phlegmatic priestly prepared is no show of Christianity; it will not shove us farther into heaven," replied George.

All looked disgustedly at Lankey George, as he ended. None cared further to attempt changing his way of looking at things. His little May, as he loved to term her, appeared momentarily downcast and sad. For the first time she now showed some little disappointment. George, in her eyes, had always been so grand and good that she never looked particularly into his religion, nor had he into hers. She felt that their religions were alike. However, she soon overcame her momentary disappointment as she looked into his honest eyes and reflected upon his conduct. "A man like him cannot be real bad, anyhow," she assured herself. Lankey noticed it, and said: "Don't worry, dear May, I will live under the order of any edict that can assume a serious aspect of true Christianity and deliver the goods in actions."

"Well, I wish to know what your belief is, anyhow," finally asked Mrs. Thornton, somewhat seriously. She liked and respected Lankey, but as a man hoping to become her son-in-law, she thought she had a right to ascertain his status of belief.

"My father was a Protestant and my mother a Catholic; between their dickering on what to believe *and* look up to, I learned what to think and look into. Perhaps I stand as ignorant as they stood, but I gathered that both of their religions were symbols of faith, fortified in the biddings and mandates of man of common clay, but garbed in priestly and clerical attire."

"Must I understand it that you don't believe in any system of religion at all?" said Mrs. Thornton, horribly disappointed.

"We all have a religion within ourselves," replied he. "It is ground in a mutual acquired and required. By performing a thorough social duty, we are living nearest the standard of a true religion, and upon it we can build a heaven."

Harry O'Neil felt it was a better plan to preserve their religious differences and to change their subject, though he privately agreed with his friend on this matter. Lankey was a splendid conversationalist, and could speak on all matters, and his talk would take a humorous turn to suit occasion, so it required but a short time for him to regain the full confidence of the good women.

For the next few minutes he devoted himself to

joking Katie about her lover. After which the evening was finished with listening to George tell some amusing tales and incidents concerning his younger days.

CHAPTER XVI.

THE DEFEAT OF JACK STEVENSON.

At last Tuesday morning came around; it gave birth to another day which went down in the history of Greater New York as infamy in politics. Voters were bought and sold by political machines, repeaters were shifted about in droves to vote in any of its weak districts. More money changed hands over the bar of gin-mills and cheap beer dives on this day in one borough, than would feed the homeless and destitute for a whole year in all New York. All was done for the sake of good government.

The saloons opened ready for business at 5 A. M., and so did the polls; as the worthy voters crowded in and out of the saloons, they would visit the polling places and cash-in their votes, leave, and again return, and, under the protection of our metropolitan police and machine election inspectors, they would vote and stuff the ballot boxes as fast as polling clerks could scribble down names. Dead, living, and unborn names were voted. To the skilled politicians it was a calm vision of victory; the less skilled were hopeful, and the voters did not care. All the districts of Greater New York shared this infamy in proportion to its gross population. Among the poor and most populated, whom a bad government system effects the strongest, there was the most corruption and ballot-stuffing.

The importance of victory in this election was as weighty to machine politicians as ever, but an insured gain with a new competing party in the field required an increase in fraud, which, however, was easily accomplished. The People's Independent Party was new and strong, and it did not have the backing of the illicit voting element nor the constituting votes from any of the many government employees and job-holders; it was natural the decent public would fall in great minority.

Harry O'Neil's firm was busy, and had decided to run on till noon, but Harry, in order not to lose his vote, at an early hour joined the rear end of a first shift of bar-room voters. Harry O'Neil, as any decent voter who must hurry to work, was measured up by the smart clans of politicians who have their crew of inspectors to detain and retard. This is a practice which very often forces a respectable man to go home without casting his vote. However, Harry had determined to cast his ballot, though he lost his job in the effort. Thus, after many difficulties, being pushed back and taking turn after every newcomer, being challenged and otherwise annoyed, finally, after an hour and a half, he was permitted to vote, and he reached his work ten minutes late.

Lankey George had no work on that day, though he went to the polling place early. He had not moved from his old district, but the same difficulty was there encountered. Lankey had long ago given up the idea of voting, and, had it not been for the sake of helping Jack Stevenson and his party, he would not have voted at all. Politics and voting system looked to him as farces. "Why not leave one or two of the bosses meet and decide the matters as they do anyhow, and distribute the tremendous cost of an election to aid the miserable, half-nourished mothers, who take to drink to deaden their torture?" was his logic on our existing election conditions. Where the only advantage of being a citizen and a voter lies only in to be handed an extra dollar and some free drinks for this one day in the year, George thought it was good economy to stay at home. "This campaign money and political outlay for display with sundries of free drinks and shoes for bums is but nominally a loan. The politicians sweat and graft the community with a usury rate so that the very debauching voter who accepts these insults is groaning under the load."

Upon casting his vote, Lankey hurried to Van Brunt Street, where he joined May and Mrs. O'Neil for the day. Both were holding small American flags, which were pinned on thin rods, as George opened the door and entered, they simultaneously waved their emblem. May, who had a sweet voice, struck up a national hymn to which Mrs. O'Neil, who began to show signs of health, joined.

"Oh, everybody says Jack Stevenson will win," said May, as she ended the last strain of the chorus. "God would not disappoint me; I have prayed so much, and I feel in my heart that my plea has been heard," said Mrs. O'Neil.

Lankey George, who was a man who believed in facing conditions, could not here withhold a sigh. May noticed it; but, without suspecting its cause, she inquired: "You don't feel so very well to-day? I think you work too hard. I'll have a cup of good strong tea and a bit of buttered toast for you in a moment." Mrs. O'Neil encouraged her to do so, and May prepared to leave for the kitchen.

Lankey George could, perhaps, have drunk a cup of tea to deceive them and hide his feeling, but he feared to lead them on to be too sanguine of success; he was afraid of the blow which would come to them, should they suffer disappointment, and he had not the heart to pierce their happy spirits and hopes without real foundation. While he questioned himself if he did not look rather dark upon the situation, he called May back. "I wish for all the world I could go a cup of tea, but truly I don't feel like having anything just yet."

May seated herself again, and dismissed from her mind her suspicion of Lankey's illness. She explained to him in detail all that she had heard in the stores and upon the street. "Good mothers are crying with joy, and bad boys are getting scarce, and the police are getting civil. It's only the bad parents whom the courts are going to deal with, and all of the officers of the Juvenile System are going to jail, and the children will be released." Such a wild conglomeration of encouraging remarks had little May heard that she could but believe it to be so, and Mrs. O'Neil was fully as credulous.

Lankey listened attentively to it all, and assumed as much cheerfulness as his conscience would permit. While he loved to be in their company, he felt relieved as they went into the kitchen to prepare dinner. Taking up a paper, he read a few columns; but then threw it back in disgust. The paper spoke of nothing but success and success and encouragement for the People's Party, and held out brilliant hopes and ideas which the editor should know by practical reason to be unfounded, for success cannot be had where the voting element is of the political office or job-holding rank with distillery-bought repeaters to fill up to a majority count. "It is good enough to show the best spirit in such matters, but it is wrong to make hearts and then break them," he murmured, thinking of Mrs. O'Neil and May, who were so certain of success for Jack Stevenson and his party that a contrary view would awaken suspicion of a feeling of opposing their interest.

The dinner was soon ready. Harry O'Neil had ended his half day's toil, and all sat together, enjoying their meal. Harry did not feel so cheerful as in the morning when he left. His experience at the polls at the early hour convinced him that political machines squandered no time. He saw corner loafers, who, on any other day, never arose until past noon hours, standing in line to keep a decent voter waiting. What would the condition not be later on in the day, when the gangs and the disorderly element, full of rum, took charge of the polls to cast the deciding ballot? Besides the general interest upon any change of administration among his fellow workers, was a shrug of the shoulders and the remark that things were bad enough as they were, and any change might make it worse. While they all held with the idea and principle of the People's Party, they felt it could be worse, and did not care to take chances; it would be losing their vote to vote with a weaker party, no matter how good principles it stood for. For these and varied reasons, and upon similar grounds, the haters of the machines joined its ranks; it drew them one cog nearer destruction.

Harry had picked up a great deal of his friend Lankey's philosophy; he hoped for the best, and prepared for the worse. Borrow trouble he would not, and, as his wife would coax him as to give his real opinion, he would only say: "The world goes round, and we must go with it, dear Nelly. Nothing is so sad but that we receive some compensation."

His wife, while she perhaps could not bear to admit it, felt the truthfulness of this assertion. She reached her hand to May, as she said: "Yes, I have been compensated by you, my faithful friend."

Their noon meal completed, Mrs. O'Neil and May

left for the kitchen. Harry and Lankey remained seated, lit their pipes, and drifted lightly in upon the day's proceedings. Their attention was suddenly drawn by a loud shouting, which sounded on the street: "It is estimated from the various polls that the People's Party will carry Greater New York by one hundred thousand majority!" was heard.

"Did you hear that, Harry?" joyfully cried Mrs. O'Neil, from the kitchen. Her husband answered; whereupon he and George again began: "I don't like to dismount until the horse has run his stretch. I fear the good women are discounting the victory; but you are a man, Harry, and when I speak to you I like to be honest," said Lankey. "A ray of sun does not make a summer, any more than a flicker of snow creates a winter. Whichever party carries the election, conditions will not be considerably the better. While the People's Party have not had a chance to disprove themselves, it is evident that we can never reach a high standard in politics where that party, like various others, is hiring halls and turning them into moving-picture shows. Why, Manhattan is full of show-lofts, where is put on exhibition live elephants, tigers, and other crude herds to discredit the one or the other of the competing parties, and all sorts of live dummies and mean caricatures are put on exhibition to ridicule the one or the other of the opposers. It is distinguishably cheap politics. Political parties who will resort to such schemes to catch a public cannot be filled with much honor, nor much relied upon to serve for the good of others. Neither can a variety of citizens, who approve of it and take in such a debauching grade of political show, be looked upon as an encouraging lot of voters. Is it not amazing that such penny variety arcades should amuse grown people, dealing upon serious social questions, upon which hangs our and our children's welfare?"

"I thoroughly agree with you, George; filter politics down, and we'll find instead of being organized society, it is organized crookedness."

"There you spoke as a judge," complimented Lankey. "The world is as a sown field of weeds with a few good grains here and there; but these are too often deprived of nourishment from the rich natural soil in which they grow."

"Your view of it is that the general people is defective?" asked Harry.

"The general people is defective, but nevertheless there is some good in all of us, which could grow on, and must grow, before we can reach higher realms. We have all reason and can think and must learn to do so. The churches and pulpits, which are now used in a false spirit, must teach and influence the weaker minds. We are all Christians and religious-ridden, but infidels at heart. The high priests and cardinals, who preach on God, are not as good teachers as the salesman who sells his goods for what they are, and extends value for worth. A good social system is the only true religion, or rather, it is the flower of religion; let that be installed, and God takes care of us all."

"Well, going back to politics, don't you think that Jack Stevenson is real honest, and if elected he would deal a blow to the Juvenile System?"

"Yes, Harry, I think Jack is thoroughly sincere, and, no doubt, we have candidates among both of the parties who can be trusted," replied Lankey. "But the dagger that strikes does not always hit the effective blow. If elected he will hold his place among the minority; he will stand helpless in carrying out his plan. Though to be candid and not to discourage you, this Juvenile System is so socially and politically connected and felt that there will, to my belief, be concocted some plot to rob him of his victory, if any such should materialize it is not that the System would fear a change in its position; it is quite safe among our present political vermin, but a man of Jack Stevenson's seriousness and ability in the Assembly might agitate the question so that, however little the public opinion figures, politicians of all grades would be forced to follow it up. It would then, naturally, mean a thorough revision of our Children's Court, and also the Juvenile System's methods."

Here Mrs. O'Neil and May re-entered and took seats. George and Harry ended their discourse on politics, and for some little while sat talking lightly upon other matters. Mrs. O'Neil discussed with May and Lankey their coming marriage, and planned the reception she was going to give them. Harry joined in and stated that his friend was looking younger every day, and was evidently trying to reach down to the age of sweet little May. Lankey was well able to face the good-natured ordeal. May did not say much, but appeared satisfied, and they often exchanged looks which spoke volumes.

The little party was interrupted in their fun by the entrance of Katie Thornton. She carried a telegram in her hand, and looked very happy. "My fellow is not too much taken up in politics to think of me. He says: 'Things look prosperous up this way, and at the end of the day there will be added to the list one man you will be proud of.'"

Did he mean Jack Stevenson or himself, or who did he mean? This momentarily perplexed them; Katie had not given it great consideration, she simply felt elated that he had been so thoughtful as to

send her some kind of word. Of course her sister
May and Mrs. O'Neil saw nothing in it but good
cheer to them. While the police were not friendly
to Jack, nor toward the People's Party, there could
in this instance be no thought that Katie's intended
would take sides against Jack, whose name was constantly upon the tongues of the family.

Harry O'Neil looked to his friend for his opinion,
and Lankey noticed it. Drawing back to his customary voice, without defining the contents of the
message, he remarked, "The most beautiful tree will
cast its shadow; let us hope the branches and leaflets
are not so thick that it obscures the rays of light."

Katie observed the doubtful in Lankey's look and
expression, and said: "You don't think for a moment
that my intended would hope to gain upon Jack Stevenson's downfall? While I did not give it a serious
thought, I am sure that he means good news to us all.
No man who shows traitor to another will ever marry
me."

"Every bugle call has its sounds, though it be far
from me to judge him or its ill, my child," he responded. "But every gain means defeat. The God-
dess glories at the downfall of the wicked. The ser-
pent squirms with joy as it crushes its prey, though,
let us hope, the victory will impel no sad burden."

The women folks for a while took up their seats
in the front room. Whereupon Harry and Lankey
again began to discuss political machines. In this discourse O'Neil grew extremely dark and bitter, and
flayed the political leaders for their greediness and the
misery they entailed. He branded the world as a
miscarriage; a grudge of Heaven. His friend inter-
posed, saying in a seriousness, "We cannot censure
the world for the doings of one. While the load of
the world is heavy it also carries with it what is beau-

tiful. The world is strewn by shame, and is streaked with human blood by the cruel courses of vampired leaders, but the sandals of Heaven, nevertheless, leave their imprint upon the earth, and this should not fail to encourage. Perfect harmony and pure politics, however, we shall not have until the body of people arise as one and single out their leaders; root them out as with brimstone and fire, bury them away within the solitary walls of prisons, which now, through their acts, are raised and filled."

"Well do you think that the people can ever so join together and lift the yoke, wipe off the earth the leaders who now drag them into the mire?"

"The keel that scrapes the bottom never reaches harbor," responded Lankey. "The people must lift themselves and seek a clear channel. These social leaders who now pilot us all upon the rocks to founder, we must discard and we must elect sounder and purer gauges to steer us thither. Not until we have reached thus far in our learning and more closely follow the one trend of carrying ourselves, will we revive from these conditions."

Here they were interrupted by loud shouting of "Extra! Extra! Assemblyman candidate Jack Stevenson thrown into Jail."

Harry, closely followed by Lankey, rushed to the front room. They all directed themselves to the window, where they saw a crowd surrounding a couple of newsboys who were loaded with extras, and handed them out as fast as they could give change. Katie Thornton quickly ran down to where the paper vendors stood, secured a copy and returned.

Mrs. O'Neil and May exhibited a distress which showed nearly a terror. "Oh, tell me what it is!" both begged before Katie had a chance to open the paper. "I hope, I hope," said Mrs. O'Neil faltering as Katie began to read the article which ran very strong and showed unfriendliness to Stevenson.

"Jack Stevenson, the veteran police officer, plying to reach higher honors," it read, "sits in the same jail into which he, while patrolman, cast others. It was established early this noon that twelve years ago, with two other convicts, he had escaped after serving two years of a five years' sentence in the San Quentin Prison in California. Pictures from the Rogues' Gallery and other various details bear out the story that this Jack Stevenson, who then lived under the name of John Rooney, and had so cleverly worked himself in as an officer on the Metropolitan police force, was a felon and a pickpocket. The credit of the discovery and arrest is entirely due to Officer James Clarmont, who——"

"James Clarmont! Oh!" Katie stopped with a sudden cry, dropping the paper upon her lap. "Can it be true? Can it be him?"

Poor Mrs. O'Neil was so overcome that she had to support herself against the table, and May sat numb and neither spoke nor moved. "Can it be Clarmont? Is it a trick? Why would he do it? Oh, I shall never marry him if it's so!" cried Katie.

Mrs. O'Neil gathered herself together in order to console Katie, suggesting that perhaps her lover did only his duty. With her own losing heart she begged her not to lose hers. Harry and Lankey looked disturbed through it all. The little company a few minutes ago had been at peace and the women folks glowing with happiness, but now suddenly a storm had broke upon their centre and darkened them all.

It had now terminated as Lankey had expected. Some political plot was in back of it. Jack Stevenson, it became known, was felt and feared more than a dozen ordinary candidates. The cause of the mothers and parents which he so admirably fought for, had stirred a stronger public interest in Greater New York than ever had been known before. The Juvenile System, like the machine parties, had realized its impending fate upon Jack Stevenson's election and the success of his party. Therefore, they had joined hands to destroy him. This method of defaming the parties' leaders was calculated to destroy his chance for election, and to weaken or scatter his party.

That this plot had been carefully prepared is evident, for upon the minute of Jack Stevenson's arrest all the boroughs were circulated with extras with pages in detail which were laid out to both discourage and shame any one showing allegiance to Jack and his party. The machine parties has resorted to this infamy as a last means upon perceiving the People's Party's progress and of Jack Stevenson's assured success.

It was also learned from a later paper that in other than Jack Stevenson's district, election clerks and inspectors had permitted a wholesale voting and ballot substitution. Legitimate voters' names were voted by this routine staff, and not only were ballots substituted, but batches of from two to five ballots were stuffed in the box at a time. Legalized voters who had thus been cheated were, under protest, ejected. The poll clerk, inspectors and the police representing the machine party all day had matters entirely their own way. But, despite all, the People's Party showed only a slight minority.

Another account read: "Notwithstanding a wholesale repeating and substituting in Jack Stevenson's district, he showed a majority. As a last resort to defeat him a long-hatched plot was carried out. This left clerks and inspectors entirely free to make ballots defective at the time of the counting of votes."

Of course Jack Stevenson did not stay overnight in jail. He had many ready friends, and was released upon habeas corpus, though the obliging mechanism of justice managed to hold him until after the polls had closed and his own district had been blotted of his victory.

This defeat of Jack Stevenson was a sad disappointment to all longing fathers and mothers whom the Juvenile System had bondaged. It was most of all a cruel blow to the little serfs who are stunting their lives by premature toil, and it gave a new lease to our Children's Court and our infamous social methods of dealing with little children. Though Jack felt it painfully, he took defeat coolly. He had been politically connected long enough to expect the worst upon any matters in opposition to standard political parties, and it was not the first plot contrived against him. Would he get redress where there was no real zeal or justice to appeal to? No, but he knew he was innocent, and his enemies knew it. While he did not have their love he held their respect, and his friends admired him and urged him on.

"My downfall will perhaps break many a good mother's heart, but I have shown to the world the infamy of our Child System. I have given Society a grain to work from," was Honorable Jack Stevenson's comment upon his defeat.

CHAPTER XVII.

MAY THORNTON'S APPEAL TO HER OLD LOVER.

The O'Neils' remained the saddest of homes. The unfortunate woman never recovered from the cruel blow she received upon election day. With Jack Stevenson's defeat vanished her last hope for regaining her little ones. Convalescing, as she was, upon the prospects of Jack's success, she suffered a severe and sudden relapse. Her disappointments had augmented her physical and mental ills so that she had been brought to a state where recovery was no longer looked for.

The Thornton family's physician had called regularly for some time, but had abandoned all hopes to effect a cure. "She may survive a fortnight, or perhaps a month, but she cannot last long, as every tissue in her body is wasting away," he declared. "Her heart is broken and no prescription, no medicine will avail."

May Thornton remained faithfully by her side throughout it all. The pretty little girl, who a few months ago was a blooming maiden, the picture of girlhood and the belle of Erie Basin, had sunk as though with age. Gay spirited and cheerful as she always had been, she now went about depressed and with a heavy heart. Her brief chapter of life appeared as though it would terminate with that of her bereaved friend.

May had long since set aside her girlish companions to slave for an impending fate. Her brothers and sisters would scold her, but she would make no reply except to sigh. Mother Thornton felt very unhappy because of this, and however much she loved and wished to help the unfortunate Mrs. O'Neil, she could not bear to sacrifice her daughter. She would reproach May and try to make her realize that she must not destroy her own life and future happiness for a cause she could not help.

The mother begged and pleaded that she would relieve herself in mind and take some little recreation, but poor May would weep and say: "I know, mother, I am doing an injustice to you; I know I am undermining my own health. I feel I cannot help the poor woman, but still I cannot do otherwise, and I would not, if I could, break away from her. I have learned to love her; she clings to me as though I was the only friend she has in the world. I fear that her end is not far off, though I pray and long that she will live on even if I were to go through my years in this suffering."

Harry O'Neil bore up bravely. He had the broadminded and cool Lankey to bolster him, and though he did not falter in his love for his wife, he had learned to look upon present circumstances as a fortune which should befall him and her. He fully did his duties and eased her where he could. He also noticed the effect which the worry had upon May, and felt sad that he could not prevail upon her to bear it with more ease. Lankey George, too, felt deeply for his sweetheart. He would not discourage her fidelity to the stricken woman, but he did upbraid her for going beyond her right in wasting her life. "You are but wasting your own life, without saving another's, my child," he would say. "We must live for others and die for others, but not lay down our life without good cause and reward to be derived therefrom. You must not sacrifice yourself to the waste and winds; it leaves but a blank memory to yourself and others. It should be a joy to me to lay down my life to save that unfortunate woman, but as it cannot be done, it is my duty to save myself."

One morning a little after eight, May was in the kitchen clearing the table and putting aside the dishes when she was disturbed by her friend's cry: "Oh, May, come—hurry, come!"

In obedience to the summons May rushed into her friend's room. "Oh, May," again said her friend, who had managed to raise herself to a sitting position, "I see my three children. I kissed them; I embraced them. Oh, the baby is so nice. Louise, Willie —" Here she halted and fell back upon the pillow. Her face wore a peculiar smile and her eyes gave a brilliant flash. She closed them and the features became deadly pale.

May Thornton had never known fear, and she was a brave nurse. Her friend she loved and clung to in life, should she fear her dead? She stood a moment and shuddered for she was alone. Had George, Harry, or some one else been there this moment, she would have felt greatly relieved. She was too frightened to become hysterical. Young girl, as she was, she feared to stay as much as she feared to leave. After a second's delay she nerved herself and tiptoed across the hall to a neighbor's apartment, and without knocking on the door entered. Incoherently and half whispering she begged her neighbor to come with her. The woman, a kind, elderly matron, understood May, and quickly accompanied her to the O'Neils' apartment.

May Thornton quickly rushed to her mother's house, explained her fears and had her little sister run for the doctor, who lived but a couple of blocks off. Mrs. Thornton threw a shawl around her shoulders and followed May, who was now greatly agitated, back to the O'Neils' house.

As they were about to enter the hall, a young lad from a few doors below accosted May and handed her a sealed note. "Here, Miss; Dan Connors told me to give this letter to you, and not to nobody else."

In all the excitement and bewilderment with Dan Connors fresh brought to her mind, it staggered her and she grasped her mother's arm for support. Her mother felt her daughter's position and realized her perplexity. May meanwhile was making strong effort to withhold tears. "Don't loose your nerve, my little child," the mother coaxed. "God is good, and will help us all." Upon finishing the last syllable the doctor hurriedly entered and preceded them up the flight of stairs.

The doctor quickly felt the sick woman's wrist. He shook his head and whispered: "Her life is ebbing away, but slowly; her end may come at any time, and she may live weeks. Her strong physical constitution and former good preservation of herself are her resisting elements. But all the medical skill in the country will not save her."

Mrs. O'Neil here opened her eyes. In appearance she was the same weak woman as before. She sent a loving smile to her friend May, who blushed and felt greatly ashamed that the fear and fright of a moment ago, should have overtaken her. Mrs. O'Neil recognized Mrs. Thornton and smiled as she reached for her hand.

The kind neighbor and Mrs. Thornton remained seated in the sick chamber, but May returned to the kitchen, too disturbed to resume the household duties. "Silly girl as I am," she scolded herself that she could be so lost in fear. As her mind began to clear she reflected upon Dan Connors' letter, which she had stuck into her bosom. Again she became nervous. "Oh, shall it, shall it be my fate to save that good woman and her little children with my own life. I shall do it," she murmured as she hastily tore open the envelope and read:

"DEAR MAY: The Juvenile System are planning to send the O'Neil children off to far western farms. You know what that means. You can save them.
"DAN."

"P. S.—You can see me any time at Flanagan's."

May crushed the letter together and threw it into the fire. "Oh, can I save him? Is he honest? Is he sincere?" she cried. With a firmness she murmured: "Well, I will see. I shall soon know. Can I save them, then I will; but shall I pay him the price of myself, his happiness shall be paid with my sorrow. Another day may be too late. These children may then be hid away in the western wilderness and my good friend die of grief," thought she, and she decided to wait no longer. The doctor had left instructions to remove the sick woman into a lighter and more airy room. Harry, who always took along his lunch, was not expected back till six o'clock, so May had her mother and the neighbor assist her in setting up a bed in the front room and carrying the helpless woman into it. Following this, May prepared to leave and begged her mother to remain till she returned, though she did not divulge her errand.

Boarding a Marcy Avenue car she reached within a block of Flanagan's home. The short distance was to her a long mile. Her heart thumped, her breath was short and she felt sharp pains in her head. Nervously and fearful she reached Dan Connors' home and dragged herself up the narrow, dingy stairs. As she reached the upper hall she halted and reflected upon her last visit there, which was at the Flanagans' "racket." She recalled the engagement she had broken off on that night and then came to her mind the eventful escape with the O'Neil children. She sighed deeply. All seemed sad and long years gone; yet she did not regret it. She had nothing to repent. She had but done her duty in helping others and she now stood prepared to do more, the cost which she could not foresee. She decided, however, to be brave, and lightly knocked upon the door.

"Walk in," was heard in response, and as May

Thornton opened the door Mrs. Flanagan and a comrade, who sat with a can of beer before them, each with a glass in her hand, simultaneously exclaimed: "Ah, how are ye, May Thornton? God bless ye," Mrs. Flanagan now alone spoke up as she bid May to a seat. "Ye look as black as a nunnery. What hive ye bane doin' ter yersel'? Sure ye was the finest gal in all Brooklyn 'fore youse broke off with Dan. Dan Connors is gettin' ter be the right looks ov a man. When you see him ye'll love all over 'gain." Her pal at every syllable nodded her head as if to verify these assertions. "Sure, sure." After having taken a sip of beer she continued: "Dan is gettin' ter be intellirgent, and looks like a jedge. He didn't get no perlice job, 'cause und that broken shoulder."

Here she halted and reflected a moment. "Oh, bad luck ter that Lankey George!" She shook her fist and pointed at a brand-new holy picture hanging above the mantlepiece. "Had he left Dan Connors elone Dan moight ter-day hive bin a perlice captain and my blessed old holy picture would never hive been broke. Sure Dan bought me this new one, God bless him," she went on, "and now he has all the luck in the world. He is a trusted agent ov the Jivernile System——"

"Sure, and Dan was out automerbalin' with the President ov the System, who is as big as Governor, and owns the foinest house o'er in New Jersey," injected Mrs. Mulligan.

"Dan'll some day be Superintendent ov the System," continued Mrs. Flanagan. "He spakes morn and night ov what a foine home he'd make for you, May, iv ye w'u'd ferget that little spat. Dan is no more a bad gang leader. He kapes up with perlititicians and other dacen company, and hive got the pull ov a jedge, and makes all kinds ov money. And he's learnin' ter be edjercated, too," she nodded, pointing at a dozen books which were strewn upon a shelf in the corner of the room.

Mrs. Flanagan continued tirelessly her loud babbling in praise of Dan Connors, and would now and then lightly scorn May for having broken off the engagement and encourage her to renew it at first opportunity. "All the gals in town are stuck on him. To be sure, he could fetch home a load ov them fer his weddin', but the poor feller hive ye in mind," she ended in a tone implying that she understood and sympathized with Red Hook Dan in his disappointed love.

May Thornton did not feel happy to hear of these strong comments upon Dan's infatuation. She now became uneasy and restless, though, while she dreaded to meet Dan she much longed to have it over. Painful as it was she said: "I must see Dan Connors on some business and would like to know where I could find him."

Mrs. Flanagan turned and looked at the dusty parlor clock. "Dan is in Court on duty fer the Jivernile System, but he'll lave the Jedge waitin' ter see you," she answered. "He would, that 'deed he would," confirmed her pal. Here Mrs. Flanagan arose from her rocker and stepping towards the window said, "I'll hive my Jimmy, who is playing crap with the lads down the street, go ter the Jivernile Court and tell Dan ye're waitin' for 'm."

Mrs. Flanagan's oldest boy Jimmy, who was part cause in the O'Neil tragedy, upon his mother's bidding, came slowly dragging into the room, smoking a cigarette. "Well, wat's you want?" he growled disrespectfully.

"Well, darlint, I want yer ter go to the Jivernile Court and tell Dan that his old sweetheart is waitin' fer him."

"Ah, I ain't got no time," remarked the lad as he ejected a secretion of saliva upon the floor. "Chase some other kid up there," he recommended as he returned to the street, taking up his game.

"Sure boys nowadays," protested Mrs. Flanagan in disgust as she refilled her glass, "aren't like boys ov old days. But sure there is worse boys in the ward than mine. When he grows up he'll hive better sense," ended she in a complacent tone as she drained her glass.

"Oh, I'll git ginny Joe, back in the alley, ter go. He'll walk his pegs off fer a penny," said Mrs. Mulligan, as she arose to send off the mesage.

Though but an interval of twenty minutes passed till Dan Connors came, it appeared hours to May. She was sick from the odor of the room, and disgusted to listen to the senseless babble of Mrs. Flanagan and her pal. How could she ever have tolerated them before? She worried and longed to return to Mrs. O'Neil, and she feared the outcome of her meeting with Dan.

Mr. Flanagan and a fellow worker had entered, but it afforded no relief. His wife began to cry and relate bad-luck stories and explain about the coal strike in all the yards around the canal, and with no work, and the beer raised two cents a pint. Pointing to a scar over the right eye of her husband, she continued: "God hive mercy on the bad people in the world; a scab hit me poor man with a brick, and he had to wear a brace 'round his head. Yes, fer six weeks at that. And poor Officer O'Sullivan, the foinest cop what ever was in this ward, the Lord hive mercy on his poor soul," she enjoined with motion of her head and an upward cast of her eyes toward the Virgin's picture, "got such a beatin' that he dies on 'count ov it a few days after. Sure 'twas a loss to the force, for a fine man he was indeed," she ended, wiping away a tear with a corner of her grease-stained apron.

Here Dan Connors entered. The color of his face showed that he had hurried. He smiled as he gave his hand to May. She returned his greeting with a touch of sullenness and looked at him distrustfully. He somewhat astonished May Thornton, though there was no mode about him which instilled great trust nor invited a reawakening of her feelings of love, he bore himself appropriately as Mrs. Flanagan had prepared her. He appeared more of a gentleman; he was clean shaven and wore a pearl stud in his tie. A finger upon his left hand bore a heavy gold initial ring. Across his waistcoat was stretched a solid gold chain; his dress was neat and tasteful. His external was pleasing, but had his soul and heart grown to match?" wondered May, half shaking with a palpitating heart.

Not a flicker of love could awake within her. Her sense of love had simmered down to respect and duty. She loved Lankey, as he possessed both of these good qualities. These good traits had grown in him so strongly and become so much a part of him that he could not conceal nor deceive his appearances. However Lankey was not just then in her mind. She had now other thoughts of love to fill her heart.

Dan bade May to follow him into the front room, which was divided off from the kitchen with two bedrooms. Instructing the Flanagans not to disturb them, he closed the two doors to insure their privacy.

"You look so awful sad May! The world is not suiting you," began her former lover gently, as he bade her be seated.

May bravely said: "No, Dan, it is not, and I came upon your invitation to see if you can help me."

Dan had seated himself close by her. "The world is not suiting me, either," he began, "for ever since that fatal night at the 'racket' I have not been real happy. You are the first girl I ever loved, and not until you broke off did I realize what real love was. I did not appreciate you at the time, but I assure you that I have suffered much and longed to have a chance to tell you so. I have a good job now, with a good salary, and lots of extra money, and though I live miserable here with my old friends, the Flanagans, I could well afford to furnish a nice home for a woman; but really I could not think of being happy with any other woman but you. And I pray you to forgive me for my harshness of that night. I speak the truth when I say that I deeply love you, and always long for you and try to improve to be worthy of you. Say you will be mine again, and I'll be the happiest man on earth," he ended, reaching for her hand, which she withheld.

May did not doubt that he spoke with sincerity, but though she felt for him, she could not aid him. "I am too sad at heart to talk of love, Dan. I came to ask you to help release the O'Neil children from the Juvenile System which you wrote you could. If it is in your power, I ask——"

May's words were not what appeared to Dan to be a rejection, and so somewhat encouraged him. Spiritedly he broke in by saying, "I can have the little ones released. I was the principal means of defeating Jack Stevenson, and the Juvenile System appreciates my service too greatly to refuse such a little favor as the release of three kids. For, at any time, I can get others to fill their——" Here he paused, but quickly changed the sentence. "In particular where the System has enough of these little ones. Say, dear May, that you will be mine and I shall at once proceed upon their release." Here again he reached for her hand, which she again withdrew and moved slightly back. This ruffled him a little, and he changed his tone: "Your eyes tell me that you don't love me, but you must. I love you and cannot live without you, and I want you to be mine always."

Though Dan Connors had heard that Lankey George had become a strong friend of the O'Neils and Thorntons and was a steady visitor in their homes, he never suspected that Lankey had taken his place in May's heart, nor did she care to betray it, for fear that it would enrage and embitter him, even though he was both in manner and speech a different personality from former days. If he held any real good impulses within him she could see, however, that he had no other purpose in view than to gain possession of her. "I told you, Dan," answered May, "that I had something else at heart than to talk love. If you love me as you say, do help me to restore the little ones to their mother, who is lying at the point of death from a broken heart."

"Say you will be mine and upon our wedding day I'll have the little ones handed over to their mother," asserted Dan in a mild, persistent tone.

"Dan, I cannot be yours. I——"

"Ah, some one else has your love?" exclaimed Dan, deeply stirred.

"Do not urge such a request of marrying and love, Dan, I can do neither. I beg you as a friend, I plead for their bereaved mother and longing father, and also in the name of Justice to the little innocent chil-

dren who are bereft their natural care, who want their
good father's advice and their loving mother's bosom
to cling to——"

"Ah! I see Jack Stevenson's speech at Cooper
Union started a spark in your heart," sneered Dan,
the first trace of his old self showing. "Why are
you sissing your head off for other people's children
when you could have a good home and be happy attending your own affairs? To be a friend," he now
changed his tactics a little, "is all very nice, but I
must be more than a friend. You loved me before,
and you can learn to love me again. Marry me and
I'll take chances of regaining your love——"

"Oh, Dan, oh, Dan!" weepingly broke in May. "Do
not speak so, do not be so cruel. While you disregard
my feelings I beg, I pray, have pity for me. It is perhaps a strange will of God, but I cannot help it, I have
learned to feel with the mother as though they were
my own children; be it a weakness, I cannot help it."
In a still more appealing tone she pleaded, stretching
her clasped hands towards him: "Oh, Dan, I implore
you, I beg you upon my knees, I ask you for the love
of me to give me the children."

Dan Connors was really touched. He arose and
walked nervously up and down. He saw that the love
he looked for was lacking. He realized that he could
never regain her affection. It cruelly affected him,
and he wavered in his feeling. In a flash, as if to
punish her, he turned towards her and said, "No, I
will not help you. You have, regardless of my feeling, stung me, and I shall have those children trans-
ported to the worst centres of the country, where they
will grow up like wild animals and forget their
names." He noticed that his cruel blow nearly con-
vulsed his former little girl. Bathed in tears, stricken
in deeper sincerity than he had ever before witnessed,

he softened to a milder tone, and now falteringly pleaded: "Can't you love me, May? Can't you say yes to my pleadings? You are breaking my heart. Say you will marry me, and your plea shall be granted," he ended, reaching both his hands toward her.

Kneeling before him, taking both his hands, and looking towards him she tearfully prayed: "I cannot love you as a wife should, I cannot marry you; it would break my heart and make you unhappy. I am suffering now, but if you have a speck of pity for me, help me. Oh, do, Dan."

Dan Connors withdrew his hands. He remained still a moment, touched but undecided. Then disappointed, he flamed into anger and cried: "No, you have crushed me and I shall crush you and my vengeance shall fall upon those children who have robbed me of my love," he ended, turning to leave the apartment.

"Oh—Oh, Dan! I will marry you, but give me the children," she piteously cried, following him. "I shall pay for their release; my heart's blood shall be your reward. I shall marry you and as your wretched slave shall dedicate my life to happiness in thought that I suffered the cruelty and injustice of the man who pretended to love me. Give me the children and I shall obey," she ended feebly as she fell fainting at his feet.

Motionless she remained upon the floor. Dan Connors felt a pang of remorse. It had touched him as he never had been touched before. The little speck of kindness within him had been kindled. It flamed into a blast. With tear-stained eyes he stared at the motionless figure. He clasped his hands as he exclaimed in a loud, faltering voice: "Wretch as I am, how could I disturb the happiness of the one I love? Heaven have mercy on me that I foster such ill nature. Shall the sins of Satan lead me on in paths of blood? No,

I shall not poison the life of that pretty, good girl, who offers her future to save others, who yields the blossom of her heart to right wrongs of theirs." He knelt beside the prostrate girl. Bending over her half-unconscious form, with tears trickling down his hardened cheeks, he cried: "Get up, May, pray get up. Forgive me for all my brutality. You have bled my heart and I shall be your slave till death claims me. The children shall be restored to you, and I shall forever bid you good-bye and bury my face with all my shame far away, where it never shall mar your happiness. Oh, do you hear me? I plead for forgiveness," he ended with a sob.

"Oh, Dan, thank you! I hear you! I have already forgiven you," she faintly replied, opening her eyes and turning her head towards him. "May God reward you, too," she added, pressing a kiss upon his hand.

Drawing her hand toward his lip, he said: "I thank you, dear May; you have at this moment made me more happy than ever has been my share in life. The faults and errors of my life have now first begun to dawn upon me. I grew up in cruel surroundings, my teachings have been raw and heartless. The only kindness that I ever felt came from my mother, who died when I was a child, and the only good that I ever saw came from you, from the heart of the one I ever loved. While I feel a sting and suffering that you cannot be mine, I shall ever love you. But worthless as I am, I shall hide my face far away and permit you to live your own happy life." Still in tears he drew himself up and gently raising the weak girl placed her upon a seat.

Much overcome May sobbed lightly. Was she in a trance or a dream? Could Dan, who had been so cruel and brutal, speak thus? Had the spirit of goodness revealed itself? her bewildered mind asked. She was awakened from her thoughts as Dan said: "Go home, my good angel girl. I swear that within twenty-four hours the children shall be at their mother's side. I admit that I aided in bringing on their ill fate, which has broken their mother's heart and burdened the good father. I belittled your love in days gone by. I was haughty, and brought evil on paths of others, and as a last resort to end my devil's bane I treaded upon and tore your heart asunder from my own. Despise me, you should; but you thank me and forgive me. God bless you. Good-bye, sweet girl. If you think of me, think of a broken man who will live and atone for the sufferings he has caused others till the Almighty at last absolves him."

As he left the room May Thornton now first fully awakened and realized that Dan Connors had spoken in deep honesty. Her heart felt for him. Though he was bad, he had shown traits of good within him. She knew that he was now sincere, she knew that he suffered. "Oh, if I only could have given him one word of cheer. If I only could have thanked him once more, and shown I had forgiven him," again she softly wept. But he was gone, her head swam in bewilderment; she did not know what to think, or how to act.

Suddenly the door opened and there entered a cabman, who approached her mildly. "Pardon me, Miss. A gentleman instructed me to bring you to your home. He said you did not feel well. The carriage is waitin' down the door, and the fare is paid, so——"

"No, thank you! I feel good enough to go hme. I'll just take the car. It will take me within a——"

"None of that, Miss," broke in the cabman. "You wouldn't offend the gentleman, I hope. He felt very sad. His eyes looked as though something was

a-burtin' him. A good Miss like you wouldn't hurt
his feelings more?" He gently touched her upon the
arm and she followed. Her thoughts reflected back
upon Dan Connors. Her feelings towards him was
now that of a staunch friend with whom she sympathized deeply. His better qualities had shown stronger
than his bad ones. He had much good within him
when awakened. To conquer it, he had to suffer. She
prayed that he would soon regain his happiness.

During the journey back to the home of her friend
her mind was a mixture of emotions. She felt happy,
and she felt sad; she worried for her friend; she hoped
and longed for the next day, when the release of the
little ones would come. She felt no doubt that Dan
would keep his word. This day had been a trial for
her life. It had been a sentence upon others. It had
afflicted punishment, and it had given reward. It was
the spirit of the Soul of man which had unfolded itself upon both plains. God the Creator of it all had
shown his wisdom of might, the value of unselfishness
and love. He had shown that the better self of man
is the stronger. He had shown that sincerity is the
strongest pleading. Within it all was a cosmic depth.

CHAPTER XVIII.

THE END.

Was the assurance of the release of Mrs. O'Neil's
children to end May's sufferings? Was their home
coming to restore the joy she so hoped and longed for?
It was a restless and sleepless night, and the morning
which followed was fully as sorrowful. The poor girl
bent over the unconscious form of Mrs. O'Neil. Between prayers to Heaven she begged her to have

strength and to live to receive the children. She fairly wore her heart out in effort to re-awaken her friend who remained lying motionless as in a trance. But neither a quiver nor a flicker was the poor girl's reward. To all appearances the end had come.

Harry O'Neil had remained home from work and Lankey had assigned some one to his job in order to remain with his bereaved friend upon the coming of the end. While George had faith in his friend as being strong and brave, he recognized that upon viewing the demise of his ,wife with all hopes to regain his children scattered, it would be more than he could bear. May Thornton had acquainted both of them with her hopes and anticipations, and both while not caring to discourage the kind girl, felt strong doubts as to the realization of her hopes.

Lankey admitted the possibility by saying: "There never was a millstone yet that crushed the corn but what left the meal behind. Dan Connors might have been a rascal, but he no doubt had some good in him. Though the life is ground out of the poor woman, let us hope and pray that the little ones will, as he promised, be returned and to nourish the spirit and heart of their worn father. Nothing can be so black but that it contains a hue of color," he would add, and then remind his friend of the lights behind the clouds.

Harry naturally felt much relieved with Lankey beside him, the load which otherwise would have crushed him, was now comparatively easy to carry. Both of them would sit and remark upon the beautiful fidelity of May. They also had some little worry regarding her health. Lankey daily loved her more because of her faithfulness to her friend. He felt she was sincere, and that her affections were genuine. Still, at the same time, he did not wholly accept it as natural. "An angelic spirit ought not to invade a physical existence so that it leaves sad footprints upon her own self. The poor girl is getting beyond herself. It is as though she strove to end her life for a cause which fate alone can account for. But there is no doubt that she is a wonderful and beautiful character. She is truly a saint in earthly disguise, and much the better would the world be were we all as she is."

"It's a grand inspiration to live for and help others," broke in Harry; "but there's not always a reward."

"Truly; but whether it be appreciated or not, it leaves a feeling of self joy. What you do for others is no waste, though it must be linked with reason. Cast yourself in front of the train if you thereby can save the crew and others, but never steer the scow on a rock unless you can see at least your own rescue. Man must not be fanatical and burn himself for pleasure or mere notions," asserted Lankey.

However, the good little May was pining away, and it was feared by Lankey and all that her death would come as inevitably as that of her friend. May, too, realized it. She admitted to George that something drew her to the poor woman; she loved her and suffered with her and would be satisfied to die with her, even though stores of pleasures were awaiting her in this life. It was, she admitted, a remarkable love and attachment for a stranger and a newly acquired friend, but nevertheless she felt it consume her. If it was a life ambition, it was none the less a worthy one.

It was close up to noon hour and the dying woman had shown no signs of life. Harry, George, and the faithful May, with her mother and the kind neighbor, sat sad and still around the bed, waiting an awaking or an end. Suddenly she gave a light quiver and with a faint motion pointed towards the wall, directly at the foot of the bed. A holy emblem, a large picture of the Lord's Supper, covered the wall. She again closed her eyes.

"Oh, merciful God, the good woman wishes to have the priest give her the last rites," sadly exclaimed Mother Thornton. "God forgive us, why didn't we think of this sooner?" in a whisper she reproached them. Harry O'Neil agreed with her, as also did May, and the good neighbor. Lankey, however, remained neutral.

"My good wife was always a good, faithful Catholic, and lived up to the order of the Church. This is the last wish of her life, and must be carried out," said Harry, as he prepared to go for Father Rex. He was intercepted by Mrs. Thornton and the neighbor, who bade him remain by his wife's side till the last. As Mother Thornton volunteered to go for the priest, the kind neighbor begged that she be permitted to go, and without a minute's delay she set off to find Father Rex.

In the space of ten minutes the neighbor returned, closely followed by a priest, an assistant in the large parish. Father Rex holds his assistants ready to go upon all calls of unction; personally, he attends to no rites, except upon extreme occasions, which are then only in appreciation of a rich donor, or some member of higher standing in the parish.

As the assistant father entered all arose with bowed head. Mrs. Thornton and the neighbor sank to their knees, showing their respect for the office of priest.

Lankey George, upon the priest's arrival, had entered the adjoining room. The good women folks stepped aside, permitting the father to perform his duties. Whatever aid the passage and rites were to the immortal soul of the poor woman, she remained unmovable, and to all appearances gone. The kind priest consoled the grief-stricken husband and offered a prayer to strengthen him, thereupon he departed. He was soon followed by the doctor, whom Mrs. Thornton had sent for.

"The good woman is gone at last," said the professional man in his customary blended tone as he felt her pulse. "She struggled hard; but it was a death that gnawed more than a cancer. A mother's heart and love for her children cannot be trifled with. Some time ago I attended a similar case of a poor woman who suffered the same fate. She was bereft her child by the Black Hand Society," he said, and expressed a few words of sympathy to the bereaved husband as he took his leave.

May Thornton still clung to the hope that the children would shortly arrive. "Dan could not deceive me. He was sincere, and he will keep his word. I have as much faith in him as I have in Heaven, for it was the spirit of Heaven that spoke through him," she murmured. "But, oh, 'she is gone now, poor woman. She was denied the pleasure of meeting them, and the poor children, how will it affect them when they arrive and find, after their long waiting, that their mother is gone? Oh, why did I wait so long?" she exclaimed, feeling a pang of guilt. She could, however, no longer weep. Her heart was heavy and she felt a depression in the centre of her body. Her eyes seemed burned out. It would have been a relief to her if she could have shed tears.

Harry, consoled and supported by the arm of his true friend, stood over the dead form of the good woman, crying and praying. Soon Lankey led the heart-broken man over towards the window and begged him to sit and rest himself. Tears trickled down his cheeks. He suffered, but made no uttering of complaint.

Kind Mother Thornton proceeded to take charge

of the burial, and prepared to go to an undertaking establishment, but was suddenly disturbed by a whizzing and loud sound of a gong which came from without the street. Harry braced up and looked out of the window. Lankey, too, peeped out. An automobile stopped in front of the building. Out of it was lifted a little girl and a boy and a child was carried in the arms of a woman. "Oh, it's my children," cried stricken O'Neil, "and now their poor mother is——" He could not speak further, his heavy frame shook with emotion. Lankey had to support him so that he could remain in a sitting position.

"Oh, I knew it!" cried poor May. "Why did I not go sooner and her life might have been saved?" Here her mother embraced her and wept over the poor girl. The door opened and little Willie and Louise flew in, followed by the woman carrying the child.

The little ones taken, too suddenly to realize the position, rushed to their father, whom they first discovered. He roused and passionately greeted them, so that all were bathed in tears. The baby had reached for May, whom she so well remembered. This responsibility awoke new life in May. She fervently hugged and kissed the little one. The women, without further word and explanation, departed.

After having tendered their father the first greeting, Willie and Louise in their exultation and joy demanded as they looked about where their mother was. They then perceived her stark figure as she lay in bed in the alcove room, and with childish quickness ran and threw themselves on top of her. Their father and Mrs. Thornton rushed to hinder them from embracing their dead mother.

"Here, leave them caress the body of their mother while it is still warm; it will lay cold long enough," commanded Lankey with a little sternness, as he drew

Harry back, and motioned Mother Thornton aside. May was too occupied to think of anything, but satisfying the prattle of the baby. The kind neighbor who had stood by the O'Neils these last days was horrified, and prayed mercy and shame as the little ones bounded on top of the extinct form of the mother.

The little ones' thoughts were that their mother was asleep. They cried, "Oh, mamma, wake up, wake, please mamma, don't you hear?"

Willie was first to realize, and began to fear that his mother was dead. Piteously he cried, "Oh, mamma, dear mamma, don't die! Live with us. Oh, mamma, I was a bad boy, but I shall never, never smoke cigarettes again." Louise also wailed and begged and clung to her mother.

It was a most touching sight. Lankey now thought it was best to break them away from their mother, and walked a step towards the bed. He startled, halted, and threw up both his hands, for he noticed on the apparently dead woman a twisting or contraction in the region of the eyes, as if with a strong effort to force the lids back.

He bid Harry instantly run for the doctor, and gently walked close to the form of Mrs. O'Neil. Restraining the little ones from caressing her further, he gently said: "Wake up, Mrs. O'Neil, your children are here waiting to greet you. Wake up, wake up," he continued forcibly but gently. He felt that her body was still warm, and noticed a slight respiration. The stricken woman was evidently alive, but too weak to command her forces.

The doctor came running, carrying his case of implements. Harry soon followed, carrying upon his shoulders a syphon charged with oxygen. The doctor had hastily decided to induce artificial respiration, and by this means bring her back to a normal condition of breathing. "The knowledge that her children are with her will strengthen her will power. Could she first be brought to a stage where she could realize it, she will live," he announced.

The doctor at once recognized symptoms of life. As he had been deceived before, he made certain not to be deceived again. After a hasty examination he applied the oxygen, though he first had the women and children leave the sick chamber. "To open her eyes and suddenly see her little ones, would be most fatal to her weak heart," he said. "She must be gently prepared, and not until she is normal must she be permitted to meet them."

After some strong exertion the doctor finally induced breathing. Her limbs twisted from light contraction of muscles, her nervous system was set a moving. A slight flush, though barely noticeable, showed in her hollow cheeks and on her temples. Faintly she drew her eyelids back. "Be strong now, dear woman; we have the children waiting for you, but you cannot and must not see them till you are strong enough," said the physician assuringly, as he lightly exercised her arm. "Rest now and sleep well and very soon you will be able to meet and embrace your little ones."

That Mrs. O'Neil had understood the doctor was evident. Weak as she was, a strong light shone from her eyes, and an expression of happiness dawned upon her face. She again closed her eyes, but this time with no pallor of death. The doctor filled out a prescription and had some medicine brought him. The kind and unusual interest which he took in the matter had influenced him to stay in attendance on the sick woman all night, and far upon the following forenoon. Upon his leaving he was satisfied that she now could be saved.

The Little Sufferers

Harry O'Neil wept for joy, and embraced his friend Lankey. Little May Thornton felt unspeakably happy. Her reward had come at last. Though she truly loved Lankey, she gave Dan Connors many a thought. Cruel as he had been, he had helped her and added to the world's happiness.

The little ones were taken over to the Thorntons, where they were to remain until such a time as their mother would be strong enough to receive them. Mother Thornton and her younger daughter looked after the children, while May remained nursing back to health her sick friend. Harry joyfully went back to work again, and of course Lankey called as regularly as was his custom. In the evenings, in his and May's spare moments, they made up for their enforced period of restraint and separation.

While Mrs. O'Neil daily improved, Lankey and May grew deeper in love, and would plan for housekeeping. George had over five hundred dollars saved, and his firm had lately given him an interest in their concern, so their prospects showed bright. Harry O'Neil was advanced to foreman at the lumber yard, and now that he had his children beside him and his wife recovering, he felt the happiest man in all the boroughs.

Truly, it was as Lankey George always said, "The brightest light casts the darkest shadow."

The O'Neil family at last were happy. All shone bright for them as it did for Lankey George, and his true little May who were to be married a week hence. But a sad shadow was cast over the life of poor Red Hook Dan. He was plainly a broken-hearted man. He deserted the neighborhood and nothing more was heard of him. Poor Katie Thornton took the treachery of her sweetheart, in his plot against Jack Stevenson, the champion of good mother and children, so strongly to heart that she never forgave him. It was her first love and she never had the heart to venture into another experience.

Jack Stevenson had fallen as others prospered. He had fought against fate and he was never discouraged. "A private institution cloaked under grand benevolence, enriching upon charity and upon the poor and defenceless," he continued, "being usurpers of laws and rights cannot forever be tolerated in a country where freedom, duty and rights are a Nation's emblem."

THE END.

BROADWAY PUBLISHING CO'S
NEWEST BOOKS
All Bound in Silk Cloth and Gilt.   Many Illustrated

Fiction

The Eyes at the Window (beautifully bound, with embossed jacket)—Olivia Smith Cornelius....$1.50

Next-Night Stories—C. J. Messer............. 1.25

Arthur St. Clair of Old Fort Recovery—S. A. D. Whipple..................................... 1.50

Barnegat Yarns—F. A. Lucas................. 1.00

Jean Carroll, with six illustrations—John H. Case 1.50

As a Soldier Would—Abner Pickering.......... 1.50

The Nut-Cracker, and Other Human Ape Fables— C. E. Blanchard, M.D...................... 1.00

Moon-Madness, and Other Fantasies—Aimée Crocker Gouraud (5th ed.).................... 1.00

Sadie, or Happy at Last—May Shepherd....... 1.50

Tweed, a Story of the Old South—S. M. Swales.. 1.50

The White Rose of the Miami—Mrs. E. W. Ammerman................................. 1.50

The Centaurians—Biagi...................... 1.50

The Reconstruction of Elinore Wood—Florenz S. Merrow.................................... 1.50

A Nest of Vipers—Morgan D. Jones........... 1.50

Religious Works

The Disintegrating Church—Frederick William Atkinson................................. 1.00

Evolution of Belief—J. W. Gordon............ 1.50

Down Hill and Up Hill—Rev. J. G. Anderson.. 2.00

A Certain Samaritan—Rev. John Richelsen..... 1.00

The Reunion of Christendom—Francis Goodman 1.50

What the Church Is and What It Should Be— Lafayette Swindle.......................... 1.50

A Harp of the Heart. (Poems)—Rev. Chas. Coke Woods............................... 1.00

The Gospel Parables in Verse—Rev. Christopher Smith...................................... .75

Who? Whence? Where? An Essay by Pedro Batista................................... 1.00

Compendium of Scriptural Truths—Marshall Smith.................................... 1.25

The Passion Play at Ober Ammergau—Esse Esto Maplestone................................ 1.00

Israel Lo Ammi—Ida M. Nungasser........... 1.00

The Eternal Evangel—Solomon S. Hilscher.....$1.50
A New Philosophy of Life—J. C. Coggins....... 1.00
Romance of the Universe—B. T. Stauber....... 1.50
In the Early Days—Adelaide Hickox.......... 1.50
The New Theology—By a Methodist Layman—
    Hamilton White........................ 1.00

Miscellaneous

Anvil Sparks—Radical Rhymes and Caustic
    Comments, by Wilby Heard................ .75
The Medical Expert and Other Papers—Louis J.
    Rosenberg............................. .50
The Little Sufferers (dealing with the Abuses of
    the Children's Societies)—G. Martin........ 1.50
Eureka, a Prose Poem—S. H. Newberry........ 1.00
Rust (a play in four acts)—Algernon Tassin (of
    Columbia University).................... 1.00
Poems by Charles Guinness.................. 1.00
Prohibition and Anti-Prohibition — Rommel,
    Ziegler & Herz......................... 1.00
Gay Gods and Merry Mortals—Verse by Robert J.
    Shores................................ 1.00
The Rubaiyat of the College Student—Ned Nafe .50
The Deluge of England, and Other Poems—James
    Francis Thierry........................ 1.00
The Dragon's Teeth—a Philosophical and Eco-
    nomic Work—T. M. Sample............... 1.00
Achsah, the Sister of Jairus—Mabel Cronise
    Jones................................. 1.00
The Marriage Bargain Counter—Daisy Deane.. 1.50
Building a New Empire—Nathaniel M. Ayers.. 1.50
Marriage and Divorce—Jeanette Laurance...... 1.00
The Clothespin Brigade—Clara L. Smiley...... .75
"Forget It"—Ida Von Claussen.............. 1.50
The Last Word: a Philosophical Essay—James
    and Mary Baldwin...................... 1.00

Travel

Eight Lands in Eight Weeks (illustrated by 90
    drawings)—Marcia P. Snyder............. 1.25
Eliza and Etheldreda in Mexico—Patty Guthrie
    (illustrated)........................... 1.25

The attention of clergymen is directed to our Religious List, one
of the largest of any house in America.
Write for free copy of our magazine, BOOK CHAT.

BROADWAY PUBLISHING CO., 835 BROADWAY, N. Y.
Branch Offices:
ATLANTA   BALTIMORE   INDIANAPOLIS   NORFOLK
    WASHINGTON   DES MOINES, IOWA

Lightning Source UK Ltd.
Milton Keynes UK
UKHW020645241218
334505UK00007B/184/P